1,205 Things I Want to Tell You.

Brody Drew McVittie

Introduction Numero Uno.

I wrote books about someone else.

I'm supposed to be writing a book about someone else, right now. 50,000 words in, and I'm running away from each and every *all* of them; hoping the day comes when I'm brave enough and far enough away from *you* and writing

*thi*s

the book I'm afraid to write, but can't seem to stop.

So I shouldn't be, but the book I'm writing right now

is *this book*

and

this book

is just for

--and all about--

You.

...

Introduction Numero Dos.

I wrote a book about boxing

and I wrote a book about bad guys.

I wrote a book about a good man

--a real, real good man--

and I wrote a book with pages and pages of pretty words describing what I *thought* were pretty girls.

I wrote a book about a writer

who I thought knew a thing or two about hurt—

--I guess I should have been a little more patient.

(More) Things you wouldn't like about me

I sold your ring and I put It on my arm,

literally,

because after three years I guess I kinda figured you weren't coming back.

There's tattoos where your diamonds used to be, and I know you hate tattoos and I know you hate me and so now you *really* would,

hate me

because I wear my beard too long and I wear my hair too long and I have the kind of tattoos you would tell me make me look like the

"crimmennal"

(*criminal)

we both kinda always figured I'd turn out to be.

I still spend my weekends back home, in the tiny little town I grew up in—the kind of from-the-mud-no-chance-of-making-it tiny little town you come from, *and live in,*

--because as much as you used to say you hated the tiny little town I came from--

your fifth-fiancée-first-husband comes from the *very same* tiny little town I come from

and you actually married him and moved there.

So my hometown isn't *really* my hometown,

anymore

and you can give it back like that Eric Church song tells you to, because of all the tiny little towns you could go and settle down in,

fate and karma

and you

decided it had to be mine.

I still write books about guys that are kinda-sorta me

and I still write books about girls that are kinda-sorta not you,

and I honestly thought that I'd never have the *patience- strength-courage* to write the one book I'm fully qualified to write

this one

but the kind of time that tricks me into thinking I can has passed, and so here it is.

Our truth laid bare,

and while I realize that everyone else is going to read this and think

there's no way these stories could actually be true

and

that's the craziest made-up love story I've ever read

the only two people who know

deep

deep

down

that every single word in these pages is true

is me

and

is you.

So here, I guess, are 1,205 Things I Want to Say to You.

...

A Little Bit About You, and—for good measure-- A Little Bit About Me.

You grew up in the mud, somewhere in a magical, made-up place called *Colombia*, where all the best things in life come from.

They are, in no particular order:

-Coffee.

-Cocaine.

-Colombian women.

-Cartels.

-Cosmetic Surgery.

*The writer in me really appreciates the first two, the way any self-respecting writer *should*. The self-styled vagabond in me really digs the nebulous moral compass of the fourth; the man in me is just really, really thankful for the third and fifth. Fake Fat Asses come from Colombia, and I couldn't care less if they're fake or not—I've heard that, in the early days of implants, they used to tend to separate from the ass they were attached to, and the saline-or-whatever-the-hell-fat-ass-implants-are-made-of would migrate down to a poor woman's ankles!

Imagine going in for a fat ass, and ending up with 'cankles?'

Oh, Colombia.

You were born in some shithole in Bogota, a couple of years before I was born in some shithole in Springfield (near Aylmer!), Ontario, Canada. I think we always kind of quietly appreciated this about one another; I think that growing up dirt-poor with no future gave us the fire in our bellies that we needed to survive.

I can't speak to your younger years, because you'd never really tell me about them—in *our* two and a half years together, Colombia stayed the kind of magical-mystery-land reserved for vague recollections and stares off into distances. I can say that you had two loving and entirely non-English speaking parents—who I came to love as well, thank you very much—and a brother and sister that, while younger, shared your intellect and your desire to build a better life for themselves.

For the sake of you not suing the shit out of me, we'll call your father *Padre*.

We'll call your mother *Madre*.

We'll call your brother *Ricardo-Gustavo,* because Colombian names are the best names,

and we'll call your sister *Consuela-Fontana.*

I've thought long and hard about what to call *you*

--and there are so very many things I could and would like to—

but let's go with

Muneca

which means 'doll;'

because you really were,

and because it's what I really used to call you.

For the record, my name will be

Mico

which means 'monkey;'

because while I'm relatively sure you might call your fifth-fiancée-first-husband the same, it's what you used to call me;

and because while

Brody Drew McVittie

is the name of the author on the front of this book,

I can count on one hand the number of times you referred to me by my real name.

I can count on one hand the number of times you referred to me by my real name

because you had trouble pronouncing it;

and while I found this to be endlessly adorable, words like

Brody

and

adorable

don't exist in Colombian; and so you really found disdain in speaking them.

I can't speak to your younger years, but for the sake of the readership that *isn't* you I'll speak to mine; I grew up, as mentioned, dirt poor in the mud of Springfield (near Aylmer!), Ontario, Canada. I was blessed with two loving parents,

Drew

and

Shelley,

who will be referred to as

Drew

and

Shelley,

because I'm relatively sure that they still love me, and therefore won't sue the shit out of me. I get my artistic side from mom—who is an artist and Chippewa Indian—so I'm pretty sure the tattoos and the crazy can be traced back to her.

I get the common sense I only sometimes have from Drew, who is Irish.

*Coincidentally, anyone astute enough to realize this is a love story between a half-Irish-half-Chippewa-Indian boy and a full-blooded Colombian girl doubtless understands the…tone…this book will contain.

 I'm blessed to have a baby sister,

Kortney

who will be referred to as

Buttons

or

Dennis

or

Denny

or any of a thousand other nicknames that don't really make sense, because I'm her bigger brother and I alone have the right to lovingly refer to her as such. It's worth noting that while I'm beautiful (--and, as the author and the hero of this story, I can describe myself any goddamn way I want; that said, I promise there is only truth in these pages--) my baby sister is drop-dead gorgeous.

*That said, I'm protective and she's happy and I have tattoos and so I think I'm tough, so stay away from her.

I grew up with Shelley and Drew and Dennis-the-future-gorgeous-girl on a tiny little hobby farm, about as far away from the luxuries of the 1980's as one could. Back then, we were too poor for toys, and my first few Christmases saw tiny painted wooden houses under the tree where gifts should be.

Now, the point of this isn't 'poor me;' hell, I was as happy as any dirty little farm boy could be. We had horses and goats and sheep and cows and, my personal favorite, pigs—and a deaf/blind black lab and a Dalmatian that was literally on steroids, but that's another novel entirely. The thing we had the most of was imagination, and I attribute playing with imaginary friends saving imaginary princesses and enduring endless imaginary swordfights to the imagination that led me to write books and make something of myself.

The point is we both grew up poor, and the fire in our respective bellies is because of it.

Back then *Colombia* was a planet from *Star Wars*, and women with honeysuckle-sweet Colombian accents only existed in whatever world *wasn't* the world of endless skies and mixing-pig-slop mornings.

I'm telling our readers this, because I'm sure it played some part, thirty-two years and the women that come with thirty-two years of relative gorgeousness later, when I laid eyes on

you

for the very first time and realized that, while dragons and my hopes of becoming a professional swordsman might not be real,

that girl from the planet Colombia *was*.

...

Day Numero Uno aka How You Look

You look

Fuck it.

There are really no words for the way you look, when you look at me for the first time, there at the desk on the first day.

*Let me paint the picture for every-other reader who isn't you, the only one this book is really for. I'm sure this recollection lives in your head, too, buried under memories attached to boys you deem better than me. So while this one is primarily for the Peanut Gallery, it's for you, as well—just in case you've bandaged this particular bleed in that pretty little sub-conscious.

I'm thirty-two and magnificent, and I'm working at this gym.

I'm six-feet-tall-*ish*, but fuck it, I'm writing this book, so I'm six-feet-tall

and I'm covered in muscles

(which you don't like)

and I've got a shaved head

(which you don't like)

and I've got the swagger and arrogance of a thirty-two year old who has risen from the mud of Springfield (near Aylmer!) Ontario, Canada.

Now, this particular gym is located in London, Ontario, Canada, which to a mud-rat like me, is about as big-city as big-city in this world gets.

*London, Ontario, Canada Population: 366, 151.

Inside this particular gym is located a desk belonging to the Personal Training Department—a Department in which I proudly work and a desk where new members like you wait to be given a Personal Training Session by douchebags like me.

For the sake of specificity, I'm proudly a special kind of trainer—namely, the kind who can perform fitness assessments for new members who request a fitness assessment…new members like you.

So, to recap, you joined my gym, and, as a thank you for joining my gym, you're offered a free

(*--if you count three wasted years as 'free'--)

assessment with a particularly suited professional assessor; lucky for us, that assessor was me.

So I'm walking up behind you, and I can't quite see your face yet, but I can see your s*o-black-it-fucking-shines* hair and I can see the curves your body both takes and tries to hide, sitting *that* ass on my stool and just waiting for someone like me to come in and try to ruin your life.

You turn, and it's just enough to see the

I'm gonna fucking ruin your life too

look on that pretty little face,

and the rumble in my balls tells me that you're pretty much perfect a half-second *before* I catch that look—the very first one—and the breath leaves my impressively-un-proportioned chest.

*Now I've written books and the pages in them describing how beautiful other girls are—the ghost of *This One* or *That One* or (for those who have read—and thank you, by the way—my shit)

This New One

…so believe me when I say that I've spent pages trying to sum up just how beautiful you look to me, here in the tiny kingdom I call my gym, on this very first day.

Sorry, baby, but I'm just not that good of a writer.

Suffice to say, you look degrees better than any-everything I've ever seen…and I've seen any-everything.

Your hair dances, softly enough around the impossible high of your impossibly high cheekbones, and they two-step in tandem, lifting just a little as your eyes smile a milli-moment before your mouth does.

*Now, bear in mind I'm trying to be professional, and, despite the connotations my work environment doubtless creates in the other reader's minds, I'm wearing dress pants and a collared shirt with, from what I can recall, was probably a fantastic fucking tie.

**This is significant *less* for painting a picture of the scene for those who weren't fortunate enough to be there to behold you, and *more* for the fact that my balls are sending high-voltage lightning blasts to the shaft of my (also fucking fantastic) penis, and my collar is completely restricting any of the air I'm hoping to have back after you stole it.

So, I'm standing there, pretty fucking fucked, and I'm doing my-best-and-probably-not-succeeding to *not* drool out of the corners of the mouth I'm turning to smile back and say anything other than

I love you

which is pretty much right when it happened,

and pretty much why I'm writing this book.

*Here I am getting ahead of myself—now, two years removed from seeing that face, live, and almost five years removed from seeing it, live, for the first time, I'll do my best to drag up the pain that comes from focusing on it, for the sake of the every-other readers who *aren't* you.

**Interestingly, around the time I was discovering your beauty, TIME magazine put out an article stating that Colombia had the Best Looking Women In The World, topping both conventional-wisdom and perennial favorite Brazil.

(I can honestly say that, due to the inherit craziness in the blood of every beautiful Colombian woman, that, were it not for the cocaine and the coffee, the civilized world would have bombed you beautiful motherfuckers right off the map years and years ago.)

***SO, your beauty is some kind of built-in Latina safety mechanism, and I'll be Goddamned if it isn't about to work on me. Now back to my inadequate description of your beauty. This is important, because when I begin to outline just how crazy you are (--and yes, I'll be sure to outline how crazy I am, too--) readers can keep coming back to this, and maybe rationalize it the way I used to.

You turn on the stool, and I'm supposed to be all

"Hello, I'm Mico"

and I think the best I can manage is

"Hello"

before you set your eyes on me, and the little bit of breath I've collected to speak to you gets stolen from me all over again.

There's a current that runs through two people once they're in certain proximity; a chemical rush, a pheromone release—some physical manifestation of love that attacks the body, and attacks it violently. I feel it and I don't yet know what it is, and, looking at me, you're feeling it too, and suddenly you're smiling even wider and I'm already cataloguing every significant and insignificant fleck on each of your painfully dark pupils.

Eventually, categorized by tiny eternities, I manage

"I'm Mico"

and before I can follow with the intended

"It's a pleasure to meet you"

I learn that

"I'm *Muneca.**"

*You *are*—because *Muneca* means doll in the magical land of Colombia, but, as mentioned and for the sake of you not suing my ass the way you probably want to, your actual identity is redacted.

And, instantly and violently,

*Muneca**

is the sweetest name I've ever heard, because it rolls thick-like-honey from your juicy Spanish lips and it's the first time I'm hearing you speak and it's right around the time I'm discovering that Colombian accents might be my *favorite-*favorite; and it's just the latest in a line of things I'm already moderately sure I'm in love with and about you.

 So here we are, Muneca* and Mico, and it's six-oh-two on some Thursday night, and, tragically, we're already doomed.

We don't know it yet, and we haven't learned to listen to the chemicals and the current exploding between us and reverberating through the walls of the gym we walk towards my office in.

For now I'm trying to ignore the hairs standing on the back of my neck and I'm telling myself that I'm not in love with you because that's crazy and stupid, and as I motion you to sit in the cheap leather seat nowhere-near-good-enough-for-that-ass, I probably even try to convince myself that I have some modicum of control of the outcome that's coming.

...

First

I'm on my way out to the tiny little town I come from for my baby sister's birthday. Its three days early, but it's the weekend, and the weekend is about the only time she and I can escape the city to visit mom and dad. *Who have moved, it's worth noting, since the time I lived with them; they've now become relative city-slickers themselves, moving from Springfield (near Aylmer!) Ontario to just outside Aylmer itself.

*Aylmer, Ontario, Canada population: 7,151.

So it's a big deal because it's her birthday and they've got a pool and its mid-May, so pool season is officially underway. After the horrors of winter, Canadians tend to be pre-mature when it comes to openings; we're so used to the torturous days of twenty-plus below that, come the first signs of warmth, it's all barbecues and backyards, *actual* temperature be damned.

Today is one of those so-perfect-we'll-do-both, barbecue and backyard, and I'll admit I'm looking forward to it as I'm driving down Wonderland Road South, heading towards the country and about as fast as a *little* over the speed limit will let me. I'll admit that while you're not the furthest thing from my mind, you're not occupying your usual spot at the forefront; I've got the windows down and the music up and I'm focusing on a weekend of not focusing at all.

I'm almost free, passing the last commercial plaza the city has to offer before surrendering to the majesty of farmer's fields, when my cell phone—riding shotgun quietly beside me—explodes in tandem with the rhythm from the speakers.

It's a text, and it's from you and it reads

What are you up to?

and I'm texting and driving, suddenly and illegally, and my text back says

Heading out of the city to see the family

and

You?

I'm stopped at a light, and I know I'm in trouble *potentially* because I'm paying more attention to my phone and waiting for the text than I am paying attention to the light and waiting for it to turn. This is a sign and not a good one—you're a client and you're beautiful and I'm supposed to be a professional and I'm finding it really

really

hard; glancing over my shoulder at the phone riding shotgun, I'll admit that, of all the thoughts I'm thinking, being professional isn't one of them.

So it's the curves your body takes as the light goes green, instead of the curves in the road—and as I approach the latest, I pay it no mind, because my phone has gone off again and this time you're telling me that

I'm at Home Depot running errands

and, miraculously, I can see the Home Depot sign through my windshield. I'm thinking it must be fate, having not quite escaped the city and the last commercial plaza it has to offer—the last commercial plaza I make an abrupt right turn into, heading directly towards both Home Depot and fate, leaving Aylmer and my sister and her birthday in the rear view mirror.

…

I spot you in the kitchen appliance aisle, and it's at least the most devastatingly beautiful sight I've ever seen. You're bent over some marble or faux-marble or almost-marble countertop, inspecting it with the kind of eye I'd imagine only a structural engineer has. For my part, I'm inspecting you with the kind of eye that only a professional-woman-appreciator has, and I'm suddenly something south of full-breath and wondering how the hell I can say hello without looking like a stalker.

I'm mid-solution when you lift your almond eyes to meet mine, and any hope I had of maintaining composure runs faster-than-maybe-I-should in the other direction. You smile and it disarms me, and I'm relatively sure I smile back, but the whole not-feeling-my-face thing I'm all at once feeling prevents me from ever knowing for sure. You move, and over the din of Home Depot I hear the sway of your hips against the denim they're tragically imprisoned in; I'm so used to seeing you in not-quite-trendy-or-tight-enough workout velour that this revelation takes time to process.

You're wearing a GUESS? tank top and I am

guessing

and about treasures that are ample and bouncing as you move to move towards me; I'm probably slack-jawed (--still can't feel my face to know for sure--) and admiring the totality of the presentation against the backdrop of Home Depot kitchen mock-ups, wishing we were in one attached to a home no one else was home in.

You're surprised and pleasantly and when your lips move to tell me so, I'm fixated on the lips attached to the mouth that moves them; thinking horrible thoughts and of exploring every molecule of them with decidedly inferior lips of my own.

I withdraw from my observation for fear of appearing a little too intense; this proves to be among the most difficult things I've ever had to do. Your voice helps, you're singing to me and sweetly with words like

Hello

and

What a nice surprise

and rebuttals to the other pleasantries I force from distracted and lesser lips. Your eyes are wild and wildly scanning mine and the smile on your face is as warm as my face *feels*, the blood underneath doubtless tired of running there and then my balls and then back to my face.

You ask me to join you, there amongst the mock kitchens in the mock kitchen aisle, and all at once I'm following you through a maze of immaculately staged faux-dwellings, heading to a desk occupied by a man with ruddy red cheeks we'll call

Red

for the sake of prosperity and this story. You join Red at his tiny little desk because, as I'm to learn, you have an appointment, meaning your visit to Home Depot is to do decidedly more than meet beautiful men like myself. As you and Red begin discussing potential renovations to your very own kitchen counters, I'm taken to studying the strands of your raven black hair, and the way they seem to trace your shoulders, only to fall wild and free some quarter-length the length of your wonderful little back. Which is arched, even seated, revealing the resplendence of your perfect breasts—breasts both Red and myself are trying our damndest not to drool over, lost instead in less-interesting conversations about countertops and countertop surfaces.

He's enamored with your voice much the way I am; there's something honeysuckle-sweet in those inflections—the tiny slurs you force against certain vowels has the both of us hanging on every word spoken from those pretty puffed up pretty little lips. Your knowledge on the porous qualities of semi-reflective surfaces is nearly as impressive as the impossibly high cut of your impossibly high cheekbones; they bounce almost as much as your breasts when you hit the part of the sentence you're speaking that excites you the most.

I listen *kinda* yeah, but I study you kinda-more; by the time you've explained that your parents are coming to visit from the magical, made-up land of Colombia I've memorized every detail of your face and counted your eyelashes at least twice. You've got a whole lot of them, and they're pretty and they're pretty long and they frame those almond eyes, and I'm appreciating them and the rest of you in ways I just can't when I'm training you and being a professional and studying your exercise form more than your *form*-form.

You're singing to Red about how your father is a structural engineer, (--which is almost as impressive as *you* being a structural engineer--) and how he's going to notice—with great disappointment—the flaws in your existing kitchen countertops when he visits, and for the first time, your new home the way he's about to.

You're wrapping up the conversation part of the conversation/negotiations with Red, and I'm stuck on the whole parents-from-Colombia thing; musing how drop-dead gorgeous *those* motherfuckers must be to have created a creature as motherfucking beautiful as you are. You settle on a visit from Red to establish a quote for some ridiculous renovations—the kind of renovations I'm in awe to learn you're perfectly capable of performing yourself.

 * This might be the two-hundred and fortieth most impressive thing about you—right after your pronunciation of the letter 'i.'

As mentioned, you finish your conversation with a clearly-in-love-with-you-also Red, turn your pretty little face in my general and awe-struck direction, and ask if I want to go get a coffee. I've got time—chances are my baby sister hasn't yet escaped the confines of the city, and chances are my poor sweet mother won't mind if the reason I'm late is because I've potentially found love—so I agree with what I hope comes across as a modicum of restraint.

And there really is none—restraint, that is—because you're wearing a tank top that reads

GUESS?

and I *am*, wondering as I follow you earnestly from Home Depot and across the plaza parking lot to Starbucks if there exists anywhere in the whole wide world I *wouldn't*.

…

We're on the patio and sipping a coffee I don't quite understand, some venti-macchiato-and-who-the-fuck-cares because it's a beautiful afternoon and the beauty of said afternoon kinda *pales*, from my vantage point across a painfully too-far-away-from-you table. The time with you today has all the qualities of one of those never-forget-it memories, the kind that only get warmer and more perfect in the subsequent recounting of.

You're laughing softly and smiling warmly, and I'm explaining why I became I writer and why I got into the fitness industry, and while I'm sure it's nowhere near as interesting as your story of how you came to Earth and Canada and how you became a Structural Engineer, you humour me by hanging on my every word.

In between the every-other thought of how beautiful I can't believe you are, I'm musing that it's *cruel* that you could be so fucking fantastic to talk to as well; accentuated by the accent, I reckon I could sit here at this table and talk with you all afternoon. And before I know it we *do*; hour five at the same table behind the same finished-hours-ago venti-macchiato, I'm aware of the subtle passage of time only by the setting of the sun and the darkening of the sky.

By now I've horribly missed my sister's birthday celebration, and though you encourage me to leave you and this patio table and this moment to somewhat salvage my plans with your mouth, your eyes are wild and wildly screaming

stay

which, as I'm sure I'll mention again, is the most powerful word in the English language. And I couldn't leave if I wanted to and I don't; and although I love my baby sister, I'm already sub-consciously aware that I desperately love you more.

It's new and it's exciting and it's absolutely electric, and so the warning signs that *should* be firing somewhere deep in my stomach are drowned out by the rumblings of just how badly I want to taste your lips when you move them to tell me

go

but really don't mean it,

not even a little bit

not even at all.

I'll learn all about ISJ--Irrational Colombian Jealousy--and how time spent with other females—even family—*even pets*—is frowned upon, when one has decided that time is better spent exclusively with said Colombian...but today isn't that day, and this is *the all-good* stage, and so my legs wouldn't let me move even if I tried.

Which I don't—and I'll always owe my baby sister a birthday for the part in hers that I'm about to miss this particular year—but I'm under your spell and if said spell was water I'd have drowned already and horribly. So we let the sun set, because

fuck it, too

and all that matters is the two of us and the intoxicating conversation. In thirty-two years on this planet I've never met the kind of person so clearly *not,* from this planet and because everything that escapes your pretty puffed up pretty little lips is as *perfect* as the rest of you clearly appears to be. We muse at the time that's passed and then mock time for passing—and so more time passes, and we only really realize this when the apparent owner of Starbucks emerges from inside Starbucks to quietly pack up the rest of the empty patio we're still only one drink deep and five plus hours on.

And I feel like I owe the owner of Starbucks something stronger than a coffee, because he kind of smiles at me from his vantage point over her shoulder, and then goes inside Starbucks and quietly turns the lights off, effectively closing up shop for the night and leaving us undisturbed on the patio, the only two chairs and a table un-packed, and I'll be damned if we're so into the conversation that we barely notice.

…

Your eyes are heavy as I walk you to your car. Your mouth is a little dry, because we haven't been properly hydrating and we've done five-plus hours of talking and with the furiousness of two people that want to get the really-getting-to-know-you part of the relationship done *fast.* Despite the dryness, your lips are still pretty puffed up pretty little lips, and as you lean against your beat up little VW Golf* I still really really want to taste them the way I figure I'm about to.

I have a theory, based on my relatively short time in the 'big city;' beautiful women—especially college age and just above—all drive beat up VW Golfs at some point. Seriously. See one on the road and pull up beside it—guaranteed there's a ten behind the wheel.

I'm reaching out, because although I'm close to you as you lean against your beat up little VW Golf I'm nowhere near close enough, and I'm taking your tiny little hand in mine with reflexes honed from years of physical exercise and powered by desperate intentions. Your hand feels warm in mine, and your eyes have not wavered once and my eyes waver once and for the first time in over five hours to fall on the lips I'm about to fall into for the first time, too.

The weather is warm and the night tells me to, and so I move in for a kiss and you stop me, softly, by moving your lips away from mine, deftly and towards the ear you find to whisper in, whispering

Not yet, Mico

and kissing me somewhere on my neck or ear; somewhere other than the lips that fumble to say something like

I understand

when we both know I really don't.

Maybe I should, as hour three veered into our pasts and the people in it; I learned that you've had three fiancées and that you've never married, and that maybe you're a little cautious of the attention that comes your way because of it. Maybe I figured you'd be cautious and didn't care, years of beautiful women and the ego beautiful women provide coupled with five hours of magical conversation telling me the first kiss was a foregone conclusion.

And it still is,

your eyes tell me, and you're smiling mischievously and bridging the distance between us, leaping from your post against your beat up little VW golf to hug me as tightly as your tiny little body will allow.

I ask if I can see you again and you say *Tuesday,* and it takes me a second and the subsequent electricity the response has generated to realize that Tuesday is our next training session. You won't let go, and I won't let go, and it's reassuring because it's making my missed kiss okay, your body telling me that this is both formality and aforementioned foregone conclusion should I follow the appropriate steps to your courting dance.

Cruelly, we separate, and as I leave you and the magic of the afternoon we bled into evening, I'm headed in the opposite direction of the birthday party I'm hours late for, heading home with a smile on my face that lasts the duration of the twelve minute drive.

...

Ending, but kinda Beginning

It's our last training session, tragically and not.

Tragically, because this is potentially the last opportunity I have to spend time with you the way I've grown excited-accustomed to; and *not* tragically, because I have every intention of asking you to dinner following the conclusion of our session.

The hour passes with appropriate tension; following our five hour coffee rendezvous I'm finding that I'm increasingly comfortable placing my hands on you in entirely professional ways—we finish with a back extension and we finish the back extension with my hand resting comfortably on the small of your back. You follow me into my office at the conclusion of the session and my night, and although we shake the hands we shake to signal a goodbye, you're standing in my office and I'm standing in my office and neither of us have any intention of leaving.

We're talking and we're laughing and we're flirting and before we know it, an hour and a half has passed. We laugh at this too, all

fuck time

again, and I can honestly say that for the first time in years, I'm not greeting the end of my shift with an immediate exit out the front door. I tell you this, and you laugh softly, running your tiny little baby carrot fingers through your hair the way you do when you're nervous and want to distract with your admittedly distracting beauty.

You move to leave, after an appropriate amount of time has tried to pass— neither of us care, and there is no sadness in your leaving, because you're asking me to walk you to your car a half-second before I get the chance to offer. I walk diligently beside you into the warm night air, and, as you lean against your beat up little VW Golf I ask you the question we've both been waiting all night for me to ask.

"Do you want to go to dinner?"

And a suggested date, unimportantly, because the details are lost on me when you immediately reply

"Yes"

offering

"but just as friends, right?"

the way you tend to, following the steps of your courtship.

I answer

"Of course"

and of course I'm lying and of course you *want* me to be lying, the chemistry between us eliminating any possibility of platonic-ness. I dance the way you want me to, and as you offer yourself off of the side of your beat up little VW Golf to embrace me, I take the kiss that comes on the neck that knows the *next* one will be planted somewhere else.

...

Dinner and the things that come After Dinner

I pull into the laneway of the house you own—and share—with your third ex-fiancée's best friend Gatto. I haven't met Gatto yet; from what I hear, he's an absolute saint, and so I have zero issue with the thought of you living with him...had you been living with your third fiancée, however, I reckon it might raise my suspicions. So as I approach your front door, I'm wondering who will answer *almost* as much as I'm wondering what you'll be wearing.

I knock and I wait and I wonder—wonder what you'll have on and wonder if what I'm wearing will be appropriate enough and wondering how the hell I'm going to find the restaurant on the other end of the city without looking lost. I'm going over the route in my head, halfway there and about to turn right onto Dundas Street when you open the door and murder my ability to string together rational thoughts.

You're wearing this tiny little red dress, cut halfway up your thigh and dangerously low across your ample chest. I'd imagine you're wearing the pumps to match, because you're taller, but I can't-see-don't-care, and couldn't lower my gaze from yours if I tried. So I don't, fixated on the flawlessness of your face and the brilliance of your smile. You run your tiny little baby carrot fingers through your black hair, and it's one of those *I'm-embarrassed-don't-look-at-me-just-kidding-I-really-want-you-to* things, and you know goddamned-well it's working.

Now, I'm a beautiful and beautifully confident thirty-two year old man; standing there on your porch however--trying to process you in that red dress-- for the first time since my formative years and the pain associated with them I'm feeling wholly unworthy. You smile at me anyways, and it's the kind of cheekbones-hiding-your-eyes smile that has my confidence crawling back from the pit of my stomach...by the time I've taken your hand and walked you the length of the laneway I'm on top of the world again.

Which makes the drive to restaurant decidedly less stressful; I navigate the streets with the confidence of a man who has a beautiful girl riding shotgun. You're singing quietly to the radio in between bouts of always-interesting conversation—I'm taking turns answering your questions and taking turns onto the streets I hope will lead us to *Auberge du Petit Prince*, the fine dining restaurant with the name I can't quite pronounce. I've never been and you've never been, but you've heard good things—as we pull up to the destination, an elegant Victorian two-story smack dab in the middle of the ghetto—I'm hoping desperately that the surroundings aren't indicative of the experience.

I'll admit I know little about French cuisine, and less about Colombian culture—as I hurry from the driver's seat to open your door for you, I'm confident that said ignorance is about to change. Rounding the hood of the car on the way to you, I'm appalled by the presence of someone's living room couch on the curb just north of you and the door you're about to exit…while the odd landmark may have helped me judge distance to the sidewalk as I pulled up, upon closer inspection, the kind of stains that adorn the cushions warn me that dining in this part of town could have been a tactical error.

As you step out of the car, I direct your attention to the restaurant's architecture, hoping you'll be focused on the craftsmanship of late-era Victorian design rather than the bloodstains adorning the slum-couch you're tragically standing beside. If you notice, you're kind enough to pretend *not to*, and so our magical evening remains magical, the fantasy unfettered by the fact that, while this is a gorgeous restaurant, it is still a renovated house on the corner of a string of still-residential houses, in what might very well be the worst neighborhood in the city.

We're led to a table on the covered porch by an enthusiastic, if ambiguously androgynous waiter; it takes the exchange of ten pleasantries and the pulling-out your chair for me to realize we're the sole patrons of the evening. This only adds to the inherit magic of the night, blood-stained couches aside; we order the most expensive bottle of red on the menu and resume engaging conversation as to the nature and definition of 'friends.*'

This might be my least-favorite word in the English language.

Sitting across the table, here on the porch of the restaurant we're magically alone in, each and every thought running through my mind includes tasting you like the wine as it arrives at the table not a moment too soon.

We drink and we talk and, after time and the first bottle have passed, so does the food we've apparently ordered. We don't notice or care, because it's cold before we've even acknowledged it's arrival--and subsequent interruption--at the table.

So engaged are we in the discussion—the verbal sparring and the laughter that accentuates it—that we're paying far more attention to the *residual*; the non-verbal elements that dance throughout the night air, enraptured as we are, there on the patio of the restaurant we're presumably still alone in.

Presumably, because neither of us interrupt our relentless gazing long enough to ascertain, and the evening is better for it. A rumbling somewhere *north* of the rumbling in my pants tells me that my stomach is yearning for the food on the table beside me. My nostrils have indicated at least a half-dozen times that the *whatever-the-hell-I-ordered* is probably worth consuming, and yet I ignore it anyways.

You're *that* mesmerizing, and, for a guy who's stuck in your *just-friends* bubble, I'm apparently that mesmerizing too, because you haven't bothered to look at, let alone taste, your dinner either. We order another bottle of wine, and I can only assume that our decidedly effeminate waiter gives the not-touched plates a dubious glance as he leaves us to our conversation.

Which has shifted to dreams, and ours and what we yearn for, and I'm halfway through explaining why I ever thought I could accomplish anything as a writer when that second bottle of red shows up, and things *really* get interesting.

...

Your *first* fiancée, you tell me, was your favorite. You met him when you were fifteen years old, in the magical, made-up land of Colombia. You tell me that he was the love of your life, but that he was poor—and so your parents didn't approve. They wanted a better life for you, so they refused when he asked their permission to marry, but you ran away and nearly eloped anyways. Three months after your disappearance, you returned with what I can only assume was a modest rock on your tiny little baby carrot finger, proclaiming that you were madly in love and that it didn't matter if they accepted him or not...and they banished you to the snowy hell of Canada as punishment. Not before, you tell me, they forced you to break it off—and, although you could never resent your parents for sending you to a land where you would be presented with greater opportunities—you never forgot him, and maybe part of you loves him still.

"I was young"

you tell me, with the best mock-authoritative tone you can muster; you repeat it between sips of wine with the conviction of someone who desperately wants to believe the rationale behind their words.

I listen with both intent and amusement, respecting the fact that you're a romantic and that you believe in love—and then it's my turn, and I tell you about the girl responsible for my first novel, the first girl I thought was the love of my life.

And you listen as intently as I did, and you smile when the storytelling requires a smile, and as I'm telling you about the first girl I wrote a novel about I can't help but wonder when I'll begin the novel I'm inevitably going to have to write about *you*.

I finish just as you're wondering when I'm going to begin the novel I'm inevitably going to have to write about you, and we're two bottles of wine deep and we still haven't touched the food that has doubtlessly gone cold and you part your pretty puffed up pretty little lips to tell me about the rest of the fiancées who failed you the way I promise myself I never could.

...

Fiancée Number Dos, you tell me, was nothing like Fiancée Numero Uno, and so you don't really tell me about him at all. From the hushed tones and all-at-once reserved body language I gather that this one was *not* your favorite. You tell me that it happened shortly after you arrived in Canada, and before you had even the slightest comprehension of the customs—let alone the language—of this strange new land, and that he took advantage of your vulnerability. I understand that he was a sponsor of sorts; someone responsible for housing new immigrants, helping them with the necessary paperwork and documentation—and subsequent education—required to become fully-functioning Canadian citizens. We speak of him quickly, in hushed tones, and then move on to decidedly better conversation.

…

Fiancée Numero Tres—following the tradition set out by the first two—is a completely different story. You were working at The Keg, washing dishes on evenings you weren't in school, and, although you had the equivalent of a degree in structural engineering, your lack of mastery of the language prevented you from the types of job opportunities that suited your acquired skillset. This all changed one night when, clearing the table for a particularly rowdy group of gentlemen, one took interest in your ravishing beauty and struck up a conversation.

His name, you tell me, was Humberto—and no, Humberto isn't Fiancée Numero Tres—but he plays a particularly important role in her meeting the eventual lucky bastard.

Over broken conversation, Humberto ascertained your educational background, and, as it so happened, as owner of a small architectural development company looking for an assistant, found your area of study potentially beneficial to his business, if not his social life. I'm sure the fact that you're one of the most beautiful women on the planet didn't hurt—either way, your days cleaning tables were through, and you caught a fortunate break at a career job.

You tell me that, despite a brief and failed romance, you and Humberto became and remain best friends, co-workers, and, as it turns out—relative neighbors. I remember noting this—thinking it of particular interest—but dismissing it in favor of the feeling your eyes give me, as they bore clear through mine and into my soul as we finish the latest bottle.

I'm dizzy now, and, although it's only *partly* due to the sweetness associated with the reds we've been sipping, I wisely switch to water; the thought of catching drunk driving charges potentially marring what has been the perfect evening.

Undaunted, you swallow the last of your latest and maybe-not-last glass, part those pretty pumped up pretty red lips, and tell me of how Humberto introduced you to Fiancée Numero Tres.

Fiancée Numero Tres came with Gatto; the same Gatto who eventually became your roommate. It was, for all intents and purposes, a package deal. You speak of Fiancée Numero Tres fondly, although you tell me that the chemistry just wasn't there—and of how, before Gatto replaced Fiancée Numero Tres as living-quarter-sharer, the two of you wouldn't even share a bed, despite potentially sharing a last name.

I glean from this that love has been…complicated…for you, and that you're decidedly guarded when giving away your heart. This explains the friendship tag so cruelly attached to the title of this *clearly-more-than-friends* encounter; I smile as I listen, and I answer and truthfully and earnestly when you ask of my dating history.

I detail my infidelities and my indiscretions and my loves and my losses, and you judge me only on the arches my eyebrows make when I mention particular names; although I've yet to realize you're filing each and every detail away in your Colombian brain, neither of us let the more potentially troubling elements of our past affect what—for the both of us—is rapidly approaching a legendary night.

Which continues, unmercifully for the waiter and the kitchen staff that would otherwise have gone home, doubtless praying for the magic out on the porch to dissipate long enough to allow the otherwise still-empty restaurant to close.

You're talking again, because it's your turn and I'd rather just sort of silently admire you anyways, when a series of events unfolds just over your shoulder that threatens the sanctity of the night I'm already writing off as perfect.

I strain with all of my might to keep my eyes locked on yours…but just to the left of them, over your right shoulder and across the patio and on the other side of the window, a thirty-something and decidedly derelict-looking man has wheeled a *clearly* baby-less baby stroller up to an equally derelict fifty year old man.

This would be odd enough—maybe even worth pointing to your attention on a date numbered *any* but *one*—but when the younger of the derelict-looking men reaches into the baby stroller and produces a handful of what certainly looks like heroin, it takes everything in my power not to interrupt whatever story you would otherwise be mesmerizing me with.

My mind races—one of a few front-runners involves such a distinguished restaurant choosing such a clearly *not*-distinguished location as host for business; another involves my memory of the couch on the curb, and the subsequent color of the stains on the couch. All the while I'm maintaining your gaze, pretending to be engrossed on the story escaping those previously-unescapable lips; the corners of my trained eyes scanning the scene unfolding over your shoulder.

There's syringes involved now, and a handful of them…the younger bum is handing them off to the older bum and receiving a small handful of what-I-assume-must-be cash in return. You're approaching the crescendo of whatever story you're telling when—just as the drug deal has finished over your shoulder—an unmarked police cruiser pulls up both rapidly and silently, and a uniformed officer leaps from the passenger side.

All at once there's a chase; a magnificent spectacle unfolding just behind you—the kind of action that begs attention, the kind that I'm used to seeing only on the movie screen. The baby carriage is abandoned, but only after being pushed in the officer's direction, and toppling sideways onto the pavement. The officer shouts and gives pursuit—the ensuing chase would be comical could I provide it sufficient attention, the chaos playing out on mute, thankfully, due to the window separating us from the action and the blight of the events and the location surrounding us.

The bums scatter, the officer follows the less nimble of the two; the undercover cruiser roars into action after the more dexterous of the runners. I'm grateful the car is unequipped with the lights and sirens that would surely influence the romanticism you're associating with the restaurant. Mercifully, the potential distraction is dispersed—your attentions unattained, I return the totality of mine to your lips and the honey that flows from them.

As you finish whatever story you were blessing me with, I'm dumbfoundedly aware of the dangers of a woman who can reduce a undercover sting operation to a nuisance…as we decide to end the evening and leave the restaurant, I'm aware of two things.

One-

I need to watch very carefully for crackheads and cops as I hold your hand on the way to the car and

Two-

I'm in completely over my head when it comes to you.

…

The After Dinner Part

It's *beyond* late as I pull into your laneway. The night just kind of hangs in waiting; there's no breeze as I open the car door, crossing the front of the vehicle in a hurry to get to you. I help you out from the passenger seat, my heartbeat quickening to the falling of your red dress against your frame. The wine isn't helping, whispering confident urges into my ears as we walk the length of the laneway to the base of the steps that lead to your front door.

We stumble a little; I catch you in my arms and you laugh, a kind of half-drunk giddiness that only lends to the pounding in my chest. You sense it because your hand is suddenly and all at once resting against the fabric of the shirt stretched painfully across my pectoral muscles; I'm grateful it didn't land lower, for fear of stretching and muscles and *elsewhere*.

My eyes catch yours in much the same way; in the half-second it takes to acknowledge that I've just saved you from falling we kinda both do,

fall,

because the other half of said second is spent with my lips against your lips for the very first time.

I'm thinking that

maybe you kiss as good as you look

or

that I'm disproving the whole 'friends' thing as passionately as I possibly can

or

nothing,

at all

because I'm kissing your lips with the kind of certainty and totality and finality of a man who never need kiss other lips, ever again.

It's a *first* kiss and it's a *fuck-friends* kiss and I press all of the tension and the longing of too many moments without kisses in them into *it*, kissing as hard as I can and mustering every technique I've ever used on the lips I've kissed that weren't yours and hoping like hell they're working.

And thankfully they are, because the only time you remove your lips from my lips is to whisper

"Take me to your place"

into my ear, there in the laneway of *your* place on the other side of the city; and I don't care if it's because you don't want your roommate to know or you don't want to bring me inside because I'm instantly back kissing your lips and separating only long enough to put you right back into the car you just so-magnificently climbed out of.

I tear through the city streets, a man possessed; you hold my hand and whisper sweetness and kisses into overly receptive ears, and

fuck a ticket

because I'm relatively sure that the sooner I get you to my apartment on the other side of the city, the sooner I can get back to kissing those pretty pumped up pretty little lips.

…

First Times, Tiny Terrors.

You're over, and we're dancing—not literally, (because, as the readers will discover later, I'm painfully clumsy) but we're moving, and our body language tells-me-without-telling-me that tonight is going to be *the* night.

Which is terrifying in its own right; terrifying because you look the way you look, and you look at me the way you look at me, and there's a *humming* between us and it has nothing to do with the wine.

Which is *red* the way I'm learning it will *always* be, and you're wearing red and moving in that dress and in between sipping and kissing I'm tasting red and maybe seeing it too; your body against sheer material rendering me *bull*.

And the china shop, tonight, is my tiny apartment—which you're kind enough to *say* you love, and maybe it's because you love me and the apartment just kind of comes with the deal.

Either way, there's music and movement and *that energy*—palpable and crackling and consuming, and we are too,

and almost too much wine for the evening to continue the way it has been, so you agree to sleep over and I agree to sleep on the couch.

You're not in that bed and one of my T-shirts for two minutes before you beckon me to join you, and it takes me two to collect myself and crawl in.

And, cruelly, there's movement as you slide your body tight against mine, and maybe time itself stops long enough to recognize that it's a perfect fit.

*Now, there's a cadence to a Colombian accent when the voice attached to it goes soft—a lull, a siren's call, one that I'm sure many a man has fallen victim to.

I'm under your spell, matador to my Raging Bull when you show your soft side, and make me promise not to touch you; touch you more than the everywhere I'm touching you as you lie as close as you can, big bed in an otherwise tiny apartment.

It's raining outside and I can't hear it

and it could be raining inside and I can't feel it

the throbbing in my head and somewhere south so loud I can barely hear myself when I whisper

I promise

and close my eyes, content to just be holding you there.

And maybe you close yours too, and maybe it's perfect for a moment or a minute or ten—

and, maybe if this book had a happy ending, this chapter would end right here.

You open your eyes, after a perfect moment or minute or ten

and you move, kind of like the way you were moving on your feet and in that red dress, but we're not; we're in bed and intertwined and you're wearing my T-Shirt and nothing else.

So I'm DeNiro in that Scorcese flick again, and when that soft, Colombian accent tells me

"You can have it"

I only have a split-second to recognize that this could be a test because you made me promise I *wouldn't*.

"We shouldn't"

I offer weakly, because

we should

and I'm in love with you already and I'm trying to show you that

yes

you can trust me

when we both know you shouldn't

and,

yes

this means more to me than just tonight, too.

I'm playing the role of the good guy, and you're moving those hips in a way that only Colombians can, and it's

"It's yours"

softly

and I'm the opposite, lying there electrified and trying to show you that you mean *more*.

We're dancing again—three am or worse, and it's metaphorical, because you're testing me and dry humping me, and I'm remembering the promise I made you and trying desperately not to taste you.

So it's a tango, or some such thing, and it's violent

because I'm hearing

"You can take it"

but I'm feeling a pain in my penis from *not* taking it

--and it's the wine or the headache the wine birthed, but I'm slowly losing both the fight and the will to.

"You can take it"

again and again, and from honeyed lips.

And all at once I'm tingling in places I've never tingled before, and, if the lights were on, I'm pretty sure my skin would be the red of the dress you've beautifully tossed onto my bedroom floor.

After not taking it for a time too many, I remember that I'm not gay (not that there's anything wrong with it) and I take it the way I'm now pretty goddamn sure you want me to.

...

The next twenty or thirty minutes pass, and pass gloriously. We're writhing in between the sheets of my modest queen bed, exploring every inch of one another in the relative blackness of the bedroom; the bedroom that *should* be an office, save for the fact that my exercise equipment wouldn't fit anywhere other than where the master bedroom *should* be. You were kind enough to not point out the ridiculousness of my interior design sensibilities—these are the kinds of things I think about as I tear savagely into you, my mind fighting feverishly against the urges my body is bemoaning. I want to continue for prosperity's sake, and so it's

baseball

and

military presses

and

anything *other* than the rigorous bouncing of your bounciest parts, all in a maddening effort to keep from releasing into you the way I so desperately want to.

Below me you're appreciative, indicating with an incoherent moan/Spanish mix that, despite telling me that you'd respect me more if I didn't proceed—and then telling me what-the-hell-you-can—you're satisfied and in your decision to renounce our friendship and your first-date barriers. Really, how could such barriers hold—the tension between us had been building since the moment we met—and, as I vigorously work to release-*but-not-too-soon* said tension, I can tell by the taste of your kisses that the decision is celebrated universally.

We continue for a duration I can be proud of; once I'm confident you've climaxed and *again*, I return from my mental baseball and military presses sabbatical, fully in the moment and assured that, should I finish, I'll have done some of my best and most enthusiastic work. Hell, if I was capable of any sort of in-the-moment reflection, I might take note of how this is the perfect end to the perfect evening—instead it's kissing and again and thrusting and more and until the moment I remove and release, magnificently, and with the vigor of a man one-hundred-percent committed to the activities that summoned physical representation of the enthusiasm unquestionably felt.

You lie there, coated in the love I've so boldly expressed to and now *on* you; you ask for and receive another kiss before urging me down beside you, holding you in my arms and breathing an exhausted sigh of relief.

For a moment we rest—I'm half way into the first of what I assume will be *many* pleasant dreams--when a shrill cry cuts the stillness of what had been a perfect and perfectly magical evening.

All at once you're dashing from the safety of the sheets and my embrace and you're screaming at the top of your lungs.

I'm sufficiently horrified, half-asleep and half-convinced that someone has broken into my modest apartment with the intent of picking up where I had just magnificently finished off...in a flash, I'm moving still-waking muscles towards the door, so assured am I that a fight is about to inevitably ensue.

It takes a moment for my still-weary mind to realize that, to my lament, no one has entered the apartment…that your screams must therefore be directed at me. I throw the light switch in the corner of the room; the illumination causes you to cower even more into the corner on the opposite side of the bed.

You're wide-eyed and alert; your dark eyes scan me furiously and without the slightest hint of recognition. The shaking of your tiny frame against the bedroom walls fills the void your screams had just finished creating; you're trembling with such an intensity that the room is reverberating.

I approach you cautiously.

The look you flash at me from between the fingers you use to hide your features tells me that this is not a wise maneuver—I retrace the two forward steps I had so gingerly made, all the while assuming from the hole now filling my insides that

Yes

this is what being a sex criminal must feel like. As the fog filling the corners of my mind and memory continues to be obliterated, I desperately search my recollections of the past hour or so for any indication that the love we made was anything other than consensual.

I'm failing at this, memories of kisses and passion and more than one

You can have it

betraying the horrible truth of you cuddled in a corner and not my arms the way you just were, some ungodly hour attached to hours previously spent in decidedly better positions.

So I'm on the other side of the room and the bed that, despite your tears and your shaking, I can't come to believe is the crime scene. I take another half-step, but not before offering a

"Muneca, what's wrong--"

"--You're scaring me"

coming well before I plant the other foot.

You're doing your best to not answer me, still staring wild-eyed and wildly from behind mascara streaked eyelids, shivering with a ferocity that makes me feel as though I'm somehow the worst human being in a world historically filled with them.

I round the last corner of the bed on my way to you, suddenly ashamed of the nudity that I was—only minutes before—so violently proud of. My admittedly well-endowed member is all at once out of place and, due to the tentative rigidity of my approach and the angle at which you're contorted, disturbingly eye-level to you. I do my best to hide him from you, reaching out my hand in a way I'd attempt to free a raccoon from a garbage pail—admitting to myself that I wouldn't be surprised if your teeth bit into the flesh of my fingers.

You *don't*, mercifully, but you bat my hand away violently before returning it to cover the delicate areas I remember you *un*covering violently minutes before.

As I recoil in terror you rise on shaky legs, your eyes escaping mine and falling firmly to the floor you're doing your damndest to stand on. You say something, but it's small and it's hurried and it's indecipherable. I respectfully move around the first corner of the bed and away from you, saying, with all due respect, that what happened was okay and that you're okay and that I'm here to help.

You speak, louder this time, and *just* audible over the sound of your body shaking against both the walls and the relative stillness of the night.

"I have to go."

I pick up the little red dress you had strewn so recklessly onto the floor, extending my hand with the same resignation as the time previous; you snatch the tiny fabric in an instant and I turn my back to you—allowing you the respect to dress without my eyes upon you and allowing you the opportunity to hit me over the head should you so choose.

The blow doesn't come; instead you blow past me, escaping the violated sanctity of the shuttered doors here in the bedroom-that-should-be-an-office on the way to the hallway and the apartment door down it.

I remind you as gently as I can that I had driven you here—and that, should I be allowed a moment to collect clothes of my own—I'd be happy to escort you safely back.

"No, I'll call a cab"

is both the curt answer you give, and the last answer I want to hear, what with the relatively-rapey vibe you've imparted on me in the minutes since the hour we spent making completely consensual love.

Clearly, you're not up to debate right now, and so I hasten my efforts to find the pants I so desperately need to; collecting amongst the debris of blankets and semen and socks what I can only hope is my T-Shirt. I'm bounding through the French doors of the office/bedroom a half-step behind you, grasping keys from counters amongst assurances that I'll drive you home and happily leave you alone after if, *as I can only assume*, you're of the mindset that what just happened *hadn't*, or in some other fashion.

You acquiesce after subsequent and significant promises, and, as I close the door to the apartment that we had entered under the most opposite of circumstances, I'm confident that despite this writer's wild imaginations, I could never have envisioned our perfect evening ending quite like *this*.

…

You're quiet the whole drive home. I'll take it over the screaming, or the crying; I keep the radio on and low, hoping the ambient noise will distract you from whatever troubled thoughts are clearly still dancing through your brain. It helps, the sound from the speakers, to drown out the still-frenetic beating of my heart—as I navigate the length of the city to your place, I'm replaying the more-horrific events of the night over and over in my troubled mind.

And still coming up empty—in all respects—when trying to find one iota of inkling that the sex we were having

and having

and having

was anything *other* than consensual and mutually spectacular. Still, the dead of this night and the precarity of the situation I find myself in demand that I both take you home and, likely, never speak to you again, so I'm getting a head-start, silently listening to the radio and winding the roads that will lead you to the safety from me you seem to desperately desire.

The sun is rising as I pull into your laneway. I leave the car in park, the running of the engine a subtle indication that I am, in fact, prepared to leave you to the safety of your homestead should you so desire.

I'm not surprised that you do not immediately exit my car only because I don't think you're capable of surprising me more than you already have.

You turn, slowly, and your big black mascara-streaked eyes scan my face for the first time since the climax of the interaction I somehow mistook for sex.

Your lips part, and they quiver in the parting…but the words that finally fall from the space in between them betray both the quivering and the intent behind the drive home.

"I don't want to leave."

I'm in shock, *probably*—at the very least, sleep-deprived and squinting against the rays of a violently rising sun. I'm ninety percent sure I heard you correctly—I'm drawing breath to confirm when you wrap your tiny, tired arms around me and kiss me with lips that stop quivering, only when pressed against mine.

I take the kiss, if not your rationale; after a sufficient and sufficiently-arousing passage of time, I separate your lips from my lips long enough to ask,

against my better judgement

if you would like to return with me, all the way across the city we just finished traversing, and back to my place and the bed within you so desperately sought to escape from.

I notice that your seatbelt is still fastened only after you tell me

"Yes"

and that you'd like to return to the destination we just departed from; and then, with a dexterity that betrays the constraints the safety harness provides, you're reaching around me again and kissing me, here in the car that is still running in your laneway. I separate only after an exaggerated passage of time; outside my windshield, the sun has become a full-blown nuisance, railing silently against the still-ongoing adventure of the now-previous night. I take it as a sign, put the car in reverse, and drive as fast as the law will allow back to my apartment.

You hold my hand the entirety of the drive home; it's all the more impressive because the transmission is manual, and you don't break contact for one gear-shift. You're purring in the passenger seat, gazing at me with still-weary eyes and whispering the sweetest-Colombian-nothings I reckon I've ever heard. We beat the morning rush back to the north end of the city; by the time I reach the parking garage and rest what would surely be a *confused-too* car, your lips have found my lips again.

And they stay there, for the most of the stumbling up the stairs from the parking garage, crashing into walls and one another, expressing passionately and without unnecessary words that, despite the drama of the evening that preceded the morning we're tragically still-awake-in, we desperately want to be with one another.

I slam you against the door to my apartment, fumbling keys and tongues, having begun the unlocking of the door and the unhooking of your painfully-restricting bra simultaneously. For a moment I restrain myself, separating my gaze from your gaze just long enough to turn the key, giving you the opportunity to stop any unlatching deemed *unwelcomed*, my mind racing back to the events that withdrew us from the apartment we're about to enter. Mercifully, my right hand is encouraged in the unclasping—you writhe from both your tiny red dress and the bra beneath, your painfully perfect breasts revealed in the hallway my left hand suddenly can't turn the doorknob fast enough to escape from.

It's dark inside; thankfully and for the first time since the night we left in. You take my hand in yours and lead me directly back to the bed I so recently considered a crime scene, climbing between the sheets and urging me to follow.

I comply with the utmost sincerity, the only hesitation coming in the amount of time it takes me to feverishly remove my clothes and maybe my common sense, diving back into a bed that--had I taken into account the events of the last time I dove into bed with you--I might have reconsidered.

Instead it's

fuck it

and

fortune favors the bold

and

the litany of other things I tell myself in the time it takes to find you beneath those sheets, falling right back into bed and sex and ignoring the rumbling in the pit of my stomach that tries to tell me you might be trouble.

...

We're in Niagara Falls, at this Fancy Restaurant….

-and it's our first time away together

-and we've only been together for a couple of weeks and the weekends within them

-and you're wearing this little black dress that has every single person in the restaurant staring at you…and the words on this page are racing as fast as the thoughts in my head.

So I'm staring at you and trying not to drool and said drool has literally *nothing* to do with the waiter walking around us shaving from-the-bone meats of various fantastical flavors directly onto our plates.

I could give a fuck about the restaurant and the people in it and the food on my plate, so enamored am I by the sight of you and that little black dress. You're barely wearing it—so wearing it well—and looking at me with black saucer eyes that scream

I want to eat you

the way I thought I might want to eat anything *other* than you when we decided to come here.

That, of course, was before you changed into the little black dress that you're wearing so well; as the waiter comes by and shaves a fresh serving of bison onto my plate, I'm beside myself with thoughts that I may have to wait the painful entirety of this meal before I get dessert.

I'm waiting, and occupying the space between mouthfuls of fantastically-flavored meats with washings of wine and an occasional fit of small talk.

You're encouraging the more abstract of my thoughts, shifting your weight across painfully-too large tables and sending the fabric of your dress cascading across the landscape that is your painfully too-large chest. Your mouth, between flavorful chewings, tends to move in the telling of things you'd like me to do to you, and, had I any inclination that I could get away with even the more aggressive of them, you can be most certain that I would move to do so.

And yet the formality of a dinner in a restaurant full of people prevents me from doing even the most mundane of the entirely-not-mundane things you want me to do to you; and so we sit, flavorfully chewing and waiting for the tediousness of an extravagant dinner to pass.

It passes, mercifully, and after far too much food and far too much wine, we're up and moving through a restaurant full of people; all of whom are staring—some, slack-jawed—at the movements your lithe little body makes as you make your movements across the distance to the door.

And the restaurant itself might be moving—*as in maybe one of those rotating-restaurants that tourist traps like the tourist trap we're in tend to favor*; might be or might not be, in part because I can't recollect if the restaurant moved in the writing of this, and in part because, if it had, I wouldn't have noticed, thanks to you and that goddamned dress.

So the restaurant is moving or isn't moving and I could care less because

fuck this restaurant

and we're leaving to go back to our room; and our room can move or not move—it won't matter in the slightest.

We make it out the door before attacking one another.

Mercifully, the restaurant exits directly into the hotel we're staying in; this is probably for the best the way we're writhing against one another. Had we been out on the street, some asshole would surely either join in or call the police—and the confines of my slightly-too-tight shirt have any potential left hooks out of commission.

Until you rip me out of it the way you're trying/about to; I press you against the elevator door while we wait, my lips tracing your lips at least as emphatically as two bottles of wine will allow. You take the kisses on your lips with the enthusiasm I've become accustomed to—so much more enthusiastically, *thank you*, than any other woman I've had the fortune of kissing and emphatically. I'm pressing my lips and you're pressing your lips, and we're moving rhythmically and sensually and everything is perfect when you *suddenly recoil in horror*

(*?)
and

push me off you with the enthusiasm only just moments ago reserved for kisses and the closeness kisses demand.

"Joo bit me!"

or something equally nonsensical escapes the lips I was just consuming-and-not-that way; I struggle to hear your exact words over the thumping of my heart in my ears. Your tiny baby-carrot fingers move to caress the area-in-question, accentuating the already-over-verbalized point you've so eloquently just made.

Admittedly, I'm not of the most rational mind at the moment, but your tiny baby-carrot fingers—despite the description—and your pretty pumped up pretty little lips, *while appetizing*, are the last things I feel like eating, thanks in part to a stomach full of fantastically-flavored meats furiously digesting away somewhere below my crazily-beating heart.

So I'm one-hundred-percent sure that I haven't bitten you, *passions aside*, and you're still checking those pretty pumped-up pretty little lips for traces of blood that just aren't there, and, had we any witnesses, I'd likely have the police called on me, given the tenacity of your instantaneous fury.

I try to calm you, words like

"Baby"

and

"I swear to God I didn't bite you"

suddenly falling on suddenly-deaf ears; you're spewing retorts like

"What, are joo some kind of sick pervert"

and

"Joo like to beat women"

in an accent that, ironically, makes it kinda sound like

"Joo like to *eat* women"

which, I suppose, is what you're getting at anyways.

I do my best not to laugh at the absurdity of this—*recalling, unfortunately and all-at-once*—the chaos of our first sleep-over together; an incident which, until this point, was isolated in its occurrence and any subsequent warnings that you might be just-*kinda* crazy.

I have only a split-second to ponder the fact that this is the *second* time you've flipped the switch on me in a passionate moment…if and only because you're suddenly lunging at me, defying the physics of what appears to be an entirely restrictive tiny black dress. Your attack is admirable, if nothing else, for passion you put into the execution of it; the trained boxer in me (--thank you very much—) could easily slip the clumsy hook you wing at my head, but I'm still somewhat in shock, and so I take the hit just the same.

Your follow up—a time-honored classic digging of the fake nails into the flesh of my back—works wonders for wrenching me from the stupor the actions of the last thirty seconds have put me in.

It hurts like hell, and so it's my turn to recoil, moving away from you and the elevator we were supposed to be waiting for as it dings somewhere behind you, heralding a timely and welcomed escape from this hallway/warzone. I inch towards it, dodging the latest of your passionately-thrown but technically unsound punches; as you back into the sanctity of the elevator with the litheness of a lioness, I can't help but feel that your movements might turn me on, if you weren't moving to kill me.

Which—*the whole trying-to-kill-me-thing*—is kinda hard to overlook right now, black dress aside; I'm filled with conflicting emotions as the elevator door thankfully traps us in privacy and unthankfully traps us in privacy. You continue your attempts to physically harm me—were I capable, I might appreciate your commitment to the insanity that is the notion that I have/would ever bite the lip I was so interested in kissing.

About four floors into our ten floor journey you realize that your physical attacks aren't achieving the desired results, and make an enlightened decision to focus once more on *verbal*. By floor six, I'm

"*a fucking loser*—I have to be seeing in public with Joo; take me to a fancy restaurant so Joo can show me off like a beeg (*big) man and then beat me—

floor eight has me labelled a

"sick fucking boy; not even a man because-a-man-doesn't-fucking-bite-the-woman-he's-supposed-to-want-to-protect."

I'm in the corner of the elevator, hurting and likely bleeding underneath the most expensive and tightest dress shirt I own; wincing from attacks just-passed and still happening, (verbally,) and wondering just what the hell is precisely wrong with you.

By floor ten I'm convinced that this is

"FUCKING OVER"

the way you've just screamed it in my ear; the door to the elevator opens and you're cannonballing down the hallway towards our expensive and just-rented room.

I'm a tentative ten steps behind; still reeling at the (second) revelation that this incredibly…interesting…relationship may very well be over for the second time in almost as many weeks. You're through the door to our room after a successful emotion-conveying slam; I'm still in the hallway and already mourning the death of passion I've admittedly never felt before.

For good or bad, and, as I cautiously turn the knob to the door of the room you're raging behind, I'm shocked (--for at least the second time tonight--) to realize you've not gone to the trouble of locking it behind you.

I peer into the darkness of the room with the caution of a man expecting a knife to the eye. It's silent—a miracle considering the voracity of your voice in the more-public of areas we've just retreated from. As my eyes adjust to the pitch, I find myself still not entering the room, despite the ever-increasing berth I allow myself. I'm half-in and wondering if you've jumped out of some window—I've certainly never seen such darkness and silence in your wake. I squeeze through the door and shut it tentatively behind me, all the while anticipating a lamp across the back of the head.

I'm thankful/fearful when it doesn't happen—danger averted, I realize that adrenaline still has my heart racing, and I'm standing, suddenly dumbfounded, in the darkness of the room you so violently disappeared into. You're nowhere to be found—at least in the hallway. My tiptoes are weighted by both the severity of the situation and the weight of my ridiculously-expensive loafers; I round the corner of an equally ridiculously-expensive hotel room, eyes adjusting to the pitch and the revelation presenting itself from the adjacent bedroom.

It is enough to land me flat-footed once more.

You're hunched in the corner, hovering over what I can only assume is your suitcase. The snarl on your lips—combined with the body language of your stance—is wholly reminiscent of an unsuspecting raccoon discovered lording over a mound of trash in someone's garage. Had I been in possession of a flashlight, I'm entirely sure that your pupils would aggressively reflect any illumination cast upon them.

Meaning you look scary as fuck, and I'm suddenly aware that I've just trapped myself in a secluded hotel room with a woman who now has access to potential weaponry. I appreciate that, while this area is decidedly bigger than the elevator, it's either out the door or out the window, and so—recognizing the futility of reasoning with you—I begin a slow and deliberate retreat.

You indicate the fight isn't over with a tenacity that—should you suddenly sprout horns or start foaming at the mouth—wouldn't surprise me. I'm dodging hateful words in half-tongues and expensive Christian Louboutin shoes; by the time the second one you were wearing explodes off the door behind me, you're crossing the distance of the room in my direction.

I'm suddenly sorry that I hadn't bit you and kinda wishing I had—and subsequently killed you—because the low center of gravity you hold on your approach has me feeling that it's either gonna be you or me. I brace, fully expecting the worst—knowing that I don't have time to escape into the relative sanctity of the hallway before you and your wrath are upon me.

The attack, I'm amazed to discover, doesn't come. You fly past me, carried on metaphorical wings of artificially-sourced and completely unjustified rage; the door behind me explodes, illuminating light from the hallway you disappear into, shoeless and exacerbated and breathing fire.

I collect myself, there in the darkness of the hotel room you've left behind. A flip of the light switch and a quick glance into the corner you were so recently cowered over reveals the contents of a half-stuffed and still-present suitcase…head swimming, I come to the conclusion that you're leaving isn't representative of *leaving*, and for good.

Meaning you'll still have to come back to the scene of this particular crime—crime because it kinda is, and that we've ruined (for the second time in as many weeks) what could have been something special.

I'm left to the hotel room and my broken and still-being-collected thoughts, recounting through the din in my head the events that have led me here—alone and battered and probably bleeding and confused and, to my abject horror, realizing that I somehow still kind of *want* you.

…

The doorknob turns, shattering the stillness of the room like a bullet from some passionately-held gun. Time has passed—how much, I'm not yet aware; judging by the remainder of the hotel room mini-bar whiskey I've been into, enough to cast the events of the evening so far into decidedly warmer light.

I rise, unsteady because of both the whiskey and the feelings the need for the whiskey created, prepared to fight or argue or hear about how I'm an asshole for letting you leave the room with no shoes or about how you're leaving which-would-be-kinda-difficult-because-we-drove-here-together or anything, really, other than the

"I love joo"

that you drop like an atomic bomb upon entering the room.

I've been drinking, and so I question it, watching you walk the length of the hotel room towards me, wondering if I heard you correctly and wondering if I should be raising guards both figurative and literal.

Your face, illuminated by the soft light of the living room that has remained on since you took off, betrays no malice or hatred or scorn. Hell, your features are softer than the bed I'm still sure we won't be sleeping on tonight, big saucer eyes burning straight through mine with a different kind of intensity than the intensity you displayed on your way out the door that closes softly, too, behind you.

You approach without caution or malice—I rise on shaky legs, mind still reconciling the chaos of the evening, circumventing pleasure and pain and longing and regret. Your lip, you should know, looks perfectly fine—tasty, yes, and yet I'm adamant that I have never chewed on it.

It moves again—the tastier of your lips quivers as it repeats the second most shocking statement of the weekend.

"I love joo."

I'm reeling, rising to meet you as you make your way to me. I'm far too tired/confused/hurt/in shock to respond the way you want me to; had my wits been quicker to return to me, I may recollect hearing that Latin culture is decidedly warmer than the cold Canadian attitudes when it comes to the claiming of such powerful emotions.

They're gone, my wits—and I'm left defenseless and standing in a hotel room with you on our second weekend together; a weekend where you've already broken up with me, again, before returning to claim your love for me.

Which is *intense*, second weekend or seventh—but I take it like the kiss that comes, full-bodied and full of the kind of passion such a statement deserves…and in the moments that follow, the taste of your lips has me forgetting all about the what-should-be-omnipresent fact that you're certifiably insane.

Because

fuck it

I'm in love with joo,

too,

and I paid a lot of money *that-I-don't-really-have* for this hotel room, and the whiskey is telling me that we might as well make the most of it.

…

You're beautiful at 2,400 feet.

We're in a Airbus H130 Helicopter, somewhere over Niagara Falls and—despite a life-long fear of flying—I could care less about the danger. Or the scenery.

Or anything, really, other than the wild look in your eyes, looking at me while you should be looking out the window, too, thank you very much. You're beside me in the backseat of a flying shoebox, careening over the precipice of one of the most beautiful/dangerous wonders of the world, and neither one of us could give a fuck.

 Had I been paying attention, I might have noticed that I actually *don't mind* helicopters—something to do with a foolish semblance of control, being able to see over the shoulder of the pilot and out the windshield. I'll reflect on this later, sometime after we land what I had initially perceived to be a sure-death flight; a sure-death flight I summoned the courage to embark on, not wanting to appear weak in the eyes of a strong and strong-willed Latin woman.

Those eyes are still locked on mine; the pilot is saying something into the microphone of his headset, and what he's saying is probably being broadcast into the headsets we're both wearing—and what he's saying probably has something to do with the unmitigated splendor undoubtedly unfolding below/all around us—but we're oblivious, staring at each other and radiating palpable sexual tension. We kiss, there in the back of the Airbus H130 Helicopter—*instantly my favorite class of helicopter*—and we spend the rest of the overpriced flight enjoying one another's company. I'm sure the pilot doesn't mind—something to watch other than the Falls for the ten thousandth time—and so we give him a show, writhing on top of one another in a way that, were another passenger on board, might give cause for concern, the way we add to the sway of the tiny cabin at 2,400 feet.

And this is relevant for a number of reasons. The events of the afternoon, in the moment, telling me that our romance is unlike anything I've experienced before--the whole not-caring-that-I'm-deathly-afraid-of-heights thing registering in my recollection—and relevant also for the fact that our second Airbus H130 ride would promise to be *nothing* like the first.

...

Your boss is an asshole.

I'm genuinely excited to see you.

Genuinely, reflecting on how fortunate I am that our initially professional relationship has turned decidedly personal, racing to pick you up from your boss's house before spending the night at your place.

It's the best idea in terms of how to spend a Tuesday night in forever; I'm navigating side-streets behind your house, looking for street signs and finding it fortunate that his house is only three and a half minutes from yours.

Fortunate because I can't wait to spend time with you; I'm expecting you're equally enthusiastic, already bracing for the now already traditional jumping-on-me-from-the-doorway you've taken to commencing our ever-increasing nights together with.

I'm not thinking about how odd it is that I wouldn't just meet you at your place, given the geographical proximity; I'm not even dwelling on the fact that your housemate Gatto, third former fiancée and your boss are all allegedly best friends and a part of the festivities I'm to interrupt.

No, I'm uncharacteristically not pessimistic pulling into the laneway of a man you spend all-day-every-work-day with; a man you've told me you even dated for a lengthy period of time, back in the day, *way back when.*

So I turn the car off, approaching the front door to the admittedly lavish home with the knowledge that you've had intimate relations with two of the men on the other side, and that you *just* live with the third.

It's still all nervous energy and excitement coursing through my body as I reach for the absurdly ornate door knocker; my anticipation outweighing a probably-growing admiration for the wealth this man clearly possesses.

I knock politely but with the confidence of a man who has arrived to take his woman home…

…and I wait.

And wait.

And *wait*.

The night just kind of settles in around me; I reckon I've been standing and increasingly *un*-politely knocking for three and a half minutes. I'm pulling out my phone to triple-check that I'm knocking on the *right* opulent door, reading through a text chain to discover that I *am* when three little bubbles appear, indicating that a response/reason-as-to-why-I'm-still-waiting is coming.

So I wait

and wait

and, after another tiny eternity, I read

just come in

across my screen, the

out back

that follows throwing the first of what has already probably been *plenty* of red flags across my consciousness—my hypothetical and probably-shouldn't-be text back might read

If you knew I was waiting at the door why the hell didn't you come answer?

I open the heavy, opulent door-knockered door, and am immediately assaulted by the sounds of some horribly dated song by some horribly dated artist. I understand why you couldn't hear me knocking for the past three and a half minutes—were I not distracted by the extravagance of the surroundings I suddenly find myself in, I might marvel at the efficiency of the home's sound proofing.

I can vaguely make out figures on the other side of a heavily-tinted sliding glass door; focusing on the opposite side of the room *totally* a near-impossibility, the pounding of the bass from the truly-horrible song blaring from unseen speakers is proving steadfast distraction.

Plus, there's a plethora of furniture to avoid crashing into; expensive-looking but horribly mismatched furniture. I recall you telling me that Humberto has become something of a career bachelor, divorced and happy and, allegedly, very popular with professional, similarly-stationed females. This explains his distinct inability to decorate; stepping down into the sunken floor of the living room, I'm tiptoeing around two gaudy coffee tables while glancing at the extra-douchey ornamental swords displayed on the adjacent wall.

Admittedly, the scene and circumstance has the hairs on the back of my neck standing; appropriately electrified by the frivolous beats and the perceived *alpha*-ness this abode and it's owner appear so desperate to project.

A trio of opened and to-the-last-drop emptied wine bottles on the kitchen table adds to my growing sense of uncertainty; I know you love your wine—and, given the forecasted personage I'm set to find on the other side of the rapidly approaching glass door, I guess the volume isn't *overly* concerning...save for the fact that, as a whiskey guy, I'm entirely mistrustful of grown men who sip wine.

(There's an honesty to drinking whiskey—an honesty unfettered by social decorum and erudite ritual...*I'm drinking this because I'm a man and I'm drinking this because the purpose of doing so is to be drunk.*)

Admittedly, my lineage might lend itself to such inclinations, but I'm resolved by the knowledge that my Irish-Indian ancestors are looking down on my from the heavens and smiling when I'm sipping something decidedly stronger than the swill that filled the three bottles I pass on my way to you.

I reach the sliding glass door as the horribly dated song reaches a horribly executed crescendo; heaving a sigh, I tell myself that I'm anxious for absolutely no reason, reminding myself to relax and give you and the situation the benefit of the doubt—

--and then I open the sliding glass door to see you sitting on your boss's lap.

...

Before I get into an overly-descriptive analysis of my feelings at this particular moment, allow me to elaborate on the macabre scene unfolding before my unblinking eyes.

Time freezes, *appropriately*, in between beats of the snare drum on the still-hidden speakers.

You're *kind of* wearing a sheer red dress—the kind previously reserved for dinner with me at restaurants I can't afford. My brain tells me that the fabric separating your healthiest endowment from the fabric of what I presume to be Humberto's ill-fitting khakis measures one-eighth of an inch; the blood rising to boil in my ears agrees with the across-the-deck measurement.

A still time-frozen analysis of said distance assures me that a healthy lunge, combined with subsequent placement of my bodyweight across the front-landing foot means my left jab could hit his fat face at the exact spot his jaw connects to his skull—with minimal chance of affecting you, perched as you are upon him.

It takes everything in my power to *not* react; the blood in my ears catches the rhythm of an unfrozen but still-slow-motion snare drum as I continue my tactical assessment.

Now, having never met the man—only hearing a now-making-sense amount of stories spoken from your *shouldn't have spoken them* lips, and having witnessed his atrocious display of perceived masculinity, I know with one hundred percent certainty that the instant and all-encompassing target of my savagery is Humberto. The other two men, seated together on a room-for-more picnic table on the opposite side of the deck, are decidedly beta and obviously Gatto and Former Fiancée number Three.

Gatto is easy because I've met him; he appears slightly concerned, as though rational enough to understand this situation probably isn't the *best* one, as far as *meet-the-other-important-and-around* men in my life.

The very lean, very tall and ruggedly-handsome-but-not-nearly-enough-to-be-relevant gentleman sitting beside him? He looks entertained by my arrival, but--thankfully for him--not in a threatening, *take this motherfucker* kind of way; no, Former Fiancée number Three has *always a good time* bewilderment written across his features that fits your previous description of a lack of appropriate cunning.

So he gets a pass—if and only because you're not sitting on *his* lap with a

Hi baby, this is perfectly normal/acceptable/why is that look on your face

look on your face.

So my focus isn't on Former Fiancée number Three and his ruggedly-handsome-but-last-years-model-rather-talk-to-the-sliding-glass-door I've just unfortunately emerged from

--hell, my focus isn't even on you.

My focus--and the totality of the murderous rage thundering rationalities in my taking-suggestions ears—is your boss.

Humberto, my instant and instantly-forever nemesis.

I catalogue the totality of his features in that moment—although concussions have rendered my facial recognition software irrevocably destroyed, the burning hatred pounding war beats into my ears tell me that I'll never forget his face and the look on it *right now*.

He's grinning/leering at me, all

I've got your girl sitting on my lap

his smile big and white and annoyingly perfect—as though his clearly deep pockets have allowed for the kind of immaculate veneers that *almost* make up for the other obviously lacking areas. He's rotund; from behind your *a-little-too-arched-back* I can make out the curves of his *wealth belly*—the kind big and round enough to be off-putting to any woman not blinded by the dollars in his bank account.

I know that hitting him to the body would clearly be a waste of time; my instantaneous, rage-filled tactical analysis has me wanting to perform emergency dental surgery on those perfect teeth. The rest of his face, crimson no doubt in part to the copious amounts of wine he's clearly consumed, emotes violently; his cheeks seem to jiggle as he laughs at some joke I've clearly arrived too late to hear. The soft lighting of the patio glistens off of the must-be-expensive moisturizer adorning his forehead—from this distance, it's impossible to discern where the product ends and the perspiration begins. He leers at me with heavily hooded eyes; heavily hooded and *telling*, both clear sign of his verified-by-interior-décor Portuguese descent and an obvious love for Botox--not even the slightest presence of bags underneath or even a *single* crow's foot adorn his somewhat oily visage.

He's *competition*, this man, her boss; although he's not a quarter of the physical specimen I humbly pride myself on being, he's not hideous--as far as portly, sophisticated older men go--in possession of a full head of *no doubt* Moroccan oil infused hair and a bank account that bends my net worth over and fucks it in the ass.

So I stare at him, this smug motherfucker, for what feels like an eternity; you *almost*-gyrate on his lap comically/tragically unaware that I have entered the man's home without the respectful decorum of an introduction or even a smile.

It takes you a full five seconds—about ten seconds too long—to rise from your undoubtedly warm resting place to greet me. Whether you realize it or not— and, truly, it is tragic either way—a primitive dance has already reached climax; the young, threatening male has invaded the band, only to be faced down by the aging silverback.

I've seen this shit on the Nature Channel a hundred times; as you sway your ample hips my way, the red of your barely-there dress captures my attentions the way it captures theirs, too, making the once-imminent punching of your boss/apparent sugar-daddy less and less a foregone conclusion.

I curse your pretty pumped up pretty little lips and the effects they have on me, still resolved in my intent to catch an assault charge on Humberto's porch. As you move said lips violently against mine I can't help but feel some of the blood pounding in my ears head somewhere just below my waist, weakening my resolve and sapping my strength.

It's *sorcery*, the way you soothe the savage beast, separating your lips from my lips after a prolonged duration, as though illustrating to the other prospective primates that you've made your mating choice. The demonstration just enough to keep my trembling rage contained, I somehow allow you to hold one of the hands better suited for punching, lead me to an empty spot on the bench between Former Fiancée Number Three and the grown ass man you *just live with.*

You proceed to sit on *my* lap, the warmth radiating from your ample bottom adding silent, further insult; through the sheer fabric of tonight's barely-there dress, I can feel the suppleness of your big fat Colombian ass as it envelops the fabric of my pants, settling over them, warmth no doubt generated from your previous resting place atop *his* pants.

Gatto breaks a chain of wildly-irrational thought, reaching out to shake my still-trembling hand with a different kind of warmth; the kind that greets me sincerely and pretends earnestly that

no

there's nothing strange about the situation I've found myself resigned to.

I turn from my right, and Gatto's warm/familiar face, to look left, and at your milquetoast Former Fiancée Number Three, who offers me an introduction and a sufficiently sincere handshake of his own, continually de-escalating his threat possibility, which settles somewhere around *just-the-idea-of-him* levels.

He smiles, I kinda smile, and it's nice—although the idea of spending any time with two out of three *that I know of* men you've bedded or let bed you, I can't really think of a nicer/less threatening duo.

Humberto, however?

I maneuver a maelstrom of your luxurious hair, straining to fix my stare on his fat, fed face through your ever-shifting presence astride me, and the follicles that threaten to annoy my attempts at intimidation. You settle long enough to un-obstruct my vision, the totality of which settles with laser focus back on the man sitting solo across the patio.

We kind of quietly assess one another for what feels like a small eternity; had I the ability to focus on anything else, I might notice that in my peripheral vision, you're chatting rapidly with equally-oblivious Gatto and Former Fiancée number Three. I might marvel at how you could have no sense of the impending danger, no comprehension of the silent battle of wills unfolding before your very (inebriated, clearly) eyes.

I might marvel at many things—your comfortability with the awkwardness of this whole goddamned situation notwithstanding—and so I'm almost grateful for your lack of interruption, focused as I am on my latest-greatest mortal enemy.

I'm not smiling

and

he's not smiling, anymore, and since you've left his lap

and

the ritual of polite introduction that allowed greetings to Gatto and cordial 'hellos' to Former Fiancée number Three has vanished, replaced by the kind of palpable animosity I'm accustomed to.

And *welcome*—I pray that, in the moments to follow, Humberto opens his fat little face to mouth something decidedly mouthy; something to justify the violence I'm counting on, something to bring to sudden end the dance of uncomfortable platitudes we might otherwise engage in.

I understand the importance of establishing boundaries during this—first, and, likely *only* meeting—already resolute in my intentions to never lay eyes on this bastard again.

Aside from the inevitable trial, should I catch an assault charge the way I'm sure I'm about to; this pompous ass is most certainly the type to call the police after losing a fight he started.

I'm okay with it

and

he's okay with it, and so we continue staring, jaws clenching and unclenching for dramatic effect as, somewhere on top of me, you begin addressing me in words I can't/don't care to hear.

This continues, unabated, for an altogether *uncomfortable for everyone else* length of time; on either side of me, the two other men on the patio, sensitive to the instinctual anxiety such silent warfare stirs in our caveman DNA, suddenly fall silent, attentions paid to the standoff unfolding before them.

You, unfortunately, remain blissfully unaware, swilling sips from a dangerously-close-to-empty wine glass, while regaling me with tales of what a wonderful friend the bastard I'm skull-fucking with my eyes is.

I can see the corners of a smile testing his once-resolute expression; by the time you extend your now empty glass dramatically his way he's practically laughing at me.

He bellows something about a celebration and heads for the sliding glass door, doubtlessly scrambling to open a fourth bottle and extend the torture this evening has quietly descended to.

I bite my tongue dramatically and, in my least-dramatic tone, urge you that

"It's getting late"

and

"We really should be going"

trying my damndest to maintain the façade of a polite guest *not* about to commit murder.

You hush me with some

"It's not even ten"

retort and, instantly, the blood pounding in my ears suggests making the forthcoming homicide a *double*.

I'm opening my painfully clenched jaw to argue viciously when Humberto stumbles back onto the patio, a freshly-uncorked bottle in his left hand, an additional, empty wine glass in his right.

This motherfucker must be joking

I rationalize as he extends his arm and the glass in it my way; he's practically tipping over top of me and muttering something along the lines of

"It's rude to deny a toast as a guest"

and smiling that

Fuck You

smile.

I take the glass reluctantly, waiting for the bastard to spill as he casually unloads the contents of the bottle into her glass, and then Gatto's, and then Former Fiancée number Three's and then, finally, mine.

He disappears again, something about wanting *more*, reemerging after a prolonged and lengthy absence with a fifth bottle, uncorked and immediately drained into his glass before proposing a toast

"To good friends and new people."

I toast because I *have to*, feigning politeness and clanging my glass against his with decidedly more force than the others before pressing my lips to the edge and emptying the contents with one determined gulp.

You're looking at me obliviously as I rest my now empty glass on the table surface behind me; I'm doing all I can to suppress my rage as you initiate conversations I have no interest participating in. The fifteen minutes it takes for you to finish your latest glass are filled with Humberto's humble recountings and of how much money he made with his company last year and of how he can't wait to sell *last* year's Jaguar to buy this year's.

The men marvel at stories they've no doubt heard before, offering platitudes and sharing specifications for a hypothetical vehicle I'm relatively sure neither can afford.

You chime in, something about buying a Range Rover this year, and the way Humberto tells you he'll take you shopping has shivers dancing the length of my spine.

There is something decidedly odd about the totality of this situation; that your employer—who you used to date—owns a house not five minutes from yours; that you're obviously comfortable sharing inebriated evenings following full days together; that you're making arrangements to shop for ridiculously expensive *essentially-just-overpriced-Fords* with a man who is appearing less and less a boss and more and more a *Sugar Daddy*.

I'm piecing it all together, here on the patio you've tricked me into spending time on—how you came from the magical land of Colombia to work at a restaurant cleaning tables with no English and managed to be hired on by an Engineering firm with only a barely-comparable Spanish certificate—how you were able to enroll in a Civil Engineering degree program at our local University while working full time as a Project Manager; how you seem to be able to come and go as you please, visiting job sites in a hardhat while wearing the kind of outfits that *just don't go with it.*

Yeah, I'm officially creeped out by your connection to this man; as he pontificates about his greatness, pouring the contents of bottle five into his rapidly emptying glass and reaching for yours, I've decided I've had more than enough merriment and revelation for one night.

I stand firmly and on sober feet, ushering you from atop me with motion belying my intent.

I offer a wholehearted

"Nice to meet you"

to Former Fiancée number Three before embracing Gatto warmly; my

"It's getting late"

a statement he agrees with, indicating that he'll see us at your/his place soon.

I move to shake Humberto's hand only because etiquette dictates I should; as I extend my arm I am entirely satisfied in the knowledge that I will never step foot on this patio again.

After a prolonged delay, the bastard takes my hand—I feel the sweat from his palm as we attempt to out-alpha one another, each gripping and shaking as forcefully as we can.

"Nice to meet you, _____"

he offers through gritted teeth, deliberately getting my name wrong in an attempt to show me just how little I matter.

I say nothing, the

I'm probably going to kill you, you fat fuck

coming from my stare and the tenacity with which I grip his plump sausage fingers, doing my best to feel his bones grind against the strength I've spent years in the gym honing. He outweighs me by at least one hundred pounds, but in this respect we are equals—we spend the next fifteen seconds shaking hands/hurting one another, neither willing to be the first to wince/disengage.

You interrupt us by throwing your arms around him, the act of which steals both his attention and the power in his grip. I watch your breasts smother against the meat of his shoulder, threatening to spill from the fabric of tonight's sheer red dress and feel my rage hit pre-wine levels; your body blocking the majority of his girth the only thing that spares him an assault.

I mock thank him and for ruining my night, moving my hand from his grip to your shoulder, doing my best to collect you as you stumble to stand.

You're drunk

and

I'm furious

and

as I collect you

I'm careful to escort you over the ridge the track from the sliding glass door makes as I open it, laying eyes on the front door and the freedom on the other side.

I'm close enough to taste it, having said goodbye earnestly and separated ourselves from the chaos of the patio; I'm about to lead you into the sunken floor of the living room when the music—still playing horribly douchey/dated party anthems from unseen speakers—rises to earth-shatteringly annoying levels.

You *squeal* as if on cue, separating your hand from my hand and turning to face Humberto, who—after following us from the patio—is grinning like a madman, clutching a small device which can only be responsible for the filth assaulting my ears.

He's exerting his dominance over you again, said song forcing you to stop leaving his home, and, apparently, commence dancing scandalously in the dining room.

The only thing more horrifying than watching you gyrate in a sheer red dress in front of your boss, Former Fiancée number Three and *the guy you just live with?*

Watching you gyrate in a sheer red dress *with* your boss, in front of Former Fiancée number Three and *the guy you just live with.*

You grind with him to the beat of some horribly douchey/dated party anthem playing from unseen speakers; were I able to divert my gaze from the horror unfolding before me, I might look at the front door before walking right out of it the way I desperately want to.

I'm thinking of leaving you and *here*; probably better off just getting in my car and driving across town to the sanctity of my apartment.

I curse my weakness, watching the curves your body takes as it grinds against the portly, sweaty mass of another man; my vanity and ego and lust making me a somewhat willing prisoner to your exotic wiles.

If you weren't the single most goddamn beautiful woman I've ever seen then I would be free of you, escaping into the night with the comfort of knowing that you're crazy and intertwined with some other man and maybe I'm not crazy because I managed to realize this and get the hell out.

So it sucks that I am, crazy and stuck and in the knowledge that I am not free of you, and may never be; watching you dance in the dining room of some place I thought I was just picking you up from.

By the time you the music reaches a truly-horrible crescendo Gatto and Former fiancée number Three have made their way into the living room, intent on both saying goodbye and refilling their already empty glasses, no doubt tired of missing the action from their former vantage point on the patio.

They look almost as astonished as I am, having thought we would be at the *gathering our things by the front door* stage of leaving; clearly the impromptu dance session has taken them by surprise—though, diverting my gaze from the horror unfolding before my eyes, they don't look *surprised*, as-if-this-has-never-happened-before.

It takes exactly twenty-seven gyrations for me to realize the bastard dancing all up on my girl has won—effectively emasculating me by way of bewilderment. My fists are clenching and unclenching, *yes*, but despite the blood pounding war beats into my sonically-assaulted ears, I lack the movement necessary to retaliate.

This kind of violence untoward me simply does not compute; I have no database of appropriate reaction. So I watch, cuckolded, as my girlfriend (?) finishes her *essentially pre-love making* ritual with the fat bastard whose living room I'm still trapped in, one of three witnesses to what can't be unsettling only to me.

It *ends*, I think, because suddenly I'm at the front door awkwardly putting on my shoes. To be honest, I'm not quite sure how I got here; a quick glance back at the living room/scene of the crime tells me that I have not painted the walls with their blood. I'm moving forcefully and with purpose, I realize; I pull my left sneaker over my heel so hard I'm momentarily afraid I might fall over, somewhat relieved to be afraid of something other than going to prison for killing you both the way I kinda want to.

As I reach for the door I'm certain I don't really care if you're following me or not, overwhelmed as I am with blind rage and a new emotion I'm acutely aware I've never displayed before.

My hands are shaking as I reach for my car door, having exited without another unnecessary word or glance behind, I slump anxiously into the driver's seat, only aware that you are in fact joining me by the sudden and entirely unwanted presence materializing in the passenger's seat. I squeal the tires on my exit from Humberto's too-long laneway; over the admittedly soothing sound I hear your voice, and the tone the words within are carried from tells me that the five minute drive to your house will be the longest of your motherfucking life.

…

It's a night of tension and horror and horrible things.

We fight, on the way back to your place.

I hear the latest of many colorful names you call me, in and around justifications for the actions I've just witnessed.

I call you many colorful names also—it is, after all, the first time I've really understood deep down that you're just not a good person.

It's also the first time I realize that, when it comes to you, I'm insanely and completely something I have never been with anyone else.

"Jealous"

you point out, right before

loser

and

insecure

and

not gonna waste my time with a thirty-two year-old child who can't understand that he's my bess

(*best)

friend,

etc.

I'm driving erratically and firing back just as, realizing with a right hand turn that, if *jealousy is a green-eyed monster*

then I'm motherfucking Swamp Thing.

(Worth a google.)

We pull into your laneway exactly six minutes and two-hundred-forty-seven insults later, and, as you unbuckle your seatbelt, I have every intention of watching you walk up the driveway and out of my life forever.

My blood is pounding rhythm to the insults you're still firing, and yet I curse my eyes for following your hand and to the unfastening of the seatbelt subtly suppressing your suppleness.

This, I realize too late, is a mistake as your wild eyes catch mine, tracing the path along the perfectness in that sheer red dress.

You smile, in between swears directed at me, and motion me to follow when you exit the vehicle, pausing suggestively as your healthiest asset leaves the leather of my seat.

All of a sudden and against my better judgement I'm following you up the laneway, freewill stolen by the sway of your hips and not unlike the manhood I know I'm about to work tirelessly to take back.

...

Expectations.

I wake in the wake of the mess we've made.

The sun assaults me relentlessly from the sliver escaping your blackout blinds; you lie uncaring around me, uncovered and covered in the testament to my manhood I spent the last *every* hour of the night creating.

I'm mad that I'm not mad at you, after last night's vulgarities and the subsequent vulgarities we performed to erase the taste of them; as I writhe out of bed, I do my best to collect myself and without waking you.

I'm reflecting on my way to the washroom, relieving myself and angry, still, at the reflection in the mirror of a man burdened, relief limited to physical and not emotional. As I wrestle with my crumpled jeans I'm wrestling the thought of leaving, weakened by your sex and the revelation of my jealousy and the cage it seems to have created.

I stumble into the shared living room, eyes still strained from entirely unforgiving sunlight, suddenly aware that the shape walking towards the living room from the opposite hallway isn't a shape at all, rather Gatto, himself stumbling, though clearly hungover from wine and not literal and metaphorical wrestling.

We make uncomfortable eye contact; uncomfortable because everything this early *is*, before proceeding silently to the kitchen and the waiting coffee pot within.

He breaks the silence after pouring two cups and offering me one—reminding me that, when it comes to other men living with you, I could do no better than the one sharing the kitchen and the relative peace of the morning after whatever the hell last night was.

"Sleep well?"

His smile betrays the fact that he can clearly see I have *not*; my smile back is without cynicism and reflects apology for the noise we've made.

"Not bad, you?"

"Enough to know I need more."

"I hear ya"

in between sips of coffee, keeping my responses short and my draws from the cup long.

"Mico, I'm glad you're here"

he offers, before offering the admittedly astonishing list of expectations that follows.

"Coffee…is something that Muneca *loves* in the morning."

I look to the drying rack for a clean mug.

"No, no…she hates instant."

I look at him, confused because instant is what he's prepared, and instant is what we've congregated here in the kitchen to consume. I'm not crazy about it either, but it's here and it's hot and it's coffee.

"She loves a Starbucks when she's getting ready for work."

Great, I think, eyes falling from Gatto to the *today-it's-instant* mug on the drying rack.

I assume the words that follow follow Gatto following my gaze.

"You know, now that you're in the picture, she's going to expect that morning Starbucks comes from you."

I look puzzled because the words he just spoke are puzzling, and because it is far too fucking early for anyone to be insinuating what Gatto clearly is.

"What's wrong with instant?"

I ask, swilling down the remainder of the cup for dramatic effect. I'm careful to sue my least-confrontational tone, having had my twenty-four hour fill of conflict on Humberto's porch.

He gives me that

Have you not met her

look, before enlightening me with her order, some ungodly complicated union of caffeine and sugar and syrup, following *that* revelation with

"and once a week, you should go gas up her car for her; you can leave it running for her when you get back."

"With the coffee."

"With the coffee."

I have to remind myself that I genuinely, really, truly *like* Gatto. The act of remembering has me swallow that last sip of coffee hard, the bitter taste at the back of my throat only partially attributed to the not-great blend.

Not that great, but good enough for us *common* folk, apparently, fuel for the journey to the only good coffee good enough for the princess still sleeping peacefully in her wing of the house her boss probably bought for her.

"And, if you could—in the winter—have it running for an extra five minutes or so…she likes it warm."

"She likes it warm."

If he senses the sarcasm escaping from between my gritted teeth, he doesn't let on.

"She'll be getting ready for work soon"

he says, patting me on the shoulder and shooting me a

it's your problem now, motherfucker

look before leaving his dirty mug in the sink and turning to return to the bed her demands have kept him from for the time between fools like me.

…

"What's *this*?"

she asks between bats of the eye she was batting, glancing from the mirror she was getting ready in and waving unceremoniously with the hand holding the mascara. My experiment, manifested in the mug of instant-kitchen coffee my hand is reaching to offer, has just confirmed/reaffirmed my ever-sinking suspicion.

Gatto wasn't kidding

and

you're an evil motherfucking monster.

You give me a *didn't you talk to Gatto* look; a *didn't you talk to Gatto* look that tells me without telling me that his little pep talk this morning was pre-meditated.

My head is suddenly swimming, drawing conclusions the way you return to the mirror and the drawing of your smoky eyes—I'm wondering if the buffoonery of the night before wasn't pre-meditated also, a test of sorts for my tolerance and my patience and my sanity.

Which must be leaving or gone—my sanity—because I don't

leave

until you bat those newly-smoked eyes my way and ask me *pretty-please* to surrender and go get the coffee everyone in this house but me knew I'd be going to get.

…

I'm walking down the laneway, having stopped only to turn on your car—not *take* it, mind you—as I head towards mine. Bathed in the harsh reality of the harsh morning light, I'm realizing that, if there really is a loser and a winner in every relationship, then I'm about to cop my first of the former, turning over engines and realizations that leaving this laneway and not coming back would be the single smartest thing I could do today.

I return, Starbucks in hand, some twelve minutes later.

Other Girls and The Complications Other Girls Bring.

She says her name is

Sugar Baby Sousa*

and she's everything you're not.

*Real name redacted—I'm moderately sure, after dating for two years and breaking up only once, that she won't sue my ass…still, she's Sugar Baby Sousa for the sake of this book and because that's what I really called her.

She smiles at me, from her perch on the same seat at the same desk you sat on when I met you, and while her

"Hello"

doesn't kill me the way yours did, the warmth in her smile is appreciated nonetheless.

*As you could guess, she joined my gym, and, as a thank you for joining my gym, Sugar Baby Sousa was offered an assessment with a particularly suited and questionably-professional assessor; unlucky for us, that assessor was me.

She's young and you're a little older than me and she's a brunette and your hair is as dark as your soul can sometimes be and she's got these big green eyes that radiate the kind of innocence sucked from yours years ago.

Now you'll tell me she's fourteen but when I ask her it's

"I'm Sugar Baby Sousa and I'm nineteen"

right after

"Hello, I'm Mico, it's nice to meet you"

and right *before* I lead her to the same office I led you to, once upon a time when the world made sense.

And as I close the door behind us, fully intent on performing the assessment required of my job and honestly nothing else, I'm completely unaware that I'm about to add another dimension to our already-doomed love story.

...

The Only Thing I Love more about You than You

There's a fucking Range Rover parked in your laneway, and it—taking the place in my heart and mind previously held by you—is the single most beautiful thing I've ever seen.

We broke up about a week ago; something to do with my jealousy over your relationship with Humberto (and, admittedly, my vocalization of a desire to murder him--) and something to do with your jealousy over the fact that there are *other* females employed at the gym.

The details, really, are hard to remember, reconciled as we are, and arriving to the laneway previously inhabited by your shitty little Volkswagen Golf, my recollections are distracted by my outright envy.

You failed to mention that you'd previously purchased a new vehicle in our *let's get back together* conversation over the phone; your invite-me-over did little to illustrate that a *whole lot*, apparently, can occur in my absence.

The details are lost on me as I circle what has undoubtedly replaced me as the bright shiny new toy in your world; it's *this year's* model and it's the *Evoque* model and, although it may or may not be simply and overpriced Ford Explorer, it's a visual representation of wealth and success and status—three traits I'll admit I envy about you, too.

So I'm slack-jawed and staring, circling the gorgeousness that occupies the space that shitty little Golf *used* to, and I haven't even got to the *it's-kinda-weird-that-Humberto-took-you-to-get-this-and-most-likely-co-signed* part when you emerge from behind your front door, keeping the storm clouds tickling my frontal lobe at bay with a flash of your perfect Colombian smile.

It's *almost* the most beautiful thing I've ever seen, your smile—and certainly enough to pull me from the outright admiration of your manifested superiority. You're on me by the time I reach the stairs to your open door, and, were it not for my honed physical prowess (about the only thing I'm proud of, having exited my Honda Civic in the laneway beside your overpriced little chariot) we might have toppled back onto the concrete I'd had such a hard time leaving moments ago.

Your kiss tastes like anxiety and enthusiasm, and I'm flattered by the tenacity with which you press your lips against mine—so much so that, when I finally move mine to catch up with you in ways *not* physical, I fail to ask how—and who helped—you attain such a prize in the only week absent my otherwise ever-present influence.

I muse that your manipulation game is as strong as your hips when they move against me the way they move against me, and in ways that have me forgetting how to muse anything, at all.

So it's less Humberto and his highly-suspect helpings and it's less about fights I can't remember and the weeks apart they resulted in—and it's more about the way you move in the darkness we find ourselves in, having ran past introductions to Gatto on the way to the lights-off blackness of your bedroom.

We spend the foreseeable future there, apologies and statements of just how much we missed one another always physical and never vocalized. We save that for later—the talking thing—over coffee consumed amongst scattered sheets, laying in the wake of the latest mess we've made, catching up in exhausted and somehow still-excited tones.

You tell me about the process of picking out the exorbitant toy in the laneway, carefully leaving out mention of the bastard who sponsors your life when you tell me about how the Porsche just didn't quite feel right and of how the Mercedes *just wasn't pretty enough.*

I listen intently and between sips of bitter coffee, trying my best to scan memories of the last week that could have come close to holding water with closing multi-million design projects in and around shopping for supercars.

I come up short, and so it's just head-nods and

uh-huh's

picturing in my head what you must have looked like sitting in some high-end dealership office, letting some man that *isn't* me and *is* your lover to every single sales manager negotiate the deal that *I couldn't anyways*—the one that landed the fucking Range Rover in your laneway.

So I swallow, bitter coffee and my questions and maybe my pride, telling you honestly when it's my turn that my week away was mostly just work and missing you.

You listen intently, feigning interest amongst kisses and reiterations that you've missed me, too—allowing me to finish my not-half-as-interesting stories before parting your pretty pumped up pretty little lips to tell me

"My parents are visiting next month"

the latest and, hopefully, *final* revelation of the catch-up, before informing me that

"we need to take them somewhere special."

. . .

We're in Niagara Falls, at this fancy restaurant.

And I can't help but wonder if we're not just returning to the scene of the crime; although it's a different fancy restaurant, with a different hotel attached and a different hallway connecting the two, it's kinda exactly the same as the last fancy restaurant, the one we left to commence fighting in, fighting over phantom bites and leading to proclamations of love.

You're wearing a distracting and distractingly similar little black dress—and although I know enough about fashion to realize it is entirely different, the result is exactly the same. Every single person in the restaurant is staring at you and *again* and, although your eyes are remaining on mine, mine can't help but wander…

…because the difference *this time*…aside from the room I can't afford and the car I can't afford we drove up in, is that there are two *other* sets of eyes to engage with tonight.

So my eyes move from yours to fall on a couple of sets of eyes entirely similar and yet different in the tenacity with which they look back at me…similar and yet different because they belong to

Madre

and

Padre

and

they're looking at me as though they can't understand one fucking word I've been saying since I met them.

Which of course they *can't*, having arrived directly from the magical, made-up land of Colombia earlier this afternoon, armed with a week's worth of luggage and absolutely no comprehension of the language they're to be immersed in over the next seven days.

We picked them up in Toronto and headed directly *here*—at some hotel I can't afford with no concrete plan other than the initial two nights we're to spend, in town and at exorbitantly priced restaurants just like this.

I suppose it would be unfair to say that you bamboozled me into this—having hastily planned their impromptu visit during our week apart and then magically reconciling just in time to have me help pay for it…hell, you innocently insinuated the Humberto had originally agreed to help shepherd them around Ontario, batting those big black eyes and not understanding how that could possibly bother me.

I wasn't in the picture, you reminded me, before assailing me with kisses and assurances that they had heard all about me and would be excited to learn that I would be joining them on this little vacation.

I suppose that I wouldn't want to confuse them—as the latest man in your life, it's only natural that any support come from me and not your de-facto employer/overlord. So I took it as a chance to gain back ground lost to that bastard in the week I let him slime his way back into your life *more than he usually is* and your laneway *because I'm still pretty sure that Range Rover is at least partially his* and, hopefully, nowhere else.

Like your legs and the space between them, the space you let me repossess in between promises I could drive your Range Rover *here*, to the hotel restaurant I find myself sitting absolutely fucking bewildered in.

Among the many things I don't quite understand?

Your dad looks like a *white* guy; meaning entirely, one-hundred-percent Caucasian. Now, prior to meeting him, I guess I just kind of assumed that everyone from the magical, made-up land of Colombia looked just like you— gorgeous, sure, but with those dark, unmistakably Spanish-almost-Native-American features—so much so that, when you started shouting and jumping up and down in the *Arrivals* terminal of the airport, I assumed the white guy walking towards us and waving back was just some dude you knew.

I learned with the first words coming from his lips as he hurried to hug you that this wasn't the case; the man's Spanish sounds even more immaculate than yours. Sitting across the table from him, smiling awkwardly and nodding my head in mock-understanding of every syllable he annunciates, I'm still amazed that you came from this man.

He's an absolute delight to be around, for one thing—heavy with the hugs and the hands on shoulders and the pretend-to-understand head nods of his own. Even on your best days, you fail to radiate the kind of warmth emanating from Padre's white-as-fuck features; I'm bewildered by the totality of this occasion, yes, but I'm sure of one thing—you did not receive your temperament from him.

Madre, on the other hand…

She's just like you.

Unmistakably so; a beautiful woman with similar dark features, she's sitting diagonally across the table from me and radiating the same palpable unpredictability that has become your hallmark.

I catch her watching me cautiously; scanning me with her saucer-black eyes, up and down and unsure, surely, of whether or not I'm the last or merely the *latest*.

She smiles pleasantly enough, and pretends to listen when I attempt to communicate with small words and grand gestures, but about the only thing not lost in translation is unmistakable feeling that she's not *sold* on me yet.

I kinda can't blame her, having sat as she has at expensive dinners on expensive trips *just like this*, diagonally across the table from boys and men engaged and not and betrothed to her oldest and most tempestuous child, each undoubetldy

the one

and

the one

for a period of time, only.

So she's reserved like the table we sit at, staring at each other awkwardly between your attempts to translate first dinner conversation/interrogations, which come between collections of the collective attentions of everyone else at this expensive restaurant; dressed as you are in some stunning little black dress.

If Madre has concerns as to your almost nudity, she doesn't vocalize them; your gestures and annunciations drawing attention and still *less* than the heaving bosom that heaves when you gesture them. Padre seems to have suggested, in Spanish and with a motion of his own, that it's cold in here and that you might want to cover up with the shawl currently warming the back of your chair— you brush him off with a smile and a batting of the eyes you've batted at me on dinners when I've suggested the same.

I'm used to it, the violent display of your beauty that comes with meals out together—if I'm being honest, more than a *little* of me appreciates the perfectness of your form, in public or not.

You're noticing I'm noticing, and it's doing something to both your smile and the suggestiveness with which you lean forward towards the table; beside you I'm stealing glances at your breasts and then scanning the room to calculate the assortment of husbands and boyfriends and fathers doing the same.

It's pretty much *all* of them, by my last count, but it kinda *doesn't*—count— because I'm the only one with your hand rubbing against the fabric of suddenly too-tight pants, sitting increasingly uncomfortably across the table from your hopefully oblivious and thus-far approving parents.

I'm about to attempt a sure-to-fail communication, laced with all three of the Spanish words I know, when you speak matter-of-factly to Madre and Padre, moving your hand as abruptly from my lap to motion me out of my chair.

I excuse myself as politely as I can, taking your hand and using the free one to dive into my front pocket, ashamed and hoping to hide the ever-growing evidence of what you were just up to under the table. Suddenly I'm following you, bewildered, and burdened by the surging uncomfortableness brushing against my trousers, traversing the restaurant floor towards the exit and— hopefully—the exploration waiting outside.

We explode out the double doors; I can tell by your pace that the elevator is your intended destination. You mouth something about

"Going to get a sweater"

and I'm halfway through

"but you had one on the back of your chair"

when your pretty pumped up pretty little lips explode across mine, making the finishing of sentences as entirely unnecessary as the trip back to our suite we're about to make.

I understand by the time the doors to the elevator open; falling into the thankfully-empty-wouldn't-matter-anyway box, I know that—since we're sharing said room with your parents—this little excursion represents our only opportunity alone together.

I am determined to make the most of it.

…

The room is dark when we enter it; the soft glow of a single bedside lamp the only assistance offered as we navigate a pile of strewn luggage. We move as one, unable to separate excited lips and tangled limbs. My ever-increasing education in the subtleties of little black dress clamps pays off; I'm relieving you of the restraint and freeing your ample curves as we traverse the length of the twin beds.

As you moan something that sounds deceptively like

"We need to go back downstairs"

I turn your face from mine and press your naked body against the pane of glass extending beautifully from floor to ceiling. Your resistance fades as I enter you roughly, words more like sounds as we perform for whoever might be gazing at the façade of the building, some thirty-something floors up.

I take my time, moving rhythmically and then not, taking out frustrations built by weeks apart and the fights that caused them.

There's a violence to our sex, an understated understanding that this time— like last time and the time before—could very well be the last time. In this, if nothing else, we are in agreement; expressing physically what we both seem to continue to fail to verbalize.

I pull your hair for emphasis; hard and almost *too* and the pitch of your startled reply betrays an appreciation for the aggressiveness. And so I continue, for longer than I should, the thought of bewildered parents waiting increasingly impatiently only adding to the force with which I attack you.

I'm thankful for the durability of floor to ceiling windows as I finish, having satisfied and appropriately exhausted you/expressed myself; we take a moment to catalogue our entirely disheveled appearance in the reflection of the glass. You retreat to the washroom, utterings of needing to fix the state my fuck left on your hair and makeup—I remain by the window, hoping a tuck and a pull will return a look you spent the last *too many minutes* destroying.

You're half-frenzied emerging from the washroom, makeup fixed and yet not, searching the half light for the remnants of your dress. We've been gone, by your calculation, for almost half-an-hour—entirely too long to leave your poor parents waiting to order a dinner that could have come and went by now. Still, you're smiling as you pour yourself into a more-wrinkled-than-it-was-when-we-left micro-dress, the thrill of our indiscretions weighed favorably against the horror of our absence.

You're ready far faster than I've ever seen, forever betraying your past and future proclamations that such perfection takes time. I take your hand, leading you out the door and back down the elevator and across the restaurant floor and to the table with your appropriately puzzled parents; realizing only after sitting down that the sweater we left to find was left behind.

...

Your parents won't let us share a bed.

Which, I suppose, is understandable—from what you tell me, they're traditional, meaning—until you're *actually, officially, honestly-for-real* married, their Colombian voodoo faith (so, Catholic) will prevent us from cuddling under sheets we'd prefer to ruin anyways.

I'm sure that returning to dinner and smelling like sex didn't help our case—so, as we return to the shared room/scene of the crime, I'm at peace with their decision. More at peace than I would be, had we not spent the better part of the evening trying to push one another through the thirty-something floor window; glancing at the glass, a full stomach and an hour removed, I swear I can still see the fog your breasts created against the reflection.

We compromise, after ten minutes of terse negotiations I'm nowhere near involved in; your parents acquiesce to letting us sleep relatively *near* one another. You take the other bed, and I pull up beside a makeshift and not-as-uncomfortable-as-it-sounds-cot. When the lights finally go out, we're holding hands across bedsheets and the gap between, falling to sleep under watchful eyes and thinking for the first time in weeks that maybe

--just maybe

--we might make it the way we both desperately pretend we could.

...

You're an asshole at 2,400 feet.

We're in an Airbus H130 helicopter, somewhere over Niagara Falls

again

and, despite my anticipation to recreate the magic of the last time, all I can think about is an overwhelming desire to throw you out the window.

Which would be difficult from my position in the backseat (*we shared the last time*) given that you're currently up front with the pilot.

Who has his hand in your lap, laughing and joking with you in English over the headsets we share…which is relevant because I'm sharing the backseat with your parents, who don't understand a word of the language.

Which kind of negates the whole *we-had-such-a-great-experience-last-time-let's-share-it-with-my-family-when-they-visit* the way they are

visiting

and getting absolutely nothing out of the supposedly informative, supposedly multi-lingual pilot currently quasi-molesting their daughter in the front seat.

So I'm in the back and enraged, and enraged quietly—not wanting to alert your unfortunately oblivious parents to the fact that the redness in my face has nothing to do with my previously described aversion to aviation. I listen to your laughter over the headphones and quietly rage, doing my very best to shoot your parents

This doesn't suck

looks between looks at your lap and his hand in it.

I'm having flashbacks of that first night at your boss's house; and starting to see a disturbing trend…I spend the next five minutes rationalizing a rather violent fantasy of throwing the pilot out the window.

Your parents are either oblivious, or—more disturbingly—used to this sort of behavior; they alternate looks out the window with incoherent yet well-intended wordings towards one another.

I do my best to remain calm—I even allow myself to appreciate the splendor of the falls from our vantage point—until you reach your tiny little hand out to playfully slap his shoulder, laughing in tandem to some whispered joke we in the back are apparently not privy to. This sort of fuckery continues, unabated, for the duration of the fifteen-minutes-feels-like-forever flight.

By the time we land I'm ready to blast off; my face undoubtedly the crimson painted on the side of the Airbus H130 you scamper from. But not before giving a warm hug to the pilot—the pilot who shoots me a cocksure grin before beckoning us to exit the helicopter; exit the helicopter so he can quasi-molest the next pretty young thing who dares sit beside him.

I do my best, again, to hide the telegraphed anger painted on my features; I'm either remarkably-and-for-the-first-time successful, or you just don't care as you make your way off the tarmac, suddenly remembering your parents and embracing them amongst declarations of how much *better* this helicopter ride was than the last one.

Revenge fantasies dance amongst my thoughts as we make our way to whatever tourist-trap restaurant we make our way to; you're doing your very best to ignore me and my seething rage the duration of the walk to the table. You sit beside me for the first time today, yet your eyes don't make their way to mine—they're locked on the potentially oblivious faces of the family you converse with in a language I don't even pretend to understand.

So I sit, alone at a table full of family, the way I sat alone in the backseat of the helicopter I've quickly come to hate. For what *can't* be the first time in our already-tumultuous relationship I'm questioning my sanity for staying, and, quite obviously, questioning your sanity for continually exposing me to such thinly-veiled emasculations.

...

This One ends bad too

. . .

I'm under covers and attack, thrashing violently against the blows raining down from above. You've mounted me here in your bed, your proposal for getting undercovers masking your intentions, intentions now laid as bare as I'd hoped you would be, fully clothed and mock-assaulting me. We're wrestling and laughing, tickling and tackling and making a mess of the bed we both probably have no intention of sleeping in.

I can't reflect on the week that was, or the events that led us *here*, third Tuesday in a row without a fight more real than the fight we're fighting, not really fighting and enjoying the path our relationship takes in the absence *of*.

So it's entirely without malice that, turning my body to avoid a particularly well-placed palming of the face, my hand—encumbered by the edge of the blanket covering my knuckles as I clasp it to aid in the assisted avoidance of your follow-up face wash—strikes you with a resounding

thud

across your beautiful face.

You burst into surprised laughter, falling from your mounted position atop me to lie across the bed, alarmed by the sound more than the significance of the strike we both know I had no intention throwing. I'm out from under the sheets instantaneously, attending to you and vocalizing between bursts of continuous and uncontained laughter that

"I'm so sorry"

and

"are you okay;"

apologizing for mock-assaulting you while making a defensive maneuver to avoid your entirely-intentioned and unrelenting mock assault.

You refrain from laughter long enough to kiss me with unblemished lips; giggling between maneuverings of your tongue and telling me without telling me that

"It's okay"

and

"accidents happen."

Satisfied and spent, you crawl under the covers and, with a flick of the lamp killing the only witness to the events that transpired, we drift peacefully to sleep.

...

Said peace lasts seven minutes.

You leap as dramatically as you can from the warmth of the bed, waking me from my just-sleep in terror, shouting incoherently in Spanish and flailing from the bedside lamp we'd agreed to kill some time ago.

I'm scanning the murdered darkness frantically, assuming that there must be a serpent in the sheets or a rapist in the on-suite, so angered are your wailings from beside the bed I thought we'd retired to.

I realize we're alone a half-second before your Spanish recedes to English, unrecognized vowels and consonants replaced with

"Joo motherfucker"

and

a barrage of colorful indignations I have unfortunately heard before.

"Joo heet* me"

(*hit)

hits me harder than you try to, swinging and for real down at my still semi-and-increasingly-not-conscious frame.

"What kind of fucking scumbag heets a woman"

you manage in between maneuvering your hand to check for swelling that isn't there and maneuvering your hand back towards my face and the intended swelling of it.

I'm dodging blows and accusations, scrambling to determine what I missed in between the alleged incident and the laughing about it and the kissing about it and the going to sleep peacefully and in agreement that it was accidental and *entirely*.

Still, in the half-light my squinted eyes can pick up the storm in yours, and so I'm out of and across the bed from you and the raging silhouette your naked form takes in the almost-dark.

"Baby"

in my most confident voice is how I start, treading carefully and choosing words *just as*, words like

"You were dreaming"

and

"we've been asleep"

doing little to calm the storm you're busy storming on the other side of the bed.

Had this been the first time you've leapt from slumber hurling outrageous accusations, I might have laughed off your wailings for the ridiculousness they most certainly are—my half-asleep mind recalls the insanity of our first night together, however, and so my tone is as serious as the situation I unfortunately woke up in.

"Get out of my fucking house"

here in your house at something just after midnight is the crux of the sentence you throw at me like the pillow you throw at me;

"Get out of my fucking house joo lowlife dirtbag before I call the police"

tells me that my night is no longer going to go as previously planned.

Foolishly—likely due to the half-sleep I'm probably still in—I offer resistance, my

"Baby, seriously"

sounding like

"That's right, I hit you and you deserved it, you fucking immigrant whore"

or something equally reprehensible to your *not-hearing-it-at-all* ears.

You pick up your cell phone in a flash, dialing what I can only assume is the London Police non-emergency twenty-four hour hotline; assume because the numbers you're pressing are decidedly more than the

9-1-1

I kinda figured you'd be picking up the cell phone to dial.

Searching for my pants in the half-light, I'm cursing Gatto for being at fucking Humberto's tonight; surely he would have had my back in this situation. His neutrality and rationality are sorely missed; especially when you graduate from pillows to once-bedside lamps, free hand fumbling for the next projectile as the phone on the other end says

"Hello?"

I figure this is my cue to leave, having known enough about Police procedure to know that, should a car be dispatched to your address, protocol demands they leave with *someone*.

So I'm half-naked and wholly bewildered, stumbling down the hallway to the door and wondering if you're bluffing, or if I can expect a knock on mine when I return home, sleep to be restricted to the cell they'll put me in, accused abuser because you've imagined it so.

I'm terrified the length of the drive home; the city streets are empty, my thoughts decidedly *not*...the time and the lack of sleep have me wondering if I'm more afraid of being arrested or the thought of not being able to trust your grip on reality.

I suppose it should be *less* troubling that this isn't the first time you've imagined aggressions and transgressions against me—and the storm passed somewhat peacefully before—but as I park the car and make my way up five sets of stairs to the not-quite-solace of my apartment, I suppose I'm really more troubled by the fact that this type of behavior is now officially a pattern.

So it's half-sleep and one eye on the phone resting *the-way-I'm-not-really* atop the bed stand beside me; waiting for the cops to call or the knock on the door to signal the coming climax to an evening that began with some perceived-innocent tickle fighting.

I'm picturing tickle-fighting with my cellmate, life ruined or at least tarnished should your delusional misinterpretation of fact lead me back on the other side of that door tonight.

I'm up for hours, waiting on a call or a knock that doesn't come—rising eventually for work exhausted and no less afraid some seven twelves on the clock later.

I spent the totality of the day that follows half-certain that I'm yet to be arrested and one-hundred-percent-certain that you think I could actually ever hurt you like that—again unsure of which is worse and wondering what it is about you that tricks me into believing this type of behavior is anything south of insane and anywhere near acceptable.

I wait a week on bated breath before daring to half-joke about the situation; answering the questions of friends and loved ones as to why I'm so miserable/disheveled/morose and still not fully feeling as though I've gotten away with the crime only one of us knows I didn't commit.

I respectfully listen to their collective urgings of

"Never talk to her again"

and

"She's going to ruin your life"

increasingly thankful as the days pass without arrest or contact; and then I think about the days without contact and the way your back arches in times of

contact

and so I do,

relieved/surprised/disheartened when you pick up the phone and tell me you miss me, too.

Relieved, because I really do miss you.

Surprised, because in the conversation and the conversation over the dinner that follows, neither of us mention the lingering abuse-elephant waiting patiently in the room behind us.

Disheartened, because even though I spend the night in the bed you'd banished me from one week prior, the last thought racing across a still-troubled mind is

this won't be the last time.

...

A Little More About Her.

Sugar Baby Sousa has big eyes.

Bigger than yours, to be sure—and while I can't imagine ever looking into a set of eyes and feeling *half* the feelings I feel when I look into yours—I admit, for the moment, looking into hers is kinda nice.

We're at the gym, and it's after my work hours, and I honestly just kinda ran into her on my way out the door thinking about you—thinking about our latest-in-a-series of never-ending breakups, wondering if I might be doomed to this kind of perpetual torture when

"Hey"

and a head-turn reveal Sugar Baby Sousa catching up impressively to my admittedly determined pace.

Sugar Baby Sousa follows with

"I've been looking for you"

and her words soothe the way her eyes *want* to; big and maybe *almost-too-big* and brimming with the kind of enthusiasm that comes with years and more specifically a lack of.

Meaning she's not bitter the way you're bitter—and you can blame it on her age—or lack of—or her experience—or lack of—but right now, following me in the gym and smiling at me with that smile and those eyes, you'd be hard pressed to blame me for smiling back.

It's a distraction and a welcome one, used to words like

"Go fuck yourself"

and

"Never gonna see joo again"

coming from the pretty lips attached to pretty girls, so

"I've been looking for you"

is a beautiful change of pace.

Sugar Baby Sousa follows me to the shake bar, and we talk about the kinds of things two people who are forbiddingly attracted to each other talk about—so nothing, really, just a series of polite and veiled flirtations masking the fact that we're both just sort of benefitting from the proximity.

I catalogue her features and the overwhelming differences to yours as we converse. The innocence in her body language contrasting the perpetual night in yours; a bounce to her kinda-red-kinda-auburn hair when I make her laugh at some anecdote I instantly can't remember reciting. Your hair, black and long and straight and mind-numbingly beautiful, only moves when you run your fingers through it, and you only run your fingers through it when you're nervous.

 So *never* in moments like this—moments without the weight of words worded in ways to wound the one listening like she is, and to every single one.

Her laughter betrays any hint of self-awareness; there's a slight *snort* on the end of it that is, instantly, stored away as classic in my memories. She bats her long, beautiful eyelashes at me, smiles in that distinct *the-world-hasn't-destroyed-me-yet* way her that age allows her to, and turns, confident that, should said flirtations run rampant, I won't be the one to.

She's wrong

and we'll get into that later, but for now *you're* the destroyer. As I leave the gym after watching her sway her ample hips away from me, I can't help but recognize that for the first time in what feels like forever, I'm thinking about an ass that isn't attached to you.

...

Christmas, and guess how it goes

It's Christmas, and you're spending it at my place.

Well, my parent's place—the place I've spent Christmas since Christmas became a thing—and it might be Christmas One or it might be Christmas Two.

I can't really remember and it doesn't really matter—all that I remember is that this is the Christmas my family learns there's more to you than impossible curves in impractical dresses.

It's going well, this Christmas, if I'm painting the picture accurately in my recollection; we've had dinner and we've had wine and we've had entirely too much of both—we're sitting in the living room and discussing the kinds of things families full of too much dinner and too much wine discuss.

I'm sitting directly between you and tonight's impossibly-fitting-Christmas-appropriate-red micro dress and my beautiful baby sister Dennis, and her beauty is appropriate both for the proud need of an older and equally-beautiful brother to brag and for the fact that her beauty is the catalyst to my parents discovering there's more to you than stunning intellect and ridiculous beauty.

So we're sitting on the couch and talking, and the talking is going the way of inhibitions, thanks mostly to the wine, and you're sharing stories of Christmas in Colombia and we're sharing stories of Christmas in Canada. And what starts as a healthy competition as to who's Christmases were more impoverished turns, in the tornado that is your ability to think rationally when drinking, into the observation that I'm teaming up with my beautiful baby sister and against you.

Sensing the gathering storm clouds, I endeavor to place my hand on the small of your back; I'm hoping physical contact will reassure you that, despite a tandem of assurances that we were in fact much more poor than you in our formative years, this gesture will prove to you that the conversation is nothing more than jovial, festive fun.

I'm agreeing with her, laughing at the memory of unwrapping kitchen pots and pans one year—well used and previously-in-home pots and pans—when the wrapping paper was the gift and household objects were repurposed expressly for the act of unwrapping—and I'm two semi-circles into rubbing your back when you disengage violently, your back from my hand, and shoot me a look that has my laughing-along Mom and Pop instantly not laughing along.

They're appropriately confused, playful banter having disintegrated over your reasonably-labelled look of utter disdain; their confusion exacerbated by your immediate removal, back and the rest of you in your Christmas-appropriate-red micro dress, from the couch we thought we were being mirthful on.

You offer a

"I'm going outside for a smoke"

more for their benefit than mine; important to note for the fact that you've previously expressed a desire to conceal your cigarette smoking from them (first impressions and all) and for the fact that you're about to venture outside, Christmas Eve in Canada, in the Christmas-appropriate-red micro dress you've just stormed off in.

They look bewildered, my parents, in the wake of the tiny little storm you've just stormed, storming somewhat quietly from the living room you've left us to.

Mom makes polite conversation, something about

"So, how's work going?"

or

"Can you believe the amount of snow this weekend"

or

anything

to dissolve the palpable tension created only partially from the too much red wine we now nervously sip on.

I'm mid polite-half-hearted retort when the violence of a text tone shatters the illusion of *not*-conflict we'd just worked so hard to create.

I attempt to ignore the electronic invasion, well aware that it's *you* and it's *angry* and it's going to preface the rest of the evening you're now intent on ruining— I'm another sip deep and about to talk snowfall when the second text rings through.

And then a third.

And a fourth.

In succession and angry, unread and yet not needed to be; implying with a sequence of volume-up blasts against the awkwardness of and awkward silence that this evening has taken the turn I thought the holiday would render impossible.

You're watching me through a frosted window; from over my shoulder I catch you peering with an almost comically malicious gaze; huddled the way you are and beside the opulent free-standing, palm-tree-shaped heater you huddle beside.

And while you're undoubtedly unhappy with your Christmas here in the countryside at my parent's house, you're at least a little grateful for my father's obsessive desire to turn his remote little acre and a half into a vacation-viable resort destination.

The crosswind, blowing snow and freely across the neighboring farmer's field, has forced your violently on-display curves to disappear, hidden behind crossed arms and a corresponding cross look, glowering at me warm and sipping wine and safe from your disdain here on the warmer side of the window.

I pretend I can't see you, slightly more successfully than the pretending I can't hear you, fumbling stealthily through the contents of my front pocket for the phone your tiny little baby carrot fingers are shaking to continually text. I don't want to give you the satisfaction of observing my reaction to your electronic assault from your vantage point, so the removal and screening of my phone happens at least as stealthily as two bottles of wine will allow.

Your first message, timestamped five minutes ago, is by far the most coherent; no doubt typed before the bitter cold of Christmas Eve in Canada defeated the heat from your Colombian temper. It's appropriately abhorrent and entirely unoriginal, calling into question both my loyalty to you and my manhood; a familiar series of colorful adjectives to illustrate your displeasure with my behavior.

Text messages two through five pertain to my sister; my sister and how my attitude changes in her presence and how it's disgusting how I flirt with her in front of you and how little you think of her and her makeup and her choice of outfit this evening.

Naturally, I find this the kind of insane it most certainly is; my reaction is tempered simply for the fact that I'm used to your particular brand of crazy. My baby sister, however—peering over my shoulder and reading decidedly less discreetly than I'm attempting to—has an entirely different reaction. She's the kind of appalled someone not used to these outbursts should be; her questions to me come as fast as your text messages, and shatter the illusion of normalcy I'd fought to maintain since you stormed off for a cigarette in the dead of night.

And so Christmas Eve is officially ruined—Dennis explodes from her position on the couch beside me, her reciting of your more incendiary texts has my mother swallowing the rest of her wine and my father pretending he's forgotten some suddenly pressing project in the basement.

I'm alone, living room on Christmas Eve, by the time you come in from the cold. Literally and not figuratively—the smug look you give me, sauntering back to your position on the couch beside me, betrays the mock sincerity in your voice when you ask

"Where did everyone go?"

knowing full well the answer, having observed the animated exit of each individual from your post by the resort-worthy stand alone space heater. Doubtless sensing that you've got me on the proverbial ropes, you decide to deliver your knockout blow; with a pursing of your pretty pumped up pretty little lips, you mention casually and between tobacco-tinged breaths that you

"Had to call Humberto, and wish him Merry Christmas"

because

"we usually spend it together"

and

"He's my family here."

This is, of course, insulting for a multitude of reasons—the fact that your exit was predicated by perceived jealousy over another female—regardless of the incredibly disturbing fact that said female is a direct blood relative—second only in temperature of affront to the fact that you abandoned my family on Christmas Eve to call a man who is most certainly *not*, all the while berating me with the kinds of texts that led to the empty living room we are miserable in.

. . .

More about Her, Less About You.

Sugar Baby Sousa doesn't understand.

"I don't understand"

she tells me, batting those big and *almost-too-big* eyes and looking at me with the kind of puzzled wonder I wonder if all *almost-out-of-the-teens* women look at men too old for them with.

"—you're such a nice guy"

I'm not

"and she's crazy and she treats you like shit and you keep going back with her. Why not find a nice girl? You're hot—"

I stick on this—the whole *'you're hot'* part—and miss the rest of the *equally-nice-but-not-as-telling* things she's telling me. We're alone in my office; Sugar Baby Sousa has come in for a workout that isn't, apparently, happening. Instead, she's talking earnestly and leaning over the chair beside my desk *just as*; and I'm trying to focus on anything other than the deep cleavage inches from my face and the sex in her syllables when she breathes them, words like

"So many women"

before words like

"die to be with you."

She's offering reassurances where none were requested; I tell myself I was simply in my office, just off the gym floor, working on spreadsheets or some such nonsense when she knocked on the door and asked already-knowing-the-answer if she could come in and visit.

I'll admit, I might have glanced at that ass as she walked by; fatter than it has any right to be, perky and youthful and resting on two legs with the kind of muscle definition that betrays a just-recently-finished adolescence undoubtedly spent on some soccer pitch.

She noticed me noticing, I'm sure, hence the deep cleavage and the aggressive leaning over my desk—breathing heavily and ensuring I appreciate the rise and fall and rise of the treasures not-so-contained beneath the shirt she *almost-* appropriately wears to the gym on the days with me in them.

I listen to her words and appreciate her body language; cataloguing the youthful beauty of her features in the manner I catch myself becoming accustomed to.

I've been loyal to you—despite the ever-increasing breakups and the admittedly unstable foundation our tragically whirlwind romance seems to be resting on— but, for the second time in as many visits here at the gym, I'm contemplating possibilities with what has to be your polar opposite.

She's youthful in both years and mannerisms, and you're not. She's Portuguese, you're Colombian. Her eyes are an ungodly mixture of blues and greens that invite staring—yours are vanta-black (*look it up) and reflect the darkness churning ever-perpetual behind them. She's genuinely happy to see me *every time*—meaning about fifty percent more often than you're happy to see me— and the conversation stays deeply rooted on the trivial, never cascading into the sorrow of your 'fucking-up-your-life' lectures.

She's short like you are—somewhere south of five-foot-five, and seeming shorter still because she's too young and athletic for the heels you constantly find yourself in. Her frame is suggestively developed in the fashion you've made me accustomed to; hips where there should be hips, resting atop long and powerful legs. Her lips move and there's a fullness to them in the moving; I'll admit to thoughts of tasting them, as she writhes suggestively in the office chair beside me.

Months ago—before the first of our constant and cataclysmic break-ups—I would have hated myself for even fathoming the kissing of lips other than yours—now, a grizzled veteran of at least three World Wars, I'm decidedly less hard on myself. So I enjoy both the company and the flirtation, laughing and *not* working and working on the possibilities of emotional infidelities with your polar opposite, resigned to the very real chance that you're done with me forever anyways.

We're in Collingwood

and we're at this fancy hotel in the middle of this ski resort village

and your parents are resting comfortably in a bedroom just a thin wooden door away

and we're fucking absolutely everywhere else.

Winter is raging outside our little chalet; inside, from our vantage point on the common room sofa and the stovetop and the kitchenette table and the spare bedroom bed and the bedroom floor, we're warm and sweating and still; when the fucking takes us outside to the balcony and the winter that rages all around us, we're as uncaring as of the threat that your parents could easily open that thin wooden door and catch us.

Maybe it was the

we can't

we told ourselves in the conversations leading up to the visit and the weekend away; knowing we would have to compromise our constant need for coitus in the presence of your parents, sacrificing sleeping together both figuratively and literally as per their traditional not-until-married views.

So they were to share the main bedroom of the opulent chalet we rented for the weekend; you were to get the spare room and I was to settle for the hopefully-pull-out couch.

Well, here we are, night one of a planned two, and it turns out the couch does pull out and it turns out that while we won't be able to sleep together we sure as fuck are *sleeping together*, already atop the pullout couch and the spare bedroom bed and all of the easily climbable appliances.

And maybe, sex position one on kinda-uncomfortable appliance one, we were the worried we should be and of your parents emerging from their supposed-and-probably-just-presumed slumber on the other side of the thin wooden door—by the time the position changed and the feel-good turned to feels-really-good we stopped worrying and thinking rationally the way we tend to when we're together.

So we're on a balcony in a blizzard, now, and the heat we're generating from the friction—combined with the heat from the bottle of wine we managed to consume in the moments after your parents disappeared behind said door--has us not shivering the way we *should* be, exploring curves and cervices lightly covered in the snowflakes we endeavor to dissipate.

We stay a little longer than we should, working to shatter the stillness of a winter night, while somewhere in the distance, tiny pretend people ski bravely down slopes we couldn't care less about.

This trip to Collingwood was for your parents, we told ourselves—that, by giving them a glimpse of the snow-covered, *this-doesn't-get-any-warmer-for-six-months-so-fuck-it-let's-race-straight-down-a-mountain-side-on-sticks* lifestyle Canadians seem so contented with, they might become enamored with the idea of you settling down with one, the way you've famously tried and tried and tried to.

I can imagine, between the thrusts I'm so diligently thrusting, that after cocaine cartels and curbside gunfights and the need to live vertically in order to avoid the dangers of habiting on street level, that we must seem a little *boring* here up north.

So we decided to expose them to the quaintness of chalets with steam-spewing chimneys, juxtaposed against the unspoken insanity of the double black diamond slopes I can kinda make out in the distance and in between the dutiful bobbing of your head.

And it might seem odd that I choose moments like this –inside you at least as aggressively as my admittedly impressive penis will allow—to ruminate on the maybe-not-quite-comparable craziness of Canadians with sticks in winter to the craziness of Colombians with straws in any season; but the shared love of powder keeps me from thinking about how fucking good fucking you here on this balcony feels, and I would prefer to keep going, as opposed to the hastened finishing your body urges me to. Still, I suppose the snow is accumulating in places I'd prefer clearly visible, and so my mind is back to the task at hand, lifting you the way I suddenly am and with the intention of carrying you somewhere both warmer and as of yet undefiled.

I cross the threshold to the interior of the chalet as cautiously as a naked and snow-covered and somehow still-performing man can; you're kind enough to remove wet and flailing strands of hair from my face so we can semi-cautiously peer into the relative darkness of the common area for signs of activity.

The thin wooden door seems to be closed and still; satisfied the way *wouldn't-really-care-at-this-point-anyways* couples coupling kinda get, we find a space on the counter right beside the can't-believe-it's-empty-already bottle of red and pick up where we left off on the balcony.

This continues unabated for the duration of the lights on the chairlift tiny pretend people in the distance and outside seem so content on riding; they blink out and the motion on the mountain is quieted long before I finish the way your body has been trying to make me. As we giggle excitedly and in tones lower than those our irresponsible wrestling created, we're scrambling for the clothes temporarily forgotten about against the stillness of a silent winter night, contented in the shared madness our proximity encourages.

We relish this—the can't-believe-we're-getting-away-with-it danger of utterly destroying a room we had no business utterly destroying; by the time you retreat to the pre-ordained confines of the spare bedroom we've exhausted the kind of romantic proclamations that can only follow the adrenaline spike our bad behavior caused.

So when sleep finally finds me, sprawled across a *thankfully* pull-out bed in the love-stained living room, I'm smitten with the idea that weekends away together—parents or not—can end the kind of ideal we'd imagined/hoped upon booking.

The big part.

"Let's go on a cruise"

you say

and, despite my better judgement, given the past year-and-a-half,

I smile and say

"Sure,"

thinking

What's the worst that could happen at sea, hopelessly trapped on a missile shooting through the Caribbean?

...

So that's where we're going,

The Caribbean,

leaving from South Beach, Miami after visiting some family (--because, aside from London, Ontario, Canada, every Colombian in the world moves to Florida--) with planned stops in San Juan Puerto Rico, St. Thomas and Saint Martin.

It sounds extraordinarily expensive and it is; as an admittedly poor fitness professional/starving writer, the idea of time off work and massive amounts of cash spent terrify me *almost* as much as the thought of being at sea with you. Still, we're hopelessly and tragically in love, and so I agree, and then I pay for a flight and a cruise I'm only half-sure I'll make it to.

Given the frequency of our break-ups; going into our second winter together, we seem to have settled into a three-weeks-on, two-weeks-off split, bookended by dramatic verbal confrontations and aggressive make-up sex.

Alarmingly, we make it to the night before we're to leave; no doubt buoyed by the excitement of time away together. Hell, we're laughing as we pack, tickle-fights and impromptu make-outs keeping me from acknowledging the anxiety already rumbling across my consciousness. It's late—almost two-am—and we're to be up and at the transportation service by six, before embarking on the two-plus hour bus shuttle to Toronto's Pearson International Airport.

Fueled by adrenaline and unquestionable physical attraction, we power through the minutiae of packing for a two-week vacation, finally wrestling onto the bed and lying in what I feverishly remember as an entirely tender embrace.

Meaning devoid of malice or malintent, which both informs and makes more tragic the events of the next two-and-a-half minutes.

I say something,

something that I promise-in-recollection was entirely well-intended, and, true-to-form, you take it as anything but.

Well-intended,

and the next thing I know you're screaming at me and calling me the names you *tend* to call me,

loser

and

poor

and

a complete and utter asshole; a complete and utter asshole who you want absolutely nothing to do with, and certainly not on the cruise following your richly-deserved family time in South Beach.

So we break-up,

really

and two-something-am before the six-am we simply had to make it to, in order to enjoy what I'm sure was intended to be a glorious vacation together.

I'm in shock and exhausted, taking punches both literal and metaphorical as we rage, twisted sheets and perspectives, in the bed we simply should have fallen to sleep in.

Three am and we're spent, the fight fought out of us both, lying and breathing heavy under the weight of the words we've spent the better part of an hour (-- an hour better suited for rest--) hurling at one another. You cry softly beside me, and I fall asleep, mercifully and *un*, to the cadence of your tear falls on your pillow.

…

We wake, exhausted and melancholy, and make our way silently to the shuttle service. Gatto drives (God Bless Gatto) and we do everything in our power to avoid his questions as to why both of our suitcases have been packed into the back of the Lexus but only *your* suitcases will be unpacked upon our arrival. You fidget with the radio in the front seat, singing along somewhat defiantly to the soulless pop song coming from the speakers, doing your best to deflect Gatto's carefully-navigated inquisitions as to our latest breakup. I just stare out the window, wondering what the hell I'm going to do with the two weeks I've painfully booked off, now that I won't be going on the painfully-expensive vacation I've got no business paying for.

We make it to the lobby, artfully dodging suggestions that we suck it up and vacation together, leaving Gatto to the car and his frustrations with us as we walk, unsupervised, towards the reception area.

We're still not speaking to each other, but the attendant gets our warmest

Hello

before the

Yes, only one of us will be travelling today

assuring her that

Yes, we understand that we're still being charged for two passengers—one body or not.

She shoots me a disappointed look,

the attendant,

reminding me in hushed tones that I really ought to make the trip, *what with having paid for it and all.*

I simply smile, fully aware of the crazy I must seem, as my used-to-be-significant-other bashfully turns away in the bashful way she's mastered, somehow making it appear to the attendant that *I'm* the asshole she spent the better part of two-am calling me.

We walk, still silently, to the waiting area and Gatto, now waiting dutifully alongside your bags, in the general vicinity of where my bags *should* be, had I been making this trip the way I was supposed to.

He gives us a moment, Gatto does, before returning to the vehicle he'll wait to drive me home in, unquestionably among the things I'll miss the most about this entire tragedy I'm one

Goodbye

away from ending.

I move my eyes from Gatto and, as my head settles from the nod I've just thrown him, I find yours for the first time since the latest war began.

They're cloudy somehow, your eyes, and the saucers that pretend to be your pupils well with *must-be* tired tears. I feel something dangerously close to resignation rise from the hole where my stomach used to be—it takes everything in my power to refrain from crying the way you look like you're about to.

The fights seem to drain us more than they used to; you're still soul-crushingly beautiful, but there's no denying the sadness has beaten your gorgeousness into submission this morning. My eyes betray my intent as I part my lips to say

Goodbye

the way the script demands I do; despite myself I'm unable to contain the

Don't go

written across my stare. Admittedly ashamed and entirely confused, I bend to lift your suitcase for you, allowing the frustration to fight the resignation on the fingertips suddenly encasing the plastic of the handle. My eyes don't move—don't move because they can't—locked on yours in case better judgment wins the day and I'm looking into them for the very last time.

The attendant interrupts, pushing a trolley and beckoning I place your lonely luggage atop it; it's difficult, but I manage the placement without breaking visual contact. You turn to leave—as much as can be allowed without leaving my gaze, and move your pretty-pumped-up pretty little lips to mouth

Goodbye

a half-second before that first tear falls from your painfully dark pupil.

Every sad song I've ever heard plays in the space between my ears, and I watch you walk away for the one-thousandth time, standing tall and fighting tears until you're seated on the shuttle and then removed from my vision entirely.

As I make my way to Gatto (God Bless Gatto) and my lonely ride home, I'm thinking less about unpacking my suitcase alone in my apartment and more about how, despite the latest war, I'd much rather be unpacking my suitcase beside you in South Beach.

...

Ten minutes pass.

I'm two sad songs into mourning the death of our relationship and maybe two streets away from the shuttle station I/we left you in—as Gatto does his very best not to address the elephant in the room, I'm about to offer my best explanation when my phone vibrates violently in my lap.

It's you, mercifully and *un*

and

I miss you

scrawled violently across the stark white background of our previously-deleted conversation string.

And it's all at once

I miss you too

typing and sending before those telltale three dots in a bubble appear to tell me

mercifully and *un*

that we're not done talking.

Gatto, peering down at the text bubbles now furiously appearing across the screen of the phone in my lap, simply shakes his head and smiles. He's been privy to most of the wars we've waged, and, as an outside party mostly removed from the yearnings and anxieties attached to the heart, sees things from a decidedly rational perspective.

"Want a ride to the airport?"

he asks, and I know he's a good enough guy to make the impromptu two-plus-hour trip. Exhausted, despondent, and probably still in shock, I decline as politely as I can, assuring him that—as of this moment—we really are broken up, admissions of longing notwithstanding.

Another headshake, another soft smile, and he leaves me to it, typing furiously and with a precision, rarely seen, proclamations of undying love escaping my thoughts just as fast as my fingers can scribe and electronically send them.

She tells me she wants me to come, and, by the time Gatto drops me off and I turn the key to my apartment door we've softly decided that I'll fly solo to Miami by week's end; I'm to arrive with just enough time to revel in the decadence of South Beach, before setting sail on a missile shooting through the Caribbean.

The door turns, and I'm alone in the darkness of my apartment, *again*

reflecting on the somewhere else I should be and, apparently, am going—when the reality of seven-something on a particularly crazy morning hit me like a proverbial ton of bricks, and sleep takes me the way it's been trying to.

…

The week passes, and passes uneventfully. We text daily,

I love you

and

I miss you

and the spectrum of emojis it takes to reiterate and enunciate one of the previous two texts; although I'm genuine in my sentiment, I can't help but notice that I'm enjoying the peace of week off without you. Thursday—the Thursday before the Friday I take the shuttle to the airport—comes faster than it has any right to. You've been gone days, enjoying the week with your family, and maybe some small part of me wonders if you hadn't preferred/planned it this way—time to converse in Colombian without the non-Colombian carry-on to translate to. I'd have been, in retrospect, just as happy with this arrangement—having called work to update them on the slight change of plans—and being assured that I need to take my holidays regardless of my geography—I had spent the nights previous to this one reveling in my tragically-won temporary independence.

Which is about to change—and, though I genuinely miss the soul-crushing totality of your beauty, I can't shake the nagging suspicion that this could be my last peaceful night. I make the most of it, re-packing recently unpacked bags—*now a week's worth of clothes lighter, thank you very much*—and drinking just heavily enough to numb the probably-pain I'm about to subject myself to.

My lifelong fear of all things aviation is battling my anxiety of fighting with you on the high-seas, my troubles wrestling one another for dominance in the worry-space of my subconscious. I can count on two fingers the number of non-helicopter flights I've taken in my life...to be honest, I'd have much preferred to travel with a seasoned veteran like yourself. Admittedly, the autonomy of shaking uncontrollably not-beside you is appealing as well—but it pales in comparison to the mounting anxiety of navigating an airport unsupervised.

For the first time in a week's worth of peaceful rests I *don't*, rest, that is, tossing and turning and thinking of all the ways the plane can go down on my way to you. The morning comes unmercifully—the morning I'm to leave—and, as I take a taxi to the very same shuttle place I (probably) should have shuttled from the week before, I'm as restless as I can recall, latest day in a year's worth of relative restlessness.

The lady working the desk at the shuttle service is the same lady that worked the desk at the shuttle service then; she looks at me with confusion before cross-checking my name in her database, realizing that

yes

I'm leaving for the same destination I adamantly assured her I wouldn't be leaving for five relatively peaceful days ago. Her heavy set features contort and resist the confines of the tiny, ergonomical chair she's confined to; after a few minutes and the half-dozen

are you sure

glances she glances at me, she stops typing furiously long enough to hand me a ticket of some sorts, and direct me towards the departure area I so painfully watched you depart from all that time ago.

I climb into the back of the van you climbed into, and, as I wait for the four other travelers—travelling in tandems, damn you—that I will be travelling with, I glance down at my phone just in time to catch the

I can't wait to see you

you've just so serendipitously typed to me.

I can't wait to see you either,

because I can't

and, as the van, now fully loaded, pulls from the parking lot, I can't help but wonder what it is about this backseat that makes/made us miss one another so very badly.

…

I survive the airport, and the flight.

Miraculously, and, to be honest, I can't really tell which part was worse—navigating the myriad of cultures and accents of the Air Canada employees, barely discerning what I perceived to be English as I followed their hastily-breathed instructions around the labyrinth otherwise known as Pearson International—or the aggressive taxying of the shoebox-hurtled-through-the-sky pretending to be a jumbo jet.

I had buried myself in thought and literature, assuring myself that I had to survive the flight in order to write *this*, the book I somehow realized even then that I would eventually have to write for/about you. Arnold Schwarzenegger's autobiography carried me through the parts of the too-bumpy ride that weren't spent thinking about you and the uncertain madness that had led me *here*, Seat 4B, cascading helplessly through the heavens on my way to you and what would certainly be our next-most-epic reunion.

I suppose I took the flight in stride, rationalizing and raving in quiet, alternating intervals—every pocket of air translating to turbulence translating to perceived certain death—and then levelling off and taking my anticipations of finality with it.

I reflect on all of this as we exit on the tarmac—another wonderful aspect of landing in decidedly better climates—and, as I make my way South of the setting sun, I'm reflecting no longer on the flight that was, and appreciating the enhanced romanticism my ambient environment suggests.

Yes, that means I'm thinking about you the way I tend to, entering the airport and searching frenetically for my luggage, and, having found it with relative ease, searching frenetically for you.

...

You're the first face I see, entering the reception area, nestled amongst your family and the throngs of families waiting for equally-and-*probably-not-quite-as* loved ones. I see you a half-second before you sense and subsequently see me, and it's worth noting the things I note in the last half-second of peace I have.

You're wearing one of those *painful* dresses, this one in canary yellow and clinging carefully to your week-without-seeing-delicious curves. You're even more tanned, somehow, as though you've spent the duration of the week without on some South Beach beach—knowing what I know of you, this is unlikely, as you tend to favor the sanctity of well-roofed shopping centers. Still, I appreciate the shine your cinnamon-kissed skin has grown, and make a mental note to tell you so, likely seventh in the list of things I've complied to say. Your eyes flirt from passenger to passenger, scanning aggressively for me, and the curve your back takes as you come up empty somehow still manages to draw the attention of at least every-other male in your vicinity.

Knowing you attain this level of attention might hurt my confidence were it not so achingly eager to see/eat you; watching you watch for me, looking all sorts of delicious in that canary-yellow dress, I feel as though I must be the most handsome, dashing man in the world.

Which I am, of course, but the time for self-appreciation will have to wait until after I've completed my current task of relentlessly appreciating you. You do the thing you do with your hair, running your tiny baby-carrot fingers through the luxurious and artificially-thickened raven-kissed strands, here in the last of the half-second before you see me, almond eyes leading the turn of your head as you search and, finally,

find

me.

You're up in an instant, dress trailing the potent explosion of your feet as they plant and carry your weight on the way to me. The onlookers onlooking in the area behind where you've stood stop and stare at the half-second of ass exposed before that canary yellow dress falls to cover it; in the moment that passes you do to, and between travelers on your way to me and the embrace that awaits you.

We're together and *finally*, and, as I take you in my arms and lift you off of your well-heeled feet, you make the tiny little noise you make when I lift you, allowing the sound to escape those pretty pumped up pretty little lips just before my lips envelop them.

We kiss with the aggression of lovers who weren't supposed to kiss, ever again—the passion and emotion of a week apart spilling over and onto our tongues and the traces they make. I'm sure that this is uncomfortable for your family—for all of the families, really, that are forced to witness this moment, your ass escaping your dress as you wrap your legs around mine—but I don't care and you don't care, and so the kissing continues.

By the time we separate, time has passed—significantly, because during said time, your father has generously collected my bags and began a trek towards what I can only assume is a waiting automobile. We disengage just long enough for me to offer assistance—after a warm handshake and a hug to your mother, I meet your baby sister for the first time, and we begin our vacation together.

Your brother, it turns out, is waiting at the South Beach apartment with your relatives/our hosts—the entire family now gathered, we will spend a weekend enjoying the splendor of Miami before departing on the cruise come Monday. I'm to take the time getting to know what is sure-to-be my extended relations; judging by the smile spread across your baby sister's face as we make our way to the vehicle, the rest of the family has already heard all about me.

I can't help but wonder what you've told them; wonder if they were looking for me the way they were *just* looking for me a week ago, when you showed up here to the *Arrivals* terminal wearing a lot more than you're wearing now and without me. Funny how our weeks' worth of texting and phone calls never really got beyond the

I miss you

I miss you more

pleasantries—now, walking alongside what could very well be my future family, I'm wondering just what darkness you've shared with them in decidedly foreign tongues. I chastise myself for my limited Spanish as you laugh with Consuela—

your baby sister—in a language I can't help but feel lost in; lost and suddenly, as the pang of anxiety rumbling to replace the adrenaline of your kiss reminds me,

alone

an English speaking alien amongst a group of individuals I can only hope to call family, should we be begin to get along the way we just kind of *don't*.

The sun has set as we reach the airport parking lot; for the first time since the plane landed I feel an uncertainty not unlike the uncertainty of being hurtled through the sky, envisioning free-falling and wondering which fate would be worse…

…the plane that carried me to you crashing

or

…seeing the storm clouds roll in behind almond eyes ten days away from home or any semblance of it.

…

The apartment in South Beach is astonishing. It's filled with Colombians, naturally; meaning we hear Latin music from the parking lot. Miami is nothing if not busy; there's a sense of life, thanks in part to the half-dozen half-drunk individuals gyrating to the music on various balconies. I'll admit, after a semi-harrowing airplane ride, and the stress/relief of seeing you, that I'm not exactly ready to go careening through the streets; you hold my hand sweetly as the car pulls into the parking lot, somehow sensing my trepidation. As we enter the building, I feel as though I may as well be in Cuba; the interior courtyard and neoclassic architecture beautifully reminding me that I'm indeed far from home.

I assume this is why so many Colombians make their way to South Beach, if not London, Ontario, Canada—as we pile into the tiny elevator, I'm wondering why the hell *any* would choose the latter if the option presented itself. We emerge on some floor north of four, and I immediately find my way to the balcony and an ocean view. You follow, sliding the sliding glass door shut behind you and leaving us alone, together and mercifully, for the first time in over a week.

I'm moderately sure your parents are watching from the other side of the glass and you're moderately sure your parents are watching from the other side of the glass but we attack each other anyways—the aggression of our kiss at the airport and tenfold; perceived aloneness causing us to kiss in the way that only doomed lovers can.

I missed you

I tell you without telling you,

tracing your tongue with my tongue and completely understanding the

I missed you, too

you tell me without telling me right back.

Your ass is out of that canary yellow dress again, and this time my hands are tracing, too, and I'm maybe not the *least* bit concerned whether or not your fairly-conservative parents can see.

By the time you've whispered the promises of what you'd like to do to me into my good ear, I'm high on the elation of seeing you and high on the magic of the South Beach breeze, and I'm telling myself that

yes,

this was a good decision and

no,

nothing will go wrong.

...

We spend the weekend the way lovers should, shopping in South Beach during the day, coffees at cafes and semi-communicating with family and the extended family that makes the trip from somewhere nearby. The nights involve lavish restaurants that I can't really afford; paying when they'll let me because decorum dictates I should, and then reveling on the boardwalk, half-drunk and taking in the living-up-to-the-name nightlife.

So I'm happy broke, dancing in nightclubs to songs I have no business dancing to, watching your writhe and whirl in the kind of dresses that would be outlawed anywhere other than the where we are.

And I'm wishing the where we are would stay, fully content to leave the cruise part of the vacation in favor of more nights here, with you and your family. By the time the hangover sets in, the weekend is dying, and we spend the last night before the ship holding hands on separate inflatable beds, still not allowed to sleep together, but doing everything we can to hold on to the moment, metaphorically, and each other, literally.

…

The goddamn boat is huge

is almost all I can think of as we wait to board,

Thank God I'm not afraid of boats, too

making up the rest of the thoughts I have that aren't about you, holding my hand beside me and likely thinking the same damn thing. Your parents point and smile, somewhere in line just ahead of us, and I nod back, communicating without communicating that I'm excited as well.

The Celebrity Silhouette, she's called, and Wikipedia on my phone tells me that she's got over 1,000 feet in length, with a beam (whatever the fuck that is) of 121 feet. I tell this to you as though it may impress you, but your reply is centered around making love on the balcony, and, as a result, my phone and the information within disappear into my pocket before I can rattle off the last irrelevant statistic.

You're barely wearing a barely-legal sundress, and so my focus is forced away from the magnificence of the barge we're waiting to board, my lips discovering new indentations on your lips as, behind us, less lucky couples likely look on in earnest jealousy.

But it's *fuck them* and because it's our world and our world alone—and, in these best-of-times and to the best of my recollection, it's always this way when you and I are working.

We board without incident and set sail; you and I find the room we're to share with your brother Ricardo-Gustavo—just arrived in time to board from some super-exclusive school he's attending in Switzerland—without incident; somewhere in one of the other thousand-thousand other cabins, your parents settle in with your baby sister Consuela.

To our credit, we remain blissfully in love for the duration of our first day and night at sea—we attend a semi-formal Captain's dinner in our finest attire, and the dress you pour into and spill-over in all the right places has us fucking in cruise ship corners, respect for your newly-arrived and jetlagged brother forcing us to be creative when he retires to his room following the meal.

The sun rises on the second day—heralding our arrival to the first of our three destinations—before I catch even a glimpse of the clouds once again rolling in behind your beautifully black eyes.

...

San Juan, Puerto Rico

the first destination is called, and *San Juan, Puerto Rico* is instantly my new favorite place on Earth. We're in a tiny van, being shuttled through the cobblestone streets by a man everyone else in the van is entirely comfortable speaking Spanish to. Meaning I miss the totality of the tourist information he's sharing—the way today's sundress has retreated from your upper thigh, revealing the treasures of your pink-today panties, I could care less.

So the architecture and the warm sea breeze creeping in from the open windows come *second* to the tour my eyes are taking of your sun-kissed thighs...from time to time you force my eyes to yours and smile warmly, the late afternoon light still betraying no hint of the malice building casually behind.

No, it's paradise, still, and as the tour van stops in front of a local tequila distillery, I revel in samples and stories sung in Spanish—again missing the entirety of the tour, but appreciating the free alcohol nonetheless. I make the most of every moment your parent's still-semi-watchful eyes aren't on us, my hands taking tours of their own and always up today's sundress. The liquor emboldens me and the chase emboldens you—by the time the tour guide gets to the good part, we're behind a barrel, alarmingly missing, and making the most of the time it takes for the group to double back and find us.

The sun is going down as we make our way back to the van, sweating *and not from the tequila* and admiring the way that the sun goes down entirely differently here, *San Juan, Puerto Rico*, from the way the sun goes down back home.

Here it lingers, bathing everything in an entirely romantic light—so much so that I catch your parents kissing the way we do, one row in front of us in a van that is making way towards the next adventure. If they're angry/embarrassed by our public displays of affection and *not* public displays of affection—and subsequent periods of absence—their faces don't betray it, smiling and kissing and hopefully-just-maybe inspired by our youthful voracity.

...

The hour before we're to board sees us at some magnificent cemetery. The light, continuing to die, seems to accelerate my anxiety to not let these moments pass. We travel between gravestones, admiring the eerie beauty and exchanging respectful-given-the-location groping. We lose your family in the twilight; I think nothing of it, our boarding time approaching and still somehow not relevant, chasing you and that sundress between rows of those who couldn't care less.

We've lost sight of the van—and the rest of your family—by the time the light heaves it's last breath. I fumble with the bottom of your sundress awkwardly; marveling at the effectiveness of the island beer I consumed in the back of the van, and my sudden inability to expose the rest of your semi-exposed ass. I figure it's the booze, not yet fully aware that you're pulling away from me and my lazy attempt at seduction. By the time my face rises from its resting place between your thighs, I'm astonished to find your usual island-happy-face replaced by one I recognize all too well.

"Joo bastard."

I mistake your slightly-under-breath uttering for something *negative*, my face just now travelling north to meet yours, figuring all the while that there is no way you could be angry with me here and now.

"Joo selfish horny bastard—where are they?"

Clearly, I'm wrong.

"What? Where are—

"My family, joo bastard! Joo drag me away from them, and joo know they have trouble understanding...what if they miss the van back to the *sheep**

*Ship. (It's adorable every single time you say it; although, given the change in your mood, my grin at your mouthing of the word is only fueling your newfound fire.)

You push me off of you and run in the general direction we had (jointly) snuck off in; I'm left standing amongst the gravestones of individuals who, should they have witnessed our little exchange, would doubtless empathize with my growing sense of

what the fuck.

But then again, the dead don't know you like I do, many moons like-the-one-that-is-rising-behind-me between us and still, although I recognize these little outbursts, they take me by surprise every time. And so I'm chasing you, off and running in the direction of the van and your undoubtedly-still-safe family, musing that of all the travelers potentially missing the *sheep*, I'm the only one who doesn't speak the Spanish you've all been communicating in all Goddamned day.

...

To spare you the suspense, we find them—your family—and we return safely to the cruise ship together...together *kinda*, because, for the duration of the half-hour van ride back, you won't speak a word, Spanish *or*, to me, or even look in my direction.

We've made up by the time you've had a bottle of wine with your dinner, and, as my head hits the pillow, I'm forced to remind myself that—although I'm in paradise with you—I'm in paradise with *you*, and so it maybe

just maybe

it's not really paradise, at all.

…

I forget easily.

Apparently, because as the sun rises on the next day, we're laughing over breakfast and preparing for the pending port of St. Thomas. The darkness of the previous evening forgotten, we're feeding each other in between kisses, discussing plans for shopping and leisure, nestled in a booth opposite parents clearly *not* lost. We disembark in tandem--by the time your brother and sister discover another local tequila distillery, dragging your parents dutifully behind them, we're sneaking off again, ducking into the nearest storefront, desperate for more time together in paradise.

The storefront, it turns out, belongs to one of five-already-passed-on-same-street diamond shops; although I reckon I'd heard that jewel sales were a cornerstone of island business, I'm astonished to discover to which extent.

You, it's worth noting, seem far less surprised.

I follow you the length of the narrow store; you move with purpose, past the various bangles, earrings, bracelets and watches. I'm wholly prepared to comment on your vigorous exploration—about to offer a reminder that you're about to lose your family again—when a heavy-set man with a healthy island tan intercepts me, offering what turns out to be a warm handshake.

He says his name is Ernesto, and Ernesto is the proprietor of this,

"The finest diamond shop on the island."

His ruddy cheeks become increasingly crimson as he introduces himself, beckoning to some unseen associate while simultaneously asking me my name.

"Ah, a fine gentleman, with a strong name. And your lovely girlfriend?"

His associate, having materialized from some unforeseen corner of the store, is kissing your extended hand by the time I'm able to respond.

"Ah, Muneca—a doll, yes. Would you care for a glass of champagne, while you browse the finest wares—for the best deals--on the island of St. Thomas?"

You nod almost as enthusiastically as Ernesto enunciates; instantly, the associate disappears again, and I'm following you once more down a seemingly endless corridor of bauble-laced display cases.

You stop three-quarters the length of the shop, having clearly found something worthy of your erudite tastes. I'm still somewhat bewildered—walking shoulder to shoulder with Ernesto (shoulder-to-hip would be more accurate, given the man's diminutive stature) and remembering that, in the totality of our tumultuous time together, we've never discussed the word emblazoned on the sign hanging directly above you.

Engagement.

I breathe a sigh, remembering that your family has no idea where we've run off to, and wondering what the hell they would think of it, should they discover. You, taking the glass of champagne eagerly from Ernesto's subordinate, couldn't appear to care less.

I turn to find him, Ernesto, having somehow misplaced the little man in the moments since noticing your interest in commitment diamonds. Had I time to think of anything other than your impromptu desire to become betrothed, I might appreciate how his height could benefit both his Gumdrop-Fairy persona and a knack for ducking into diamond-strewn corners. His absence allows me to catch up to you—I'm timidly about to discover what it is that has you so transfixed when he materializes once more, offering me an just-uncapped bottle of beer.

"It's domestic, sir....best on any island you'll visit."

I accept his generosity; given the potential gravity of the situation unfolding before me, I'm sure that some part of me greatly appreciates the gesture. I partake, long and deep, before thanking Ernesto and joining you, already motioning for a second glass.

"Look Mico"

My eyes fall tentatively to the glass display case, only after swilling deeply from the bottle once more.

I know absolutely nothing about diamonds...except that the ones I'm suddenly gazing upon are certainly above my budget. They're beautiful, sure-- as Ernesto's associate replaces your already-empty flute with a full one, I can't help but be reminded how *you* are, as well.

In fact, I'm suddenly and totally enraptured; you're annoyed at my inability to focus on the diamonds, or the engagement ring you're ordering Ernesto to remove from the case, or anything, really, other than the curves your body takes when you bend slightly to point at your favorite.

I've abruptly forgotten about my concern for your family's whereabouts and I've forgotten about my concern for your interest in rings and I've forgotten about just about everything, save for the taste of this mysteriously delicious beer and intentions of showing you my appreciation.

Ernesto, intent on exploiting my lowered inhibitions, presents me a preposterously large rock.

"Ah, a fine choice, Muneca. Sir, your girlfriend has exquisite taste. Princess cut, 3.4 carat center stone, with another 1.7 in the surrounding circle."

"It's beautiful."

It is.

"Ma'am, would you like to try it on?"

"Jes."

I've handed the ring back to Ernesto, who doesn't miss a beat in placing it on your finger. I finish my beer, and notice his associate materializing beside me, fresh bottle in his grasp.

In the time it takes my eyes to divert to the necessary exchange taking place in my left hand, yours is adorned with the comically large diamond. I clutch the fresh beer, appreciating the coldness in my palm almost as much as the look of all-encompassing joy spread across your features. I toast your elatedness with a strong sip, feeling lightheaded as the bottle escapes my apparently-starved lips.

I tell myself that I can't be drunk—after all, I'm a bottle and a half deep—but the sensation of elation rising up from my stomach has me reeling. You're radiant, smiling at me while waving the ostentatious bauble between us, a palpable manifestation of perhaps the latest barrier to your undaunted happiness.

Maybe I tell myself that this is what it would take—to finally separate our undeniable love from the constant storm that seems to encircle it—a symbol of my commitment to you and you alone. I'm rationalizing what would be the most monumental impromptu-purchase of my life…

…and realizing in an instant that

yes

I am *completely* inebriated.

You're looking at me, and in my moment of drunken self-realization, you read my thoughts the way only someone completely separated from reality believes they can be read, and you tell me that

you're drunk too

and that

yes, this is a good idea.

So I'm relatively certain that

yes

my absurdly good island beer is laced with something and that

yes

I'm all at once aware that marrying you—despite all of our well-documented problems—is a great idea.

Ernesto nods, his best

I agree

smile stretched across his lips; he's clearly reading my mind—another side effect of whatever hypnotizing drug he's laced the contents of this bottle with.

I part my lips—for the first time in four partings, not to partake from the Devil's bottle—but to ask the most dreaded of my four questions

How much?

when the clarion call of the boat-boarding bell shatters the illusion of the moment.

As if on cue, you slam your champagne flute on the display case, removing the ring with a ferocity I—unfortunately—recognize all too well.

...

"My parents!"

I'm drunk, but I distinctly feel as though I've heard this before.

The ring is back in Ernesto's sweaty little palm before he can open his mouth to protest; you're half the length of the store before his

"Wait, I can offer you an additional ten percent"

follows the way I am and out the door, hitting the cobblestone street a dozen steps before you and the fury of your wake.

I can barely keep pace, trailing you and your exposed ass, cheeks winking at me from the intermitted raising of your sundress as you careen wildly between not-nearly-as-panicked cruisers returning to the vessel.

And they all notice, too; the males of the species staring a touch too long for the liking of the females they're travelling with. You're out of earshot by the time the arguing inevitably begins, illusions of blissful matrimony shopping together in paradise wrenched away by the stampeding of a drop-dead gorgeous Colombian, plentiful heaving on approach mirrored by a symphony of jiggling as you painfully retreat from sight. I hear you, shouts of

"Mama"

and

"Papa"

ringing out over the din. Were it not for the honeysuckle sweet of your voice, the cries could be mistaken for the wailings of a little girl separated from her family; despite the calamity of the situation, the inebriation allows a smile to trace my lips at the absurdity of a thirty-six year old woman lamenting the way you most certainly are.

I'm struggling to keep up, and so the smile fades as quickly as it came on, my concentration certainly compromised and still somehow focused on corralling you long enough to ensure a safe return to the ship before departure.

You take a left up ahead, away from both the boat and the cobblestone path clearly designated to lead us back; I offer a sigh and a quickened pace as I fight through the hordes of methodically moving shoppers to join you.

As I round the corner, I realize in abject horror that you have, too…and another one, meaning you're farther from the boat and the path to it, and, additionally, now absent from my admittedly blurry sight.

I'm running, as fast as the fog in my head will allow, and, reaching the next corner a half-step slower than I should, I'm faced with probably the *second* most important decision of the past ten minutes.

Left,

down a particularly tourist-unfriendly looking side street, accented by a series of dumpsters and an aggressive looking alley cat, clearly perturbed at having his sunbathing and garbage-picking interrupted—or

Right

and at least parallel to the direction we're *supposed* to be returning in; the direction that hopefully ends on the deck of a big goddamn boat.

The booze in me tells me to go right; behind me, the aggressive looking alley cat agrees with a hiss.

Looking to avoid street fights with natives of *any* species I acquiesce; assuming, had you ventured left, the alley cat would be lying dismembered in the aftermath of your interrogation as to the whereabouts of *your really-not-missing* parents.

Really not missing the way you're *trying* to be, apparently, disappeared from sight and sound and down some street just north of the last acceptable street for tourists such as ourselves.

So I'm off to the right and running, now, and not running well, too much island beer and the problems too much island beer creates, all blurry-vision and stutter-stepped as I feel desperation welling up inside of me.

It's fermenting, this feeling, the way I imagine the beer must be, my guts a chaotic representation of the despair my head is increasingly feeling; projecting whispers of

hurry

into ears better suited for listening, and for your cries to momma.

...

I hear another bell in the distance and quicken my pace—the thought of being stranded here on this beautiful goddamned island only slightly more appealing than the thought of the 'conversation' we're sure to have should I find you.

Still, I find myself resigned to my fate and following, half-a-fool for falling in love with you and half-a-fool for remaining that way, knowing deep down in the pit of my stomach it will ensure a lifetime of chasing you down alleys just like this one.

I'm somewhere just north of exhausted, heading south down some tourist-untraveled back road, when I spot you on the horizon. Your shape is whirling, details obscured by both distance and debris, but over dumpsters and between decaying building facades I catch glimpses of you, conversing with three equally obscured shapes.

'Conversing' I catch only because I can hear you, *yelling* in the distance, echoing off of the otherwise uninhabited street. As I approach the corner you're rampaging on, I realize—much to my lack of surprise—that the three shapes you're talking towards belong to appropriately-aggressive looking local men.

Who notice me, thank you very much, but remain primarily interested in *you*; you and the parts of you peeking from beneath the perpetual motion of your barely-there sundress.

My Spanish isn't great, but I recognize the more colorful of the insults you're hurling at them; the looks on their faces does little to quiet the growing sense of dread in my stomach. So I reach for your hand upon reaching you, short of breath and patience and time—you're

"Get away from me, *loser*"

does little to convey that we're together to the locals you're so keen on provoking. My temper tells me I could take them, should it come to conflict; the beer swilling in my stomach and fogging my thought process heartily agrees. The rest of me surely realizes that I'm horribly outnumbered and likely to be severely beaten or stabbed—or severely beaten and shot—let alone the fate that would befall you should I fall, too.

And so, missing the boat is suddenly the *least* of my currently-three-and-growing problems; fighting to maintain a grip on your arm before possibly fighting three possibly armed locals a half-a-mile from where the rest of the tourists boarding the cruise ship the way we *should* be.

You call me names in Spanish and they call me names, probably, in Spanish, and yet my grip on your arm remains—the beer and my foolish Irish pride assuring me that

yes

I'm ready to miss the boat and whatever pieces of me they're about to remove.

I'm sure there's some twisted part of me that figures this is romantic or heroic, my mind already chasing analogies of wolves and well-endowed sheep. I offer you one *what-I-assume-will-be-final* look and the beer tells me you're beautiful; maybe beautiful enough to justify getting on the boat in the first place, let alone the tragic and tragically comical events of the day.

Given the nature of our relationship, this back alley and these three locals aren't as dangerous as Ernesto and his diamond shop anyways…and so I turn the totality of my attentions to my assailants for the first time since catching up to you.

Two of the three are somewhat diminutive; in a one-on-one situation, given my aforementioned temper an penchant for punching things in the face, I'm reasonably certain I could best them. Part of me probably wants to, frustration and inebriation creating a rationalization for the more violent of my inclinations.

Yeah, two out of the three—instantly classified as Simon and Theodore in my still-hazy head—represent the '*wish-a-bitch-would*' demographic.

The third?

Alvin?

Alvin looks like he would fuck both me and my cantankerous would be/almost bride at the same time. I figure it's got something to do with his size—still mounted atop a milk crate, he's easily eye-level with you, meaning two heads taller than his fellow Chipmunks, and *eclipse-the-sun status* should he rise to tower over me. Maybe it's the roadmap of pockmarks zigzagging his tanned-leather face giving him such an aggressive countenance; having wrestled the acne-monster once or twice, I can understand a pent-up frustration form having to face *that* reflected in the mirror every morning. He's more heaving than breathing, there atop his throne, his eyes now removed from *your* animated heaving, breasts seemingly now less-desirable than whatever those charcoal marbles he calls pupils intend to do to me.

I watch the striations in his naked shoulders, telling myself I'm telegraphing movement, should he lead with his right the way the percentages tell me he most likely *will*—in reality, my boxing training is really masking a sense of admiration.

Hell, maybe being stranded on paradise island would work wonders for my deltoids and my tan, too—I'll admit the temptation of leaving you and the boat to go catch some sun sounds about right, *right now*, as Alvin opens his mouth to announce my doom.

His dental situation gives me pause—in between syllables collectively promising my imminent death, I catch a total of six teeth in the entirety of his maw; instantly my aggression is replaced by feelings of pity, and for the poverty Alvin and his Chipmunks must be resigned to.

Six yellow, decaying teeth are all it takes to snap me to my senses. I tell myself that my sudden lack of interest in the violence to come has *nothing* to do with the shadow he casts as he rises from the milk crate.

I can't imagine the sadness of his existence, one street north of happy, rich tourists buzzing ignorantly amongst shops he would never be allowed to enter. The contrast of everything and nothing, separated by a building and the odd alley-cat, fighting for scraps and dying in the shadows of the storefronts that exist to placate fools like me.

And *you*, still mouthing off somewhere to my left, now less resistant to my grip on your arm then you were *before* milk crates and risings off them.

I almost can't blame these men for clamoring at the moment of happiness your unconscious-required takings would allow; still, I sigh and give thanks that it's my right hand holding your left arm, my southpaw-ness and preparedness to swing first our one and only chance to escape the illusion-shattered reality we find ourselves in.

I clench my for-the-moment still full of teeth jaw and brace for the worst of it, allowing the all-too-familiar surge of adrenaline to coat my pain receptors, as beside me your tone finally changes.

Enough to tear Alvin's charcoal marble pupils away from me for the first time since his supper became *male*; still bracing, I'm a half moment from hitting the big bastard when the mouth surrounding his six teeth moves and

"Go"

escapes his lips—in English—where

"You're dead"

or

"Estas Muerto"

should be.

He points, echoing the universally understood if phonetically-challenged rumbling of his command, pointing in the direction I was--before this all-encompassing distraction--reasonably sure our boat is.

I can hear now, the blood pounding in my ears subsiding enough to tell me that you've gone from insulting to pleading, and probably for our lives.

Although my pride won't allow me to admit it, I'm reasonably sure I'm glad you did, the thought of being murdered on this island just a little less appealing than staying on it forever or being engaged to you.

So I take the loss as a win, the whole *escaping-with-our-lives thing* bringing back the buzz my imminent stabbing had threatened to ruin. You take off as fast as your ridiculous and ridiculously expensive heels will allow; my last glimpse of Alvin, Simon and Theodore has more compassion and understanding than violence in it. Had I time to marvel at my in-the-face-of-danger maturation, I might call dodging refuse and your resumed and *now-totally-directed-at-me* insults, I'm just glad the intoxication has hold of me once more.

"Joo fucking asshole"

and

"If my parents mees (**miss*) this boat"

and

the threats that follow have you exhausted by the time we hit what must be a main road. Despite the savagery of your words, the adventure and the endorphins have you almost-smiling in between the hurling of them; insults are intermittent with laughter by the time you flag a truck driver carrying what must be supplies to one of the fleet of cruise ships now visible on the horizon.

Your face betrays a lack of elation as I lift you into the cab—you take my hand in yours as I rise to share the bench with what turns out to be 'Steve,' our latest savior.

We laugh at his jokes in broken English, listen earnestly as he assures us that we are not the first tourists he's had to escort back to the boarding port. We learn that our *perceived* danger was in fact *just* danger—and that although the locals are hesitant to disrupt the source of income the tourist industry affords, they're not above the occasional stab/rape. He assures us that such incidents are isolated, sensing our reactions must mean we were closer to his previous sentence's statistics.

A conciliatory offering of more island beer—from the cooler he keeps just behind his seat at the steering wheel—has us drinking and laughing the rest of the seven minute drive.

We disembark Steve's supply truck just in time to catch the final boarding whistle—we're past the obligatory security check and subsequent race to your parent's cabin by the time the sun sets and the ship sets sail.

We find them safely within—to my utter and total lack of surprise, and to your complete and utter surprise. You throw yourself at your poor mother, who looks appropriately shocked at your apparent enthusiasm to see after what could only have been a couple of hours absence.

You begin recounting events in foreign tongues, alternating between fits of elated laughter and dramatic gesture. Your father joins you both on the bed, interrupting moments of intense listening with what could be looks of disappointment or understanding—the buzz hasn't worn off enough for me to tell.

After an eternity of standing polite and silent in the doorway, I offer a modest interruption in a language only the two of us understand.

The look you shoot me in return defies description.

In my exhausted, adrenal-depleted state I fail to question the reasoning for the sudden return of your vitriol; recognizing the storm in your eyes, I merely slump my shoulders and retreat from your view.

On my defeated walk back to our cabin I pass your baby sister, burdened by a half-dozen brightly colored shopping bags, beaming brilliantly the length of the hallway. Consuela seems unbothered by the fact that, according to hurried recountings, she not only managed to lose every member of her family moments after we dove into that diamond shop, but was the very last tourist collected before the ship set sail.

I weigh her laissez-faire, admittedly refreshing lack of worry against your

"It's all your fault"

approach,

wondering as she separates from an impromptu hug and subsequent skip down the hallway towards your parent's room (and the whirlwind within) if—based on personality alone—I hadn't fallen for the wrong sibling.

I'll admit that I contemplate this—amidst reflections over the latest insanities to befall our romance—the length of the labyrinthian hallways to our cabin.

I'm spent by the time I reach our room; I can barely find the energy to required to recount the happenings of the day to your brother, himself returned peacefully from isolated explorations some time ago.

At his urgings, we hit both the balcony and the alcohol smuggled aboard prior to our initial departure; by the second sip of something strong *and-still-not-as* that damned island beer, I'm grateful for the ability to communicate in shared tongue with members of your family.

His insight is both profound and appreciated; having almost become fiancée number four, I find it refreshing to learn I'm not the only one close to you who recognizes a distinct and troubling pattern.

Your inclination to both love and conflict—coupled with your unparalleled beauty—have made you the object of desire, devotion and damnation for men of equal bravery or stupidity.

He nods in appreciation when I speak of my exhaustion, assuring me that you've been a source of nothing *but* for decades and to everyone in your path. He's kind when he tells me that the intensity with which you bare your fangs has been reserved for me, and me alone—that previous men were lucky to elicit feelings of resigned complacency, if not outright boredom.

I take it as a sign that I'm not completely insane—not yet—and that all the love we share is real, even if we both wish it was not.

We finish both the whiskey and the evening, retiring to bed before seeing you return to our room.

As I lay my troubled head on the pillow, before gently lulled to sleep by the subtle rocking of the ship in the sea and the not-so-subtle rocking of the alcohol in my system my last moment of self-reflection burns across a troubled self-conscious—despite your brother's assurances that I am indeed special, all I can think before sleep takes me is

Thank God I didn't get engaged to you.

...

The Very Next Day.

We're on a different island

and

we're in a different diamond shop

and

the sun is shining and I'm drinking island beer

and

I'm thinking *Why Not?*

and

before I know it, I'm on the phone with my credit card company and, despite their thinly-veiled cautions against making irrational purchases on beautiful islands, I'm authorizing a seven-thousand-eight-hundred dollar purchase for the ridiculously large rock resting currently on your ring finger.

...

I can't really hear what today's diamond salesman—Esteban—is saying,

something about

"Worth twenty-two thousand"

and

"pick it up in an hour"

because I'm looking into your beautiful little black-hole eyes and I'm marveling at how, for the very first time, there is not a trace of a storm brewing behind them.

I'm in love and

fuck it

and the blood is pounding in my ears like I'm about to take a right on the chin from Alvin, and I'm not thinking *at all* and about how I might very well be just as insane as you are.

...

The wait for the boat is considerably more pleasant than yesterday.

We take our time, stopping outside storefronts and inside stores containing items that only marginally catch our interest, distracted as we are and only partially because of the alcohol. We whisper to one another, separated by the clothing racks we feign interest in, already making grand plans as to how we will reveal our decidedly big news.

In the time it takes for Esteban to size the ring, we've decided that I'm to ask for your hand in marriage—honoring tradition and *your* tradition and all that— and that I'll have the better part of an evening to come up with a suitable, if unsurprising, proposal. The former concerns me more than the latter—the whole '*not speaking Spanish thing*' making communication near-impossible; given my booze-induced elation, I'm reasonably sure I can come up with a creative way to ask you to marry me—technically, for the *third* time in twenty-four hours.

Drunken joy and endorphin release carries us the duration of the allocated excursion time; we pick up the ring and return to the boat undetected. The only time you're wearing the brilliantly gaudy bauble is through the security checkpoint—as we board and begin the now-daily search for your parents, I slide it into my pocket, already contemplating some grand design while you float down the hallway beside me, decidedly less worried about your missing-*again* family than you were yesterday.

Unsurprisingly, we find them in their cabin—the same cabin you banished me from, recently and now feeling some million years ago. Given the look on your face today, beaming brilliantly as you join your mother on the bed to discuss *all-but-one* of today's purchases, I almost can't fathom the thought of fighting with you, ever again. Removing myself quietly (and, today, without resignation) from the room, I've half-convinced myself that the events of today will be enough to cleanse the palate of yesterday, and prevent the storms of tomorrow.

My head is swimming—again, likely due to the consumption of dubious island beer—as I race the length of the boat, assured that

yes

I've already formulated a plan to ask her father for his blessing and

yes

I've already formulated a plan to come up with a suitably entertaining proposal—as I reach the always-bustling cafeteria, the last thing I tell myself is

yes

my parents are going to be absolutely thrilled at my decision to blow my savings on some island in the Caribbean, all to propose to a woman I can't spend more than a month with.

…

Luis looks at me with dead eyes; dead eyes that can only come from serving chicken-fried rice to gringos like me for far, far too long.

"Hablas espanol?"

I ask him, the only Spanish, aside from elaborate cursings and cute pet names, I've managed to retain in our tumultuous time together.

"Si?"

he answers, with absolutely no enthusiasm at all.

"I need your help."

Nothing.

"Joo want some rice?"

"No."

Luis looks—or would look, were he capable of human emotion—overly confused.

"I need you to translate something for me."

"So, no chicken-fried rice?"

He's fucking with me, the way I would imagine fake-happy cruise ship waiters love to fuck with passengers they've perceived won't be tipping. He's wrong, Luis, and the twenty dollar bill I pass him over the chicken-fried rice heater instantly changes his stoic demeanor.

"What do you want to say boss?"

Luis' grin threatens to envelop his face. His eyes, half-disappeared between painfully robust cheekbones, suddenly display the kind of put-on enthusiasm that surely landed him behind the chicken-fried rice counter in the first place.

Still, I admire his presentation and so I begin, describing my verbose professions of love for 'your' daughter while Luis listens, amused, and offers a silky-smooth translation.

A translation I butcher, writing phonetically what I pray will be authentic and *sound* that way, coming from my decidedly uncultured tongue.

By the time Luis fake-enthusiastically asks me to speak the words I've just written back to him, a small army of equally-unimpressed but undoubtedly-amused cafeteria staff has joined, appropriately placed

Ooh's

and

Ahh's

arming me with enough false confidence to believe I might actually pull this *off*.

I thank them with a greater sincerity than anything pantomimed my way; as I turn to leave, Luis assures me that a gluttonous portion of chicken-fried rice awaits the happy couple, should we return to his station.

...

"I have something to ask of you"

"Tengo algo que pedirte"

sounding sweeter in Spanish—even my broken facsimile—as I look your father in the eyes and commence with the saying of it.

He motions me onto the bed—the only suitable sitting space in the tiny cabin—with the kind of patient grace he's exhibited the totality of our time together. Resting uncomfortably at the edge of the bed, I study his features as he leans back against a well-worn pillow.

His body language assures me there is no rush, although, beside him and sitting completely erect, your mother may beg to differ. He smiles at her softly, the extension of his hand assuring her that the news to come *can't* be bad.

He looks as though he may have been in this situation before—seeing as I'm now, officially, the fourth man to make this presentation, I can understand his languid expression.

He smiles at me, your father does, and the crags of his weathered skin trace a roadmap extending from the corners of his upper lip all the way to his eyelids. Housed within are probably the warmest, kindest eyes I've ever seen on a man of his age—they instantly remind me of yours, on *good days*, rich and dark and expressing varieties of your seventy-seven emotions all at once.

I take this recognition as a good sign, draw breath to continue my hastily-scribed and poorly-rehearsed request, noting the cut of his razor-sharp cheekbones and realizing form where you got yours.

He's *whiter* than I figured Colombians could be, your father; with his plume of *still-all-there* cotton-candy white hair and the thick designer frames, he could pass for Caucasian. Until he opens his mouth *the way he's about to*, and the urgings to continue he urges ring out in foreign tongues and with accents just slightly stronger than his features.

"I love your daughter very much"

"Amo mucho a tu hija"

Your mother gasps, her hand rising dramatically to rest against her chest. A petite, sturdy-framed woman, there's little doubt as to where you received *those* endowments from. Seated on the bed next to your father, their differences are vast—she's nearly the color of the chestnut headboard behind her, and darkening by the second. *Her* eyes, large and expressive, distinctly lack the warmth of your dad's—I've learned from which side of the family the storm behind them comes from.

She's a beautiful woman, if a touch *icier* than the other half of your genetic contributors; I have little doubt that, at your age, she turned just as many heads as you do, now. She braces, indicating by a return of her hands to her lap that, despite her theatrical interruption, she's ready for me to continue.

"I'm grateful for this time away together"

"Estoy agradecido por este tiempo juntos"

"and I would like to take this opportunity"

"y me gustaria aprovechar esta opportunidad"

I falter a little, doing my best to look them both in the eye, the act of straying phonetically-transcribed notes causing pause at inopportune times. I curse the restraints of the aggressively too-tight button-up I've selected to make this little presentation, favoring a slightly-more respectable look at the expense of comfort. I pull at my collar, clear my throat, and clench my jaw.

As if urging me on, the ship sways, cresting some unseen aggressive wave.

"to ask for your daughter's hand in marriage."

"pedir la mano de tu hija en matrimonio."

There's more written haphazardly on my page—eschewing preparation in favor of emphasis, I let my tongue finish the complicated phrasing of the sentence, resting my eyes on your father.

He sits, silently, for an eternity wrapped in an instant. Your mother, more befitting of her personality, does the same. Locked in the weight of the question, I allow my mind to retrace every single encounter with either of them, searching frantically for any moment in our times together that would betray my assumptions of overjoyed acceptance.

Did I fail in my efforts to hide my disgust at your behavior with that goddamned helicopter pilot? Did I overestimate the language barrier on one of our trips to Collingwood, arguing in English with you while they sat presumably unknowing in the backseat?

The alcohol in my system, now having painfully receded enough to allow doubt to creep in at the corners of my consciousness, isn't blanketing my nearly enough for this moment to be bearable.

I swallow hard, consider opening my mouth to utter some sort of follow-up and off-script urgings, imagining how to cast them in some form of recognizable cadence when the stoic illusion your parents' collectively maintain crumbles.

And crumbles brilliantly, chased back into the realm of apparently misguided assumption by the smile stretched once more across your father's handsome face. Your mother kind of *yelps* from her side of the bed, lunging to embrace me with a vigor betraying her years. I take the hug and the kiss on the cheek that follows her

"Si"

Yes

echoing—and maybe beating—his to my ear and my comprehension by a half syllable. She's crying what I very much hope are tears of joy, speaking to me rapidly and using words I couldn't hope to understand, despite their tempo. Finally, she withdraws, still smiling, and offers her

"Jes"

Yes

with a nod of her head, symbolic in that I've never before heard her attempt *my* language. I rise from the bed to embrace your father warmly—truly thankful for the warmth your culture allows. My interactions with my own father—who I love more than just about anything in this world—are usually limited to a terse handshake and the occasional grip on the shoulder. We're a little *cold*, us Canadians of Irish-Native American descent, and so I welcome the opportunity to join a family as outwardly loving as yours.

(It helps, to be honest, in the moments when you're displaying your *stormy* side, to understand the violence you're pre-inclined to display may be more chemical imbalance than genetic hardwiring.)

So I hold him, your father, for longer than the ice-blood in my veins would normally deem appropriate, enjoying the moment and feeling both empowered and respected in my decision, thinking again of my own family and hoping/praying their reaction to the big news will be anything remotely comparable to *this*.

There are tears in his eyes when we separate from a prolonged embrace; the cynic in me can't help but wonder if they're not both relieved that *another* man has been brave enough to attempt to tame the shrew that is their tempestuous daughter.

Had I clarity, I might marvel at nature's inherit defense systems, granting you ridiculous beauty. Still, I'm half-drunk and on a boat in the middle of the goddamned sea, having chased you halfway around the world to end up *here*, in a tiny cabin with your parents having just promised to be with you forever…in actuality, you may not be the only half-crazy one.

Which makes the moment mean that much more, validation that the storms have been worth it, justification as your father extends his hand to shake mine, physical manifestation of a *different* voice than the voice in my head that whispers

run away

and more often than not.

I've always been the fuck it type, and, after spending another five or fifteen minutes hugging it out with the future in-laws, I leave them to their cabin and the conversation-I-can't-understand-anyways. I'm off to complete the second part of my mission; the proposal to cement the latest and undoubtedly most daring/potentially damning/undoubtedly foolish decision of my *too-old-to-be-playing-with-fire-like-this* life.

…

There's a theatre on the boat.

Naturally, given the three days at sea—it's only fitting that a ship so grandiose and opulent would be outfitted with a two-storey, lavishly-furnished, opera-esque stage. We've already taken in a *Cirque du Soleil* act, and some fifties music retrospective during our voyage—between sips of whatever I was drinking, I distinctly remember marveling at the architecture of the floating auditorium.

Given the time constraints—and lack of viable options, what with being on an oversized boat in the middle of the sea—I figure it's the perfect place for my pending 'surprise' proposal.

My hopes are temporarily dashed, having reached the double-doors leading to the theatre and finding them locked—I suppose they want to avoid drunken passengers careening down flights of auditorium stairs in between performances. Through the fog of adrenal-overload and between pangs of pain the headache my ever-increasing and unfortunate sobriety is starting to cause, I remember a listing for '*Director of Entertainment*' on the playbill to the show we attended—the playbill now resting on the end table beside the bed of the room we share.

I head back hurriedly, stopping only at the cafeteria for some much-needed caffeine; hoping *those* hunger receptors will keep the pain occupied for the time it takes to complete my endeavors. Mercifully, you're not in the room when I return—though I'm thrilled at the prospect of our engagement, my idea is somewhat time-sensitive, and I'd just as soon not be bombarded with questions concerning the result of my meeting with your parents.

So it's a quick stop for the playbill, opting to use a common area phone *just in case* you return from the ship casino or the ship shopping floor or wherever it is your excitement has taken you to.

Finding a suitable, *private* space in the all-but-abandoned ship library, I place a call to concierge services, and, miraculously and after explaining my idea to a thankfully-impressed voice on the other end of the line, manage to learn the Director of Entertainment's name,

Bill

and, *just-as-if-not-probably-more-importantly,*

his cell phone number.

I dial his number with almost-shaking fingers attached to suddenly-sweaty palms; after all, this is my one and only option for securing a suitably viable venue.

Bill, kind enough to pick up after the seventh ring answers with the kind of gruff

"Hello"

that tells me he's not used to having this particular number called.

I start softly, all

"Hello, Bill, you don't know who I am, but—"

before hitting him with the proposal-for-the-proposal; buoyed by the confidence of my successful delivery to whoever it was that gave me the private number I've dialed to speak to him.

I talk and talk *fast*, hoping to stick the landing before he can open his mouth to protest; after all, what I'm asking won't require anything more of him than breaking one or two of his steadfast cruise ship policies.

Bill is still being kind, breathing into the phone aggressively and rhythmically but not interrupting, allowing me to plead my case before creating an overly-pregnant pause between the time I finish speaking and he starts.

"Fifteen minutes."

The tone of his voice tells me it's non-negotiable; the timeframe I will have to successfully pull this thing off, before his rigging crew begins entering the theatre to set up for the night's circus performance. He assures me that the theatre will be accessible during this window, and that my additional request will be accommodated, should I not bother him for further concessions.

I find his terms more than agreeable, and so we strike a deal, leaving me with just enough time to write the most romantic proposal the twenty minutes before I'm to collect you will allow.

I thank Bill sincerely, and he just kind of *sighs*, reminding me that, like Luis behind the chicken-fried rice counter, part of a cruise-ship employee's existence must be occasionally acquiescing to passenger requests as outlandish as mine.

Before hanging up he reminds me half-politely to never contact him on this number again; all I can do is thank him once more before returning the phone to its resting place in the middle of the abandoned library, before starting off towards what will surely be the only other unpopulated area on the whole damn boat.

...

"Where are you taking me"

she asks between wiggles in this evening's cocktail dress; nineteen of the twenty available minutes before my window of opportunity begins spent fussing over the implications of wearing the *really-dark-blue* dress instead of the *navy* one.

The *really-dark-blue* dress won out, and the time between the first three changings was spent ironing out the hastily-written proposal now burning a hole, metaphorically, in my nicest button-up shirt's pocket.

The *second* pocket carrying precious cargo; as we race down cruise ship hallways towards the theatre and it's *should-be* unlocked double-doors, my free hand dives into the one in my pants, quadruple checking that the ring hasn't escaped it's cotton-blend prison. Thankfully, it remains—and so my other hand—the one ushering you down the never-ending hallway—sweats just a little less than it was moments before, when I placed it on your back to assist in the hustling.

I'm nervous as we reach the double-doors to the theatre; should they be locked, I'll be left with no alternative plan suitable for the kind of proposal I promised. I know that, should I reach for the handle the way I'm about to and find my access blocked, I'll incur your wrath and that Bill will incur mine—meaning there's a distinct possibility that either one of us could end up overboard.

I feel a familiar bead of sweat forming just north of my left temple; that particularly overactive gland gearing up production just the way it did reaching for the door to your parent's cabin. Between my brow and palms I'm *wetter* than I have any right to be—again I'm picturing sea water replacing perspiration should you throw me off the boat.

You're beaming *now*, sure—the past twenty-four hours having done wonders for both your mood and the pleasantness of my vacation—but I'm pragmatic enough to realize there is a good deal riding on this. After all, my proposal is competing with three previous, and I'm relatively sure my prep window has been the shortest…

I'm contemplating possibilities and consequences, free hand moving gingerly from ring-in-pocket to door. The familiar brass of the handle welcomes my grip with a pleasant cooling sensation augmented by the tiny flood now tracing the grooves of my palm.

I close my eyes to the soundtrack of your gentle *cooing* over my shoulder, draw the deepest breath my *too-tight* shirt will allow, and pull with all of my might.

The door opens.

"Mico—

So do my eyes; I allow my shoulder to appreciate the weight of the heavy oak transferred to the brass handle in the palm of my hand as it traces a grooved-in-carpet path away from my body.

"—are you crazy?"

You ask the way you do when you're uncertain and I'm up to something potentially *pleasing*; as you tremble with reserved anticipation, I find levity in that you're the one who uses the 'c' word when referring to *me*. I realize I'm probably half-crazy for being here and in this situation, and lying when I tell myself it's the *good* kind. As I look out into the black of the amphitheater, pierced solely by the spotlight shining violently upon an empty stage, I know that there's no way a completely sane person could have cooked up a proposal as brilliant as this one.

Bill came through; honoring the second part of my request, and leaving a light on center stage—a key part of the proposal I'm ushering you down stadium stairs to recite.

"Are we allowed to be in here?"

you ask, heels click-clacking tentatively and in ever- increasing octaves, your Colombian accent echoing throughout the abandoned theatre.

"I called in a favor"

I answer because *why not*; so far, my plan is being executed without a hitch—acting as though I'm some sort of cruise ship VIP seems a natural extension of the inflated ego my adrenaline high has manifested. The echo rings hollow as the validity of my statement, but I don't care and you don't care. We pass rows of ergonomically-designed and richly-accented brown faux-leather seats; empty tonight, they'll nevertheless be a stoic audience for the entertainment to unfold.

As we reach the bottom edge of the stage, you remove your tiny little hand from mine and turn to stare, appropriately awestruck, at the enormity of the amphitheater we have all to ourselves. You run your tiny baby carrot fingers along the surface of the wooden platform of the stage, head still facing out at the must-be-twenty-deep rows of seating, offering glances at the two-tier balconies before coming to rest on the elaborate, gold-lined floral tapestry emerging brilliantly from the hooded stage covering to extend the length of the ceiling.

I usher you *stage left*, grab hold of the railing and take the six stairs leading to the light in two. Meaning I'm *flying*, blood pounding in my ears once more as the reality of the moment I'm about to create sets in on me. You follow slowly, taking six stairs in eight steps, barely holding my gaze as I retreat backwards into the brilliance. Back-pedaling until I feel the warmth beat down on my head and shoulders, I step further into the heat the spotlight exudes, stopping only after ensuring I've left room for you.

I watch you cross the stage, command my memory to retain every single motion in the moments and many it takes you to reach me. You're beautiful in ways too painful to describe, looking the part of some important film star on awards night, hand reaching to nervously brush some imagined-unruly hair back into place, about to accept your prize to the chorus of applause from adoring fans and faux-leather observers.

You glance out at them, your audience, forced to squint those big expressive eyes, and yet you retain all of the two-hundred-forty-seven colors I've come to love counting when you allow them to fall back on me.

I extend my hand, feel my body begin a calculated descent, knee bending to my will despite the cavalcade of nerves and endorphins and pheromones assaulting my ability to part the lips I'm about to.

I watch your thigh jiggle softly against the fabric of a too-tight really-dark-blue dress, and all the blood in my body threatens to pool just north of the knee I'm bending.

I watch your raven black hair sparkle in the light of the light I fought keep on for you, and my parched lips can't part to recite the words your radiance threatens to make me forget.

I watch you look at me as though I'm the only man you've ever loved or *will*, and my knee hits the stage so hard I forget I'm number *four*.

"Muneca"

Your tiny little baby carrot fingers move to your mouth and the covering of it; I catch watercolor versions of the two-hundred-forty-seven shades in your eyes, tears attempting to attacking my vision, too.

"Our love is dramatic, like a play."

The first explodes from the corner of your left eye, catching and carrying a significant amount of the significant amount of mascara you're wearing across the spotlight-illuminated racetrack of your impossible cheekbone.

"Our love is ever-changing, like the sea."

We're on a stage in the middle of a goddamned ocean. I couldn't be more pleased with myself.

"Our love is wild, a ship in a storm—"

You're enraptured, gazing down on me as though my words and the gentle buzz of the light are the first sounds you've ever truly *felt*. The dance of the dust particles around your head forms a halo; as I move into the bones of my speech, I'm emboldened by the execution of a masterfully-executed plan.

I'm some syllable south of

"I promise to weather any weather"

when the shotgun blast of an auditorium door opening kills your attention span dead.

Somewhere over my left shoulder—the shoulder attached to the hand just extended with an engagement ring on the end of it—Bill's rigging crew barges into the theatre, their buffoonery raping the moment you could suddenly care less about.

I do my very best to continue, keeping my eyes on you and rhyming off important promises of forever, while your eyes—suddenly and completely dry—trace their movements down twenty-some rows of faux-leather seats that have apparently stopped paying attention, too.

Their ghastly procession continues the length of the theatre; tracing our steps all the way to the base of the stage I'm performing on, their own crude conversations competing with my spoken-softer-now continuations. We're competing for both echo and your attentions; tragically, I'm losing on all fronts. It takes everything in my power to remain on bended knee and continue a proposal you're no longer invested in; as the troop hits the base and approaches *stage left*, I'm foaming at the mouth.

Meaning the words aren't escaping my lips unmolested; I'm suddenly struggling with syllables and forcing consonants that once felt flawless. Mercifully, they pay us no mind, climbing the six steps in twos and in tandem, and disappearing behind the heavy lavender curtain some six feet to my right, doubtless headed for some rigging apparatus that apparently couldn't wait the fifteen minutes Bill had promised me.

Had they appreciated your beauty with a cat call or a whistle or a lingering glance, I'm moderately sure this boat would be on fire right now; instead I'm the only thing smoldering in a silent-again amphitheater.

When your eyes fall back into mine they betray no hint of apology and for allowing attentions to be wrestled away—and so I bite my tongue as hard as I can and cut seven brilliantly-crafted lines to settle for a

"Will you marry me?"

pushed through a clenched jaw; your

"Jes"

back is a *jes* less enthusiastic than it should have been, before Bill's henchmen violated the terms of our little understanding.

I place the ring on your second tiniest tiny baby carrot finger, rising to kiss your lips with lips probably bloody from the tongue I've just bitten and *almost off*.

Your look has both love and bewilderment in it; parting lips it looks as though bewilderment has won the day and so I take your hand, settling for the fact that it now weighs a little bit *more*, and hang my head as we exit Stage Left.

...

There's this guy on the boat.

I've hesitated in bringing this up for many reasons; the most relevant being that there's generally at least one *this guy* everywhere I go. To give you some background, before it becomes an important part of our impending first evening as an officially betrothed couple: men of my physical *outstandingness* and men with my overly-inflated ego generally spend a great deal of time noticing similar qualities in other males.

Meaning—for lack of a better team—the wandering eyes you've accused me of possessing are more-often-than-not directed at the detection of *other* alpha males; competing lions vying for the prize of your companionship. The fact that you're a creature of remarkable beauty ensures my head is on a near-constant swivel, regardless of my self-esteem; the cruel reality of the animal kingdom states that threats are omnipresent.

So when we arrived on the boat, I spent the first afternoon on the sun deck scanning the faces for a suitable challenge—needless to say, I found one.

Hence,

there's this guy on the boat.

We discovered one another, thanks in part to our half-nakedness; welcoming the deadly rays of a South Florida sun, we had simultaneously been parading our granite-chiseled superiority around the perimeter of the barge when our ever-wandering eyes settled on one another.

Separated by a swimming pool, two tiki-bars and one hundred-thirty *not-nearly-as-in-shape* travelers, we sensed the other's claim to *alpha-ness*, and the necessary instant dislike that comes with it.

You pulled me away after an uncomfortable and not-unnoticed duration; in the days since, we've interrupted moments of vacation-induced bliss to appropriately mean-mug one another.

Given the ridiculousness of the voyage so far, it is without surprise that *this guy on the boat* would factor into what should be one of the happiest nights of my life.

...

We're celebrating.

I'm sandwiched between you and your parents on a sofa in one of the many lounges on the ship. The fabric of this evening's red micro-dress pressed violently against the flesh of your near-indecently-exposed thighs stirs the excitement in me—I have a hard time focusing on the toast your brother is toasting, having returned from the nearest bar with a fresh bottle of champagne. Your sister, rising from the bookend of the sofa next to your father, is the first to echo the sentiment, threatening to escape the confines of her nearly-as-scandalous-and-not-quite-as micro-dress as she throws her arm around her latest-potential-brother.

We're appropriately drunk—the way we have been, more or less, the entirety of the voyage—tonight, however, we're celebrating something worth celebrating, and so the champagne is going nearly as fast as it's coming.

Your sister motions for the riotous conversation to pause, indicating with a nowhere-near stable wave of the arm with the flute in it that another toast is approaching. Just as she opens her mouth to voice what is sure to be an interesting appraisal of our torrid love affair, the elevator over her left shoulder

dings

and, emerging shirtless from the slowly opening doors, is

this guy on the boat.

His necktie is wrapped strategically around his head, a bandana of sorts, doubtlessly absorbing the copious amounts of sweat the *whatever-drugs-in-his-system* have him perspiring. I can tell he's medicated not only by the sheen stuck to the various ridges and ripples cascading his admittedly *second-best-on-the-boat* body, but by the wild of pupils I can tell are *pinned* from my vantage point across the room.

Pupils which, naturally, fall on me—I catch his jaw clench and unclench violently in recognition, watch his course correct as he notices my almost-as-intoxicated bride to be.

Courtesy has me nodding my head enthusiastically as your father, seated beside me blissfully unaware, pats me on my shoulder—all the while, I'm studying *this guys on the boat's* movements as he approaches enthusiastically.

The vodka bottle in his left hand—half-empty I might add—tells me to watch out for his right; between this and yesterday's drama with the Chipmunks, I'm wondering what it is about 'relaxing vacations' that has me so precipitously close to fist fights.

Punching him in the face is something I'd love to do, watching him shirtless and in dress pants and loafers and clearly high and likely drunk—and yet I remind myself that this is a celebration, and so I don't rise to meet him.

"I'm having a party"

he yells as he violates the sanctity of my personal space, looking at me with the kind of hatred that comes when one is only about five-foot-nine, and I'm six feet tall.

I recognize this look, do my best to ignore him when he follows, all

"I've got free booze and drugs in my cabin"

as his pinned eyes shift from mine

--to those of my *almost* as intoxicated bride to be.

"*You* should come."

The answer you give him might be

Love to

or

Jes

or

even just *maybe*—

the blood, pounding in my ears again, prevents me from hearing your exact response. All I know is that it's not

No

or some suitable variation

the way it should be

and so, by the time he unfixes his eyes from the fabric of this evening's red micro-dress, pressed violently against the flesh of your nearly-exposed thighs, and extends the same douchey invitation to your equally-receptive sister, I un-grind my teeth long enough to inform him—quietly and in my least-aggressive octave

"We're celebrating our engagement."

His wildly pinned eyes fall back on mine; I can sense his body temperature rising in tandem with my own.

Peripherally I catch your father and mother smiling at this buffoon, doubtless unaware of his entirely un-friendly intentions…before my tunnel vision blocks out absolutely everything in the world except him

and the middle finger he raises six inches from my face.

Time stops.

I can imagine that, despite the language barrier and the cultural differences and the world of difference, really, between us, your parents can understand the universally recognized symbol to *go fuck myself.*

I can project, reasonably, that they might even understand, should I rise from the couch the way every fiber in my being—plus the fibers in the too-tight clothing I'm semi-restrained in—tell me to commence with the *hitting* of *this guy on the boat.*

I can even extrapolate that, somewhere in the animal kingdom hierarchy hard-wired into our simian DNA, they might respect the re-claiming of my superiority with a barrage of ultra-violence induced thrashings—the whole 'protect our precious daughter' thing.

And still, despite evolutionary allowances to the contrary, I simply sit and smile through bleeding-again tongue and tightly clenched teeth; my respect for you and your family and the significance of the moment we're *supposed* to be celebrating keeping me from indulging the more primal of my urges.

Now, any reasonably sane woman would appreciate the presence of decorum in the face of evening-ending eventualities; any rational fiancée might put her family first and commend an absence of couch-topping transgressions and the limb-flailing's that come with it.

Of course, you're neither—reasonably sane or rational—and so, as I quietly command my oppressor away, I catch you rising to follow him the way your sister does.

My hand finds your hand *almost* as fast as my hand was about to find his face; I rise from the couch to reason with you, while below and beside, your brother remains seated to attempt to explain the situation to your poor parents.

By the time your sister has entered the elevator with *this guy on the boat*, headed to whatever party my engagement celebration is apparently keeping you from, you've called me every possible soul-crushing name you could call me in English, and are settling in on Spanish as you storm away as fast as the confines of tonight's micro-dress will allow.

…

I'm chasing you down cruise ship hallways.

I suppose I wouldn't quite call it *following*, the way you're waving me off with fingers and words, wiggling away from me as fast as the confines of tonight's red micro-dress pressed violently against the flesh of your nearly-indecently exposed thighs will allow.

I feel like I've done this before, back when you were *just* my girlfriend; I figure it means more now, the ridiculous bauble on your finger weighing you down as you do your best to escape me, using the finger beside the weighted one to tell me to

fuck off

for the ten-thousandth time, writhing aimlessly down the latest interchangeable corridor you're writhing aimlessly down.

I'm thinking of/feeling sorry for the bewildered set of non-English speaking parents I left on a couch some three interchangeable corridors back— appreciating the weight of them *witnessing* the kind of behavior that seems to magically occur only in their absence. I know you're appropriately intoxicated, but I still can't help but wonder if you recognize the fact that you're running away from your fiancée and the engagement party you coordinated—I find either possible outcome equally terrifying.

Yes

I'm engaged and again and for the fourth time and panicking, or

No

I'm just screaming and swearing and running away because it's kinda my thing.

You didn't grow up playing sports, but you're moving like an athlete in those heels—between the blood doubtlessly tired of pounding in my ears, the swilling of the alcohol in my stomach, and the confines of my too-tight shirt, I'm struggling to keep pace.

It's probably *better that way*—I have the distinct feeling that, should I enter striking range, I'm likely to end up with a fist in my face. Had I time, I might marvel at how said possibility is almost omni-present here on my supposed 'vacation'—instead I'm laser-focused and gaining ground on you, having apparently slowed in order to adjust the mini-dress that just flashed your ass to passers-by.

Sighing at the prospect of this—the potential rest of my life—I'm just about to reach out and corral you when you stop, suddenly, and beside a heavy hatch door leading to the entirely-restricted crew's quarters…

…a heavy hatch door left *just* ajar enough for you to writhe through.

Which you do—writhe through—escaping my outstretched fingertips with lithe movement and a maniacal dissertation of my *lesser* qualities, spoken in multiple languages as you squirm.

Admittedly, the concept of you, drunk and in *that* dress, happening upon a lecherous party of tourist-fucking crew worries me *almost* as much as the concept of you, drunk and in that dress, happening upon a lecherous party in *this guy on the boat's* cabin, and so the blood, already tired of pounding in my ears, pounds a little *harder.*

Mercifully, you're having a hard time closing the heavy iron door behind you. Recognizing your intentions of leaving me trapped topside, I launch my arm at you, managing to encircle your strained bicep in my grip as you flex it in your endeavor to abandon me.

I pull you towards me as politely as possible; your overly dramatic cries for help doing little to help me from feeling that

you're entirely insane

and

despite the fact that you're entirely insane, I still feel like the abusive asshole you're calling me

and

despite the fact that you're entirely insane, everyone else in earshot will think I'm an abusive asshole, too.

So there's an urgency —despite the politeness of my restraint—to my pulling and of you from behind the heavy iron door; you're jiggling and wiggling and flailing, but *coming*, though not without considerable effort otherwise.

Two not-quite-as-forceful-as-they-could-be pulls and you're back, reminding me with a fresh slap to my already-red face that it is not entirely willingly.

It snaps me to my senses, the caress of your five fingers against my undeserving cheek—the blood pounding in my ears slowing in rhythm as I take stock of my current situation.

I'm flashing back to the last time I told myself that continuing to be with you

--let alone marry you—

was a bad idea

so yesterday

and, once again, despair hits me like your tiny little hand.

As I follow you, resuming your determined pace in any direction *away* from me, the familiar rumble in the pit of my stomach tells me that you might not be the *only* entirely insane engaged individual on this goddamned boat.

…

You finally stop on the stern of this goddamned boat.

Flagstaff, to use a nautical term—you're pressed up against the pole, apparently exhausted after a small forever of unsuccessfully eluding me. I'm sure the night air helps, your heavings thankfully not attracting the attention they would were the sun up, and the deck populated.

It is not—and even though you're not swearing at me multi-lingually at the moment, I'm sure you'll be drawing breath to resume in a moment.

You look at me with wild in your eyes, some goddamned breeze moving your hair dramatically in the warm darkness.

You're framed, standing under the deck lights, illuminated brilliantly against the backdrop of the night air.

You're beautiful

tragically,

and I catch that hint of

save me

buried somewhere in the black of your black little pupils, and the fucked up thing about it is that it makes chases down cruise ship corridors somehow worthwhile.

You reach for me, and maybe your reach has a little more

fuck me

than

fuck you

in it; and so I take the kiss that follows the fingers you place across my face with the enthusiasm usually reserved for your slaps.

Now, I may be drunk, and that might even make the events of the evening (and, by extension, every evening of our relationship) somewhere approaching okay—still, I'm trying my damndest to resist the irrational urge to wholly lose myself in this moment.

Something happens in between the transition of your tongue from behind my teeth to the cleft of my upper lip; the aggressiveness behind your latest attack brings the blood rhythm back to fever pitch. I push my lips against yours, and we're *competing* again—endeavoring to prove to the other one that we care more, flagstaff on the stern of some boat in the middle of the sea.

So we're fighting *even when we're not*, this time agreeing on the theatre of war, neither willing to relent or show lesser enthusiasm.

All at once I'm not blaming *this guy on the boat* for competing for your attentions and I'm not blaming you for running away from our engagement party after not listening to my proposal and I'm thinking about reciting my proposal right here as soon as my lips leave yours

the way they do

and because you're suddenly pulling away from me, as violently as you possibly can.
I shouldn't be surprised at what comes next

"Joo fucking beet (*bit) me"

even though, of course, I did not and *again*; feeling as though I've been down this road before. I'm a touch desensitized to the accusations and the renewed yelling that follows your initial proclamation; I'm able to expertly slip the telegraphed right you throw at my face before using your left to scan the surface of your lips for blood that simply isn't there.

Somewhat resigned to the rest of my life I seem to have so foolishly chosen, I simply submit to your game, following when you take off running, yelling to anyone within earshot about how—of the two of us—*I'm* the abusive one.

Your cries for help catch the attention of the lone security guard patrolling the perimeter of the deck; he stops mid-stride, opening his mouth to utter some sort of command, but you blow right past him, offering a wave of your hand and a retort in a tongue he thankfully doesn't understand.

The look he gives me, trailing a familiar ten steps behind me, says

good luck

and so I nod, feeling like a storm chaser foolishly endeavoring to catch a tornado—this one in a really tight dress. The night of my engagement ends this way; I'm thankful for the cardio, if nothing else, hitting the pillow after another lap around the boat, exhausted and alone, having given up on consummating the special occasion or even sleeping together.

Your adventuring ended at your parent's cabin, and I'm relatively sure—having hosted a ten minute vigil outside your door—that you won't be venturing back out; it's the one worry not currently assaulting the lobes of a massively stressed and entirely over stimulated brain.

I'm still up some hours later, when the door turns and your brother stumbles in, doubtless returning from *this guy on the boat's* party—the same party that ruined what was otherwise a relatively drama free evening. I suppose I should have known better, musing that the events of the day had been going a little *too* smoothly—the request for permission not denied, the door to the theatre not locked. I reckon I could forgive the intrusion of Bill's rigging crew, *almost* understand *this guy on the boat's* drunken buffoonery—as your brother begins snoring voraciously from the adjacent bed, the troubling thought that haunts my near-sleep is that I may not be able to forgive *you* for ruining my *very first* engagement.

...

It's our last day on this goddamned boat.

I find you before breakfast, hair wild and makeup smeared, somehow still looking perfect as you emerge from your parent's cabin wearing one of my oversized hoodies. I don't remember leaving it there, but *fuck it*, because you assure me with a smile and a wave of the hand still weighted by the gaudy bauble that the storm has passed. You're sober, albeit hungover, and so we mutually agree to start fresh, the events of the previous nightmare blamed on the celebrating, and maybe a little *too much*. Our kiss hello tastes like whiskey, and although my stomach churns at the familiarity lingering on non-bitten lips, you're punching me in the face with your pheromones again, and so I'm living in denial by the time your parents emerge bewildered behind you.

It's a small miracle, but breakfast passes without incident; we speak of schedules and packing our bags and plans for goodbye—anything, really, save for the universally troubling events of last night. You're worried about our vacation coming to an end and I'm looking forward to our vacation coming to an end; I'm sure we can agree that we will miss your parent's mediation. Biting into an oversized mouthful of chicken-fried rice, I'm relatively sure I would have thrown you overboard had it not been for their near-constant supervision.

Instead, we're engaged—I nearly choke on my rice, wondering if the end of this magical vacation will change my perception of that particular and peculiar reality. I suppose I'll have the remainder of the day to reconcile this predicament; one more day of sunshine and fantasy before returning to a world of winter and what I'm sure will be shocked reactions to still-settling-in-my-own-mind news.

I watch you, exchanging pleasantries with your siblings—having stumbled to breakfast understandably late, given their recountings of the *epic-ness of this guy on the boat's* party—and marvel at your ability to seduce even the most rational of men, your ethereal, contagious madness and my complete and total inability to resist it.

I think of the moments I'm almost free of your thrall, and then you look at me, the black of your black little eyes pulling me back into the void of being your latest

--and, with any luck, greatest—

victim.

I wash my internal monologue down with bitter toast and black coffee, finishing breakfast on the last day aboard this goddamned boat lost at sea both figuratively *and* literally.

...

The sun is setting; we're minutes from disembarking.

I find myself on the stern again; you're somewhere below, tearfully saying goodbye to a family you'll not see again all year. I relish the time to reflect, removed from the admittedly astounding warmth Colombians display during all such occasions. For once I'm grateful for the coldness of my Irish-Indian blood; although I long to be enveloped in the loving culture I'm to join, at this particular moment, I prefer the temperature of my introspections to be as cool as the sea breeze stinging my frequently slapped face.

Preparing to face the reality of a return to some semblance of routine, I make a mental checklist of your virtues and damnable qualities, hoping home is met with reconciliation regarding my island-influenced decision to marry your crazy ass.

You're hot

and

unnervingly insane.

You're incredibly, wickedly intelligent

and

clearly more so than myself; while my foolish male pride can handle the emasculation of your clearly better and better paying job, I do take umbrage with your overly-affectionate boss.

You're capable of displays of incredible warmth

and

you're capable of displays of incredible cruelty—though the physical abuse is tolerable—even comical—the mental and emotional has effectively broken me down to the point that I'm on the deck of some boat, lost at sea only minutes more, making checklists and questioning the futility of it all.

The breeze kicks up, urging me to continue, and so it's

the perfect, indescribable radiance of your raven hair

vs

the indescribable agony of a week apart from you, knowing I'm due one in every *four* or so.

I'm engaged to you

the thought sobering

meaning you love me *more* than your boss and *this guy on the boat* and all of the other constantly-seeking affection men in your radius

but

I'm the fourth; meaning you loved three more men *more* than your boss and *this guy on the boat* and all of the other constantly-seeking affection men in your radius, and yet still not enough to actually go through with it.

...

I *win* the flight home.

Meaning I'm less scared, amazingly, than you—for all your vaunted talk of fearless frequent flying—and for all your claims that I'm a pussy when it comes to all things aviation—*you're* the one gripping my hand tightly at the first romp of turbulence.

I suppose I'm resigned to it, the whole *I'm fucked anyway* return to Canada; rationalizing that plummeting to earth from thirty-thousand feet is only *marginally* worse than the remainder of my life loving/fighting you.

It's a competition the way *everything* is a competition—I'm taking solace in the victory of our first flight together the way you're taking Ambien, and just to tolerate the remainder of this voyage.

We're mid-flight *maybe* and the pills have you almost sleeping; I'll admit I'm somewhat envious, fully alert and allowing my mind to travel at least as fast as the flying shoebox we're trapped in. For what I'm sure will be the only time in my life, I'm kind of hoping the flight will take a little longer to land than it normally would; I can't shake the feeling that reality *and* the ground will be rushing up to meet me soon.

Spending my savings in paradise seems like a great idea when void of the consequences of home; sun and freedom soon to be replaced with snow and cable bills and rent and parents who may not *quite* share in the enthusiasm of my latest endeavor. I'm thinking of the hours I'll need to work in order to make a dent in the debt this almost-avoided voyage cost me—turning my head to face you, sleeping peacefully, hand resplendent with the sum of my life's savings heaving against the just-inhaled elevation of the breasts it rests on— I'm thankfully offered some semblance of reassurance.

You really are beautiful.

Deceivingly so, pristine features accentuated by the distinct lack of facial contortions I'm used to seeing when you yell at me—I'll admit, it's views like this that remind me why I allowed madness to become my new rationale in the first place. I allow myself to live in the moment for the precious few that remain in my voyage; as I see the promise of winter reflected in the lights of the Toronto skyline, I know that the Monday to follow will be the first of many that I'm engaged and maybe damned and home and—bank account depleted— *years* away from being able to escape the new reality I'm about to touch down in.

...

"You're *what?*"

I've known the both of them, *literally*, the totality of my life. I'm relatively sure that I learned everything I know about human emotion and interpretation from studying the various looks on their faces, ever since the result of such study yielded nourishment and sustenance and survival.

I know them better than I know anyone or anything on this planet

--so why, as I scan the faces of my parents, immediately after informing them

"I'm engaged"

do I have absolutely no fucking clue what they're thinking?

I had a feeling—a sinking, gravel-in-your-guts premonition that this might be the case—and so I brought you as backup, figuring parental niceties might mask the aggressiveness of their true reactions.

"I *knew* you were going to get engaged over there"

my mother claims—which means that she had no idea we were going to get engaged over there and means that, while she secretly may not approve of our *probably*-pending nuptials, she'll never admit it in your company.

She *ooohs* and *aaahs* appropriately, the artist/dreamer in her believing in true love, overlooking the obvious

there's no fucking way you can afford this

reaction written all over my businessman/*not* dreamer father's face.

He's remaining the kind of quiet I feared the entirety of the drive to my hometown; oblivious to my right, you spent the duration admiring the way the light of the sun caught the biggest of the too-many diamonds on your ring, hand out the open window as you sang along to whatever country song came through the speakers.

You're blissfully unaware, offering your hand the way I imagine some Spanish Queen might, not noticing or caring that my father's expression is more

you're fucking crazy

Both of you

than

Ohmigod, congratulations.

He says it anyway,

"Congratulations"

pressed through gritted teeth; and while he would never ever utter *Omigod* about anything, I can imagine he's praying to whatever deity he believes in that this is some elaborate prank.

Still, we're good people and so they maintain the illusion brilliantly, not wanting to hurt your feelings and not wanting to hurt my feelings in front of you. They spend the next several minutes collectively marveling over the intricacies of the admittedly astonishing design; mom mentions more than once that it's far bigger than the ring my father waited too many years to produce.

Her repeated attempts at emasculation do little to improve his mood; I count a half-dozen times in the half-hour that follows where Dad seems precariously close to shattering the illusion and sharing how he *really* feels.

He takes it on the chin because he loves me—although he'd never come out and say it, a lifetime of patience in the face of suspensions from school and stolen cars and the police visits late at night that resulted from them have taught him that being disappointed in his only son is nothing new.

The wild in me comes from mom; I'd imagine that decades of being married to her have taught him to just kind of grin-and-bear-it. So I get away with it, this little presentation, and by the time my mother rises excitedly to hug you and offer her warmest

"Welcome to the family"

my father is a half-step behind, a terse hug of his own telling me without-telling-me that

yes

we will discuss this—in private—later.

...

The dinner that follows fills me with a satisfaction I have not felt since returning from vacation a week ago. I'm dreaming again, sitting around a fire with my family, the newest member of which is curled up tightly against me; you purr softly from your vantage point in my lap, exchanging *colored* recountings of our time away over long sips of wine and stares into the sun setting over the open field behind us.

You tell me that you love the country, and would love to move out here someday; I know you to be the consummate city girl, but I appreciate the sentiment. My mother, filled with equal parts whiskey and love, offers to have us married out here, backyard of their ranch, in between assurances that we could all live happily together.

We laugh, softly and in tandem, knowing full well that a week of sharing a household would reveal not only the worst aspects of *our* torrid love, but theirs as well.

The illusion is nice; I pour a fresh whiskey and allow the dream to linger like the light over the empty field, happy to be home and with you and maybe even buying into the notion that the ring on your finger has quieted the storm behind your eyes.

...

We're in Toronto

We're in Toronto

and we're at this fancy restaurant in the heart of Maple Leaf Square

and I figure that a lavish weekend away—alone—is just what we need to calm the storm that is time spent together in the confines of routine.

So it's a weekend and it's *away* and from the influence of your boss/sponsor and it's a weekend away from the four walls of my modest apartment and it's a weekend

here;

the St. Germaine

soon to be my favorite and your favorite—and therefore likely most expensive—hotel in the city we've escaped to. We pull up in your Range Rover—the only thing I love more about you than you—and the doorman who opens your door introduces himself with the kind of earnestness that comes with working at what might be the most expensive hotel in the city.

He says his name is Dejan; Dejan the doorman, and, noticing that you're one hundred percent Colombian, Dejan the doorman informs us that

    a)   you're beautiful

and

    b)   his beautiful wife is Colombian, also.

We share enthusiastic conversation as Dejan the doorman goes for the bags in the back of the Range; as he lifts the heaviest and what he no doubt hopes is the final of your three oversized only-gone-for-the-weekend bags, the look he shoots me assures that this is common practice for beautiful Colombian women.

We make small talk as we traverse the opulent lobby to the check-in counter; you walk with the purpose of someone who has stayed here before—you're holding my hand tightly and leading, a half-step ahead and immune to both my conversing with Dejan the doorman and my frequent head-turnings.

I'm taking it all in; recountings of which celebrity DJ's and sports figures are staying here this weekend, wondering if they're as impressed with the electric neon lighting accents embedded in the marble floors. Admittedly, this industrial urban chic décor is right up my alley; as Dejan the doorman finishes informing me which dinner spots are the *hottest*, I'm starting to believe this ridiculously expensive weekend away will be money well spent.

Your Colombian assertiveness takes care of the check-in; I'm standing that same half-step behind and, narrowing my gaze from what looks to be a Banksy behind the counter, I find myself enamored by the curves your body takes in today's (white) minidress.

Beside me, Dejan the doorman is admiring also, sheepishly presenting some random and probably true fact about the origins of Colombian beauty. Yeah, he's going on about Slavic peoples crossing the Bering Strait; all the while his eyes and my eyes are crossing the lines in the soft horizontal pattern doing work to conceal the ridiculousness of the ass threatening to consume it.

So I'm preoccupied; the look you shoot me, following the head turn that followed the command to produce my credit card, has equal parts playfulness and impatience—in the moment it takes me to collect myself, I'm aware that you're both amused by my rampant desire and annoyed at the effect it seems to be having on my ability to participate.

I do, participate, and in the paying of today's little extravagance—at least, the pending paying of today's little extravagance, my credit card on file as we're suddenly saying goodbye to Dejan the doorman and travelling hotel hallways towards our ninth floor room.

There's a shower in the middle of it—our room—and, having turned the knob on the ninth floor door to enter, this is immediately all I care about. You enter a half-step behind, and, as you and that ass saunter ahead of my holding-the-door like a gentleman-ness, I can't help but note your seeming indifference, and to the outright splendor of the room unfolding before me.

I mention this, something that sounds a lot like

"There's a fucking shower in the middle of the room"

maybe hoping to elicit some sort of shared response in regards to appreciation of the ostentatious nature of the space I step into; instead I'm greeted with the sort of flippant

"Uh-huh"

response that reminds me you're accustomed to lavishness.

I'll admit that, from a social-climbing standpoint, this turns me on; that a kid from the mud could end up in a place like this with some Latina Goddess; the kind that looks like the barbarian queens Frazetta (worth a google) used to paint on the covers of the *Conan* dime-store novels I was too poor to afford.

This appreciation inspires the undressing of you that follows the closing and *just* of the door; you've yet to unzip your many suitcases and I've yet to observe the rest of the room and yet today's (white) minidress is suddenly the on-the-floor it should be.

We're in the shower in the middle of the room immediately; the fogging of the glass prevents inspection of the rest of the room I could suddenly care less about.

It'll be lobster at *e11even* and the tourist shit that follows dinners at restaurants named after times in time; for now it's unnecessary mid-afternoon showers and the kinds of things unnecessary mid-afternoon showers become necessary to rinse away.

We're in Toronto

and we don't need to be; but it's the weekend and it's ours and it's one without a chance of metaphorical rain—and so it's the kind of weekend away that makes the other kind bearable.

...

Valentine's Day

It's Valentine's Day and I'm appropriately horrified.

I glance at my watch, ten am on a Tuesday, this year, and not even two weeks removed from a particularly life-changing and ridiculously expensive cruise.

The preposterous bauble adorning your ring finger—the one cementing my status/damning me to hell as Fiancée Number Four—drained every last dollar form an admittedly humble savings account. Still, Colombians love romance, and the calendar has declared today the most romantic of days, and so I'm scrambling to satisfy what are sure to be lofty expectations.

I had booked a dinner the day we landed back in London and, woefully, reality; a dinner at the best and therefore most expensive restaurant in the city, figuring foolishly that the extravagance of the trip would still be weighed favorably against a modest gym salary when forecasting your mood.

Looking down at the desk in my office...

the desk now adorned with a dozen long-stem red roses and my favorite Starbucks creation and a ridiculously emasculating stuffed monkey and, most shockingly, a *thousands-of-dollars-at-least engagement* ring for a man--an engagement ring for a man, which--mysteriously and never having tried one on or had a fitting for or an idea about— happens to be a perfect fit

...I realize I'm horribly mistaken.

I'm picturing you measuring my finger in my sleep, the feeling only slightly less disturbing than the fear of finality washing over me as I slip it on, the stuffed monkey smiling wickedly from his perch above my delicious and not-soothing-enough beverage.

It fits perfectly; I spend the next five minutes getting used to the weight of it— literally and figuratively—finding subsequent keyboarding and favorite-Starbucks-creation-sipping impacted by the sudden and overwhelming aversion to banging it off of something.

Meaning I value it—that, or I'm recognizing the intrinsic value of the ring itself—not used to admiring myself with anything decidedly more expensive than I can readily afford.

The monkey I hide—while the sentiment is appreciated, the emasculation I'm sure to experience if discovered by one of my testosterone-enhanced co-workers humbles the emasculation I'm *already* experiencing, having received flowers and a ridiculously-expensive engagement ring for a man on *this*, the most romantic of days I'm suddenly remembering we had previously agreed to not be more romantic than the aforementioned dinner on.

I'm scrambling, suddenly, having realized you'll be expecting decidedly more than a dinner in retaliation for your romanticism. I curse my inability to forecast the intention behind your honeyed *dinner-is-enough* words, reach for my phone with a suddenly-weighted left hand, intent on ordering a better-than-yours bouquet from one of the dozen local flower shops.

...

An hour later, I'm understandably panicked.

It turns out that, by noon on Valentine's Day, every other similarly-stationed male in my three-hundred-eighty-eight-thousand city has made the phone call ahead of me—meaning there are literally no elaborate bouquets to be sold.

I find myself sweating more than the next three clients I guide through pre-booked fitness assessments, my mind entirely removed from body fat analysis and strength tests.

It's three pm before I'm able to steal away to the grocery store one plaza away; I practically collide with the doors, a half-step behind my pace in retraction.

If grocery store flowers are a step down from flower shop flowers, then three-pm-Valentine's-Day-flowers are lower still; of the dismal selection left, I select the *least* atrocious, returning to the rest of the work day as deflated as the stems I'm holding.

The rest of the workday passes painfully; you text, excited and often, and of how you're to pick me up in your new Range Rover—the only thing I love more about you than you—and of how you're to drive us to the dinner that tradition and my foolish masculine pride dictate I should be driving us to. I can tell by the onslaught of your love-filled messages that you're doubtless expecting similar extravagances to those I've received—and so, deciding my grocery store flowers are nowhere near enough, the last half-hour of my shift is spent one plaza over and again, sifting through ransacked rows of Valentine's Day cards for one with space to inscribe more promises that I can only *probably* fill.

...

I'm emasculated in the passenger seat, watching as you navigate rush-hour-on-a-holiday traffic, leading to our destination at the most expensive and therefore best restaurant in the city.

I'm five minutes removed from meeting you in the parking lot of the gym, four-and-a-half from catching you as you hurled yourself into my arms and showered me with the first of seven appropriately-aggressive kisses. Things went well for the thirty-nine seconds between appropriately-aggressive kiss seven and the presentation of my humble, grocery store bouquet—I even counted the thirteen seconds you entertained the idea that they might be some kind of elaborate holiday joke.

Five-minutes-ten-seconds later—now—I'm sitting silently in the passenger seat, weighted by the realization that my grocery store flowers were nowhere near sufficient and weighted by the weight of the ridiculously expensive bauble adorning my ring finger and weighted by the realization that I really should have known better.

You're uncharacteristically/characteristically-when-you're-mad-but-not-too-mad-yet silent, navigating cluttered streets and sticky thoughts, turning the last of three lefts before our destination/doom.

What makes it worse is that you're all the way *extra* tonight; a literal twenty on your usual ten scale, fake hair extensions where none are needed and elaborate and freshly extended/adorned nails and the kind of makeup contouring that could have your cheekbones cut glass. Yeah, you're drop dead tonight, the curves your body takes in tonight's navy blue barely there dress making/adding to the feelings of outright inadequacy I'm feeling over here in the passenger seat.

And don't get me wrong I get it; your willingness to go all in on a crazy love and go all out in your efforts to show/shower the lucky bastard/recipient; I wish that I had the money and the job and the age and the status to shower you with the things I *can't*, foolishly believing that crazy love and *only* would ever be anything close to enough for you.

So I'm lamenting on this—the happiest of romantic holidays—the entirety of the search for a parking spot in a crowded restaurant parking lot, maybe welcoming the diversion the hunt for a *stop*, literally and metaphorically, would provide.

You skip the conversation but go for the customary hand-holding, navigating a treacherous and icy parking lot and navigating a treacherous and icy relationship with *this*, the first glimmer of hope that our evening might be salvageable since I wiped the smile off of your pretty pumped up pretty little lips with my grocery store flowers.

We're shown to our seats moments after entering the must-be-mahogany double doors; one of the advantages to dining on a reservations-or-you're-fucked day at a reservations-or-you're-fucked restaurant.

Making our way through a myriad of candle-lit and expensively adorned tables, I take my eyes off of your ass in that dress long enough to appreciate the ambiance of *this*, the most expensive and therefore best restaurant in the city. I also take note that you pass by indifferently—my knowledge of your three-nights-out-at-dinner-per-week demands meaning this is nowhere near your *first* foray into this dining room. Probably not your first foray into this dining room on this particular holiday, either—the weight of my new engagement ring against the hand you're still holding reminds me of at least three other men you've emasculated/adorned the same.

And as we're walking the length of an appropriately-long dining room I'm thinking *less* about the beautiful playing of the beautiful lady playing the beautiful Baby Grand Piano in the corner and more about how I actually appreciate the ring and the gesture—hell, like it even, a physical representation of your devotion back to me; my feelings of emasculation stemming more from the fact that my ring to you and this dinner have drained every penny from an account I spent a decade building and from the fact that you throw thousands around as afterthought.

We reach our table—elevated from the main dining room in a cozy little alcove beside a beautiful fireplace, surrounded by strategically placed tables containing couples or dates and *only*.

It's a little quieter than the din rising from the main floor below us; placing my jacket—the one containing the grocery store card with the hastily inscribed message—over the back of my chair, I appreciate the view of the still-being-played-beautifully Baby Grand, and the romantic overtones permeating the air.

As I settle into my seat, making eye contact for the first time since I presented my admittedly-off-the-mark bouquet, I'm figuring I'll need all the help I can get.

"How was your day?"

I lob across the table, a peace offering masquerading as semi-serious inquiry.

"Fine—

with an iciness to rival that of the parking lot; your eyes fall to the diamond-embedded silver ring now decorating my dominant hand

--how was yours?"

I take a moment to inspect my prize, using the delay to quell the desire to reply

"Valentine's Day isn't a fucking competition"

before replying

"Baby, I love it"

instead, and diving into an investigation of just how you pulled this—the most expensive/elaborate of surprises—off.

Naturally, you're more than willing to discuss this—how you'd sized my finger in my sleep the way I'd feared/imagined/figured—how you'd visited three jewelers before settling on one who could customize the price-tag-roughly-mentioned piece now weighing my finger and my conscience.

I offer extravagant and not-untrue descriptions of how much I appreciate the gesture and of how thoughtful and unnecessary it was; attempting an earnest

"But it's my job to spoil *you*"

and not allowing steam to escape my ears when you scoff in response violently enough to draw the attention of the couple dining behind you.

As if on cue, the waiter arrives to delicately—apparently sensing a touch of hostility at the table—go over the featured extravagances and the outrageously expensive wine list.

Despite the dread my bank account statement is sure to induce, I'm grateful at your animated response; selecting for us a bottle of Cabernet-Sauvignon that is sure to either greatly help—or horribly retard—this evening's progression.

Mercifully, he's back with the bottle—the bottle you sample and smile favorably after indulging—before our tension-filled banter can escalate into name-calling.

You're done the first glass before our entrees are selected; I've only half-paid attention to the menu, settling on roasted duck—I think—while parrying jabs at my opportunities to plan something more significant than the woefully received flowers likely withering at your words from their resting place on the floor behind the driver's seat of your Range Rover.

The wine seems to enhance your volume if not your mood; as our conversation inevitably escalates so too does your enthusiasm, leaning into once-whispered words like

"supposed to be a romantic day"

and

"Jeecus"

(*Jesus)

and all of the colorful phrasing in and around your persistent intent to remind me of my Valentine's Day failings.

You pause when the meal arrives—sensing a break in proverbial cloud cover, I savor the first bites of *turns-out-I-did-order-duck*, further attempting to lighten the mood with mutterings of surprises to come;

surprises

being an equally-shitty grocery store card.

Your mood lightens, detected only by the jiggling your breasts do as you bounce playfully in your seat, humming along to music in your head and only, chewing a healthy mouthful of pasta and completely oblivious to the notes from the beautifully played piano.

This activity enlightens me to *two* realities; one, you're really feeling that third glass of wine and two, in addition to being insanely beautiful, there's a tiny chance you're insanely insane.

I ponder this between sumptuous chewings; relieved to be chewing fowl amongst somewhat pleasant conversation, a welcome turn from chewing my bottom lip amongst admonishings.

So maybe I don't see the danger when you order that second bottle of red, despite the fact that I've stopped drinking or at least slowed to a crawl, not really a wine guy but foolishly relishing the reprieve that the fermented grapes seem to be allowing.

I'm a tiger in the tall grass, waiting full and fed for the perfect and least dangerous opportunity to present you with the present that isn't anywhere near the inflated expectations you doubtlessly have made since I announced it's pending arrival and since you started really going in on that wine.

So the time might *not* be now, but you're back to looking at me favorably and dinner—if not the drive to—has been going reasonably well, and so I reach nervously into the jacket pocket on the back of my chair and I pull the card sealed in the holiday-appropriate red envelope and I read your look of momentary approval as you're presented a mysterious and therefore not-yet-judged present…

…and I even get to enjoy the moment for a few moments more.

You tear into the envelope with the fervor of realized and delayed eventualities; I see your big, black, hungry eyes scan the handwritten contents

--the ones outlining a promised vacation to some sunny getaway, at a time of your choosing

--and I study the fallout; gauging the subtle vibration of your cornea as sign that maybe I did okay this time.

I mean, it's not a *thousands-of-dollars-ring* (--like the one you received weeks ago) and it's not the retaliatory *thousands-of-dollars ring* I received hours ago—and it's not a stuffed monkey—but maybe

…just maybe

…it's enough to roll back the storm that had previously threatened to ruin this, the most romantic of holidays.

As you proceed to violently tear the card into pieces, however—

--I'm learning just how foolish assumptions can be.

…

I'm scared to take my eyes off of you; I can tell by the animated flailings you're flailing across the table that you might not be finished with the launching of things in my direction.

Despite my inability to turn, I'm entirely aware that your theatrics have attracted the attentions of every other restaurant-goer in the immediate vicinity. I'd like to say that I'm in shock, sitting half-covered in pieces of torn Valentine's Day card, but tragedies like this are comically commonplace in our relationship.

So I'm dumbfounded and entirely embarrassed, face undoubtedly the crimson of the card stock attached to my beard, frozen and watching you rage beautifully in a restaurant full of people fortunate enough to experience this for the first time.

And fuck them anyways, I'm sure you would say were your mouth capable of vocalizing anything other than my failures as a man—surely their respective *most-romantic-day-of-the-year-because-Hallmark-says-so* dinners aren't worth half of yours, ruined now by my promised vacation card. I allow you to continue for the time it takes, half-hoping the waiter with the pitcher of water shaking somewhat rhythmically in his hand will grow the balls to come over to our table and interrupt our little episode with a timely top up.

I'm foolish enough to remove my eyes from yours, fully aware that said action leaves me open to a throwing of whatever your little Colombian temper deems throwable and in my direction; still, I take time to scan the faces of the restaurant-goers, committing to memory the sizeable number of meals we're ruining. To her credit, the lovely woman playing the Baby Grand Piano *keeps* playing the Baby Grand Piano, distracting the patrons on the lower level—their reservations below paying dividends now, unaware as they are of the turmoil above them.

Further angered by the insolence that is my lack of eye contact, your rage reaches fever pitch; I resume my gaze just in time to catch the ring I paid my soul for, removed as it was from your tiny little baby carrot finger and hurled with ferocity in my direction.

So I'm sitting stunned and *single*, apparently, here on Valentine's Day and in the best and therefore most expensive restaurant in the city, fourth victim of your troubling desire to get engaged and then destroy the fool foolish enough to try to tame you.

…

There's clouds in your eyes—metaphorically, anyways; the dim restaurant lighting makes it hard to tell in the literal sense—and maybe they're lifting or maybe you're simply spent, your rage reduced three octaves as, mercifully, the rest of the restaurant returns to collectively private conversations.

For a moment that might take ten we're silent, simply studying one another from across a table unbothered by dinners we won't touch. I watch you heave said table and worlds away, maybe wondering what could have damaged you so significantly that behaviors like this are a reality, maybe wondering nothing at all. The shock makes it hard to tell; I'm more reacting than participating, collecting thoughts and card stock from pieces of what I'm imagining was probably delicious eighty-dollar duck.

You watch me intensely, the way you always do when the fight lacks significant fight back, doubtless discerning if it is weakness or lack of appropriate passion that has me so restrained *here*, in a restaurant full of horrified people who deserve better.

And the clouds might be parting or they might not be; sensing the approach of the timid waiter with the still-quivering pitcher of water from over your still-tensed shoulder, you part your pretty pumped up pretty little lips to mouth

"I have to go to the washroom,"

the first words in English, entirely, and the first words without some overwrought description of the man I'm *not* since words were the only things left to hurl.

I'm as taken aback by the lack of violence in your voice as I was taken aback by the violence in the words preceding these *seven*; embattled but still amazed you can change directions as fast as you seemingly change them.

"Will you come with me"

quietly and next and, astonishingly, devoid of any awareness that the last several minutes included sentences about never going anywhere with me, ever again.

So it's not the destination vacation I promised on the card you peppered my entrée with, and it's not the *anywhere else* my embarrassed and emasculated and utterly humiliated ass would rather be--but, despite the voice called common sense screaming at me to *not*, I'm all at once holding your hand and walking the direction of the stairs, as bewildered as the rest of the audience our impromptu theatre created, collectively aghast at the latest turn this performance has taken.

...

I'm waiting patiently outside the washroom we walked to; walked to past astonished and angered topside tables of couples who would also probably rather be the anywhere we are not.

Downstairs—miraculously unaware of your assault, in part due to the playing of the Baby Grand Piano—we made our way through a sea of blissfully unaware and uninterrupted diners, navigating the bustle of the floor on our way to the ladies room you've disappeared into.

Posted against the wall opposite, I fumble with your ring in my pocket, feeling it crash periodically against the elaborately expensive metal of mine. And I suppose I should remove it—mine—single now and not for the first time, *off again* in the middle of the best and therefore most expensive restaurant in the city, here on some holiday Hallmark can go fuck itself for creating.

I have time to collect thoughts like this—collecting sympathetic glances from wait staff who've doubtlessly whispered tales of just-transpired events a floor above—while I wait the six minutes and counting you've been hiding on the other side of the door I'm resigned to staring at.

I'm in shock, still and surely, having experienced your storm yet never in so public a place—wondering how I'll brave the walk back up those stairs, to collect a bill for at least two meals I've had hand in ruining.

I notice my hand is trembling as I remove it from the pocket your ring swears it's sorry for inhabiting—and I can't tell if it's from rage or embarrassment or adrenaline, or some tired and true cocktail of the three, as I bring it towards lips parched from a lack of the wine that led us here.

...

The ladies' room washroom door opens some six or seven or eight minutes later, and the sight of you in that dress—the same dress you took off your ring and threw it in my face in some six or seven or eight minutes ago—momentarily makes me forget that you threw anything, words or rings, at all.

You're breathtaking in ways that makes random acts of violence okay; maybe I blame my animal ancestors for carnal instincts, maybe I tell myself it's the byproduct of too many hits to the head—either way, when you extend your hand towards mine I know I'm weak enough to take it without a fight before reaching out and taking it the way we both know I was going to anyways.

We walk together, heads raised defiantly, marching across the floor and up the stairs and then across the wreckage we've created on the way to our table.

The waiter, still trembling somewhat, offers his best confused look at the sight of our interlocked fingers; we do our best to ignore scoffs and subtle curses from still-displeased patrons as I pay—and tip generously—for food that won't be digested tonight.

…

The funeral march towards your Range Rover—and the cold and the snow and the night it is encased in—occurs in slow motion, and yet I process nothing. You collect your coat on the way out the door, *I think*; admittedly, it isn't until the winter outside the heavy double doors hits me that I return to the reality I'm trapped in.

We're traversing the still-treacherous parking lot and you're thumbing for the remote starter when I realize that you're far too intoxicated to drive the way you're about to.

I stop you, my hand leaving yours to rest against the handle of the door you had mind to reach for and *do* moments later.

And with this, we're back in rings metaphorical, boxing the twelfth round tonight and over who should pilot your Range Rover—the only thing I love about you more than you—home. You're unrestrained by the constraints of walls and the civility co-presence with civilians creates, and so you fight harder than you have been, hurling insults and hands no longer range-restricted by dining room tables and no longer reaching for doors, settling for resting on *faces* instead.

So yeah, you slap me and maybe mean to again, calling me a pussy for worrying about silly little things like blood-alcohol levels and police; I parry your verbal jabs with assurances that you're in no shape to drive.

Still, you're steadfast in your resolve to take me back to my snow-buried car *and never see me again* and so, after another six or seven or eight minutes of fighting a losing battle in the cold night of some holiday I'm reasonably sure is now ruined forever, I crawl into the passenger seat, resigned to my fate and figuring this night has already undoubtedly reached the apex of awfulness.

...

I was wrong.

Earlier, when I crawled into your passenger seat and ruminated about awfulness and apexes of—musing under a chorus of

"Joo fucking pussy"

and

"Never let you drive my car"

that this night couldn't get worse.

The drive—given the time of night and the less-than-ideal weather conditions currently being less than ideal outside my passenger side window—should have taken us twelve minutes to get *here*, Commissioners and Wonderland and six stop lights from the left turn into the sanctity of the gym parking lot.

It's taken four.

You run the red at Commissioners, howling the way you have been and at my horrified urgings to obey the fucking traffic signals, if not consider the patches of black ice we've been skating on, far too fast on streets that plead us not to be so far too fast on.

You turn the music up, diverting your eyes from the road far too long to fake sobriety, thumbing carelessly through radio stations that don't care back, drowning out the

"Joo fucking pussy"

you call me for the sixth time in four broken traffic regulations. You're speeding along and singing along between breaks—not brakes—and taking the time between this chorus and the next one to remind me that I'm not a man.

I'm contemplating this—wondering if the glass of wine I got through before your latest/greatest World War is causing me to question my manhood as you come dangerously close to striking the curb I'm subsequently considering tucking/rolling out onto—

--and then all at once, and far faster than we should be

--we're making the left turn into the sanctity of the parking lot I thought we would never make it to.

And maybe it's sick and yet maybe some part of me admires it; having spent the better part of thirty years endeavoring to be the bad boy you and your Colombian recklessness beat me at (--except the boy part--) so effortlessly, turning parking lot corners to my far-safer car and howling at me all the while.

I get out in a hurry, shame washing over me as I realize I'm really not as advertised; that my wild can't match half the wild in your weakest eye—and it looks a little lazy tonight, from the too-much wine and the too-many hoarsely shouted words you hoarsely shouted at me this evening.

Still, you're a slightly diminished vision of the beauty you were when you picked me up here; leaving me breathless once more as you swing your Range Rover back and away from me, rolling down the window before putting it in drive.

I brace for one last forthcoming obscenity, knowing that the key to winning this latest war hangs on the last hoarsely shouted word.

So I'm a combat veteran, decorated and surrendered and lined up against some proverbial wall, waiting to be executed by the firing squad hiding behind your pretty pumped up pretty little lips. I'm expecting something about my lack of masculinity, or my withering and suddenly-insufficient penis or maybe even some dissertation as to the latent vulnerabilities of Canadian-born men...

...as you pull off, lowering the just-thumping bass from tired and expensive speakers, the

"I love joo"

you squeal before squealing tires hits me harder than the ring you threw at me at the dinner that kinda led me to believe *otherwise*.

...

I bet that I stand in this damned parking lot for five minutes, watching the trails in the snow your tires made, the lightly falling flakes soothing my inflamed temperature and gently urging a return to the reality I still kinda can't believe I'm coming back to.

I'm replaying the events of the evening, still-heightened temperature fighting off the reminder that it's cold as fuck out here; thumbing not-yet-frozen fingers nervously through pockets containing rings I couldn't foresee being there for the keys to get me the fuck away from this night and this cold and this fresh set of memories.

I remove them gingerly from pockets holding decidedly more precious cargo, baffled by the juxtaposition their contents and your last words have left me swimming in.

The drive home has me feeling the drunk you most certainly were/are—and maybe I wonder if you made it home safely or maybe I muse that I can't wait to call my father and tell him this story and that it's over the way he desperately wants it to be—either way within two troubled minutes of my head hitting the pillow I'm soundly sleeping and *off* this latest and *most public* dangerous disaster.

...

Bad Decisions, for Good Reasons

Sugar Baby Sousa looks at me with eyes that *aren't* yours.

In color or clarity; hers shine bright and innocent and pure—and, although she's young, she moves towards me with sex in her hips and intent in her steps that betray her relatively *lacking* years—all grown up as she pulls me closer to her.

Those lips, *almost* as fat as yours and maybe just as tasty, move against mine for the first time, pushed forcefully and by someone resolute in their desire to show me just how much they care.

It's refreshing and it's wrong and—even though we are technically on one of our seemingly regular bi-weekly breaks—I can't help but feel as though I'm cheating on you as I kiss her back, almost as hard as she endeavors to continue kissing me.

I know that there's a chance that we will end up back together, your

Never wanna see you again

and

Why don't you fuck off and die

really more half-hearted suggestions that outright proclamation. Sure, it's been four weeks since you shouted those words and more my way—and sure, you've probably deleted my number and not contacted me; although Sugar Baby Sousa and her fat little lips would beg to differ, I can't quite shake the you or the feeling this latest

goodbye, forever

might just be more permanent than the last three.

So *not*; I'm contemplating this and the perpetual exhaustion of it, while a drop dead gorgeous nineteen year old kisses my lips with a tenacity designed to make memories of you melt.

She's less seasoned than you, her lips landing with a lack of nuance—she's forceful in her explorations, tiny tongue scanning wildly the contents of my *swear-I'm-resisting* mouth. The tactile differences send electricity surging through my body; in my ever-advancing age and after what feels like years of emotional abuse; my ego appreciates the unadulterated adoration this nubile young woman is showering me with.

So I take the kisses that come and the thrusting of her body against mine with increasingly *minimal* fight back; altogether thankful that she came to my apartment tonight to

help me through it

the way we both knew she intended when she called on the phone an hour ago to make the offer.

You should know I fought the urge to invite her—even said

"No thanks"

a couple of times,

but she told me she needed help with an assignment she subsequently forgot to bring.

She made it through the front entrance without buzzing up, and so her knocking on my door snapped me from whatever melancholy haze I had undoubtedly fallen into in the time since she hung up the phone to begin the drive over.

I answer the door and my eyes meet her eyes…

and

Sugar Baby Sousa looks at me with eyes *that aren't yours*

and you pretty much know the rest.

...

I wake up feeling guilty

and

I wake up feeling great

and

she's still sleeping soundly beside me, exhausted after events containing a tenacity and a fury and a series of complicated movement patterns she's doubtless just experienced for the first time. I took it out on her, somewhere in the middle of our first tangling—expressing with honed physicality my frustrations at the circumstances I've found myself enclosed in. She took it with admirable resolve, writhing away underneath and then on top and then the everywhere else we ended up as I valiantly attempted to forget all about you.

You should know that I did not—forget about you, even for a moment—although her youthful exuberance did wonders for my resignation and perpetual melancholy.

So I wake up feeling guilty and I wake up feeling great, rising from the bed I used to share with you, having shared it with her, and wondering as I stumble over to the coffee maker if I haven't just fallen headfirst into the first and next best thing to ever happen to me since *you* did.

...

She's *easy*, Sugar Baby Sousa.

It's been a month since you broke off our engagement—and while this isn't the first time you've called it off forever, it is by far the longest.

I'm starting to think it's real—this separation thing—and Sugar Baby Sousa has me worried less and less about the soul-crushing potential of never seeing you again, all kisses where there should be sadness and *presence* when there should be none.

She's laughing, often and loudly, and keeping her hands on me when we're together; and so the failure of taming you is tempered by the attentions of a mouth-wateringly beautiful, non-jaded *new* adult.

She doesn't chastise me for the kind of music that tends to pop up on the random playlist playing in the background of my apartment.

She doesn't require elaborate dinners out on multiple nights; she even cooks a thing or two, and doesn't complain that I can only cook a thing or two.

She likes the kinds of movies I like, cowers adorably when something startles her, curling up closely into a chest she doesn't mind if I go a day or two without shaving.

She converses easily and often, hangs on every word I say, listens attentively to stories of my past, even if those stories are about you.

She offers advice in gentle octaves, tells me not to hurt her with her eyes and not words in multiple tongues, her defense a little more defense and a little less offence than what I've become accustomed to.

She's comfortable in public spaces, maybe not as used to drawing the attentions of everyone in whatever room we walk into, but adjusting marvelously to continually developing radiance.

She tells me she likes me and without any weight or consequence or darkness; I find myself letting my guard down with each passing day, having strung together a few without a single sign of storm.

She's beautiful in every opposite way that you're beautiful, young and red-headed and rosy-cheeked, freckled and fair and kind of treating me that way too.

So why, after she's closed her eyes and rested her head on my chest and reduced her breathing rate rhythmically, am I wide awake with a pounding heart thinking about you?

...

Sugar Baby Sousa is *here*, my apartment, for what might be the thirty-first day in a row and what may be the thirty-fifth day since you *haven't* been.

And so, when my phone screen lights up from a resting place beside the bed we're both resting in, it takes me a half-second longer than it should to rub the half-sleep from my tired eyes and realize the message displayed across my screen is

mercifully and *un*

from you.

I reach for it—the phone *literally* and the communication from you *metaphorically*-- doing the best I can not to wrest her from the kind of peaceful sleep new adults who haven't yet been damaged by boys like me tend to sleep, fingers shaking and nearly failing at both lifting the phone from the end table and leaving her blissfully unaware beside me.

I can see, illuminated against the darkness of a midnight-black room, that the text is from you and that it's not a text at all—it's a photo.

My adrenaline—returned instantly after a well-deserved month long sabbatical—has the blood beating a familiar rhythm in my ears as I fumble my thumb across the screen, eager to illuminate the contents of the thumbnail photo my still-tired eyes can't quite discern.

It's a photo, yes—and while it isn't the kind of photo my half-sleep would selfishly hope you'd choose to send me after a month of non-communication, it has the same effect.

Meaning my heart skips a half-beat, looking at a photo of a wrist with a hospital bracelet attached to it. The bracelet has your name on it because it's your wrist wearing it—in the time it takes me to read the inscription bearing the hospital name, I'm out of bed and half-dressed, leaving Sugar Baby Sousa in bed and dreaming beautifully about boys who won't hurt her the way I'm about to.

…

It's late by the time I reach St. Joseph's hospital.

Like two am late, which means that—although the streets I speed down were relatively void, including, thankfully, the presence of police—visiting hours are long since over.

Paid parking never sleeps, and so—even though I'm one of the only cars in the lot—the card I punch has a ten dollar price tag, money spent regardless of whether or not I'm able to gain access to you. One more thing to curse as I rub my tired eyes, navigate the empty spaces for one comfortably close to the entrance, and kill the engine. I feel my blood, pumping the way it has been since I received your cryptic message some twenty minutes ago, kick up a notch as I exit the car. The cool, not-even-close-to-morning breeze assaults my should-be tired senses, does little to calm newly frayed nerves, woken with the rest of me and from a month long, anxiety-free sabbatical.

The feeling is both troubling and familiar; I suppose I'm too tired and too wired to catalogue what this might mean for my state of mind, approaching the sliding glass door and noting anticipation where feelings of reservation *should* be.

There's a security guard posted on the other side of the doors; from my vantage point opposite the condensation-coated glass, he looks decidedly less than alert, seated as he is at a folding table in the center of the lobby.

The soft mechanical *whir* of the opening door wrests him from half-slumber; I offer a warm hello, hoping my hopefully casual body language suggests to him that post-midnight hospital visits are something that comes naturally to me.

He gives me one of those

No

It's not natural for someone to come strolling in at two am

looks;

I beat him to the punch by saying

"Just had to run home to let the dog out"

hoping he's half the animal lover I am.

"Who are you here to see?"

he responds, decidedly un-warmly; it could be the time or the intrusion, but Bill—as I gather from the name tag on Bill's security uniform—isn't particularly interested in talking *breeds* at two am.

"Muneca _____"

He leaves his eyes on me for a moment; I curse my clearly-just-woken-up appearance and the contrast it lends to the story I cooked up. Since we're staring, I take stock of Bill, cataloguing his features for storytelling reference; the square-jaw*ness* of his square jaw, the competing bushiness of his mousy grey moustache to his mousey grey eyebrows. Everything about him, from the high-and-tight haircut to the scowling jowls screams *unsuccessful-but-not-over-it* police services applicant; judging from the depth of the crags in his crag-laden face, he's been resenting not being a cop for decades. The once-over he continues to give me lends credence to his palpable need to project authority; blood pumping and two-o-five now, I'm in no mood to lower my gaze.

I came here for confrontation; sensing my unwavering stare and the *make a decision* written across my dilated pupils, Bill rubs his with his free hand, the other holding the clipboard he lowers his eyes to scan. Apparently, your name is on *Page Two* because that's where he stops; eyes raising again behind really, ridiculously, bushy eyebrows, Bill offers a terse

"And you are?"

"Fiancée"

and not a heartbeat later, deciding Bill doesn't need details about how I'm actually the fourth and only, apparently, every other month or so.

I'm expecting him to say no; at the very least, regale me with some rhetoric about adhering to clearly outlined hospital visiting hours—instead he kind of half-yawns, and, apparently having decided that I'm not worth the effort it would take to throw me out, motions me in.

I have absolutely no idea where your room is—not wanting to press my luck— or shatter the illusion of just having left to let the dog out—I figure I'll take my chances, giving Bill a

"Thanks"

where

"Room number?"

should be.

…

I regret my decision almost immediately.

The goddamned hospital is even bigger than I remember it; having wrestled a particularly nasty bout of Spinal Meningitis two decades prior, I called this place home for over a month in my formative years. Understandably, I've developed a bit of an aversion to hospitals as a result—which makes navigating its near abandoned corridors even *less* ideal now. My post-two-am fog is worsening; the blood pounding in my ears is beating almost rhythmically as I turn continually left corners on my way to you.

There's a quiet desperation setting in; I'm sharing it with sanitized walls and no one else, alone and tired and doing the kind of ridiculous thing I tend to do when it comes to you. I contrast this with how my night was supposed to end—warm and in bed with someone who, in the times between times with you, hasn't left me or threatened to once.

It's sobering the way I kind of guess it should be; I'm lost and in thought, rounding my seventeenth corner before laying eyes on a graveyard-shift populated nurses' station.

I'm expecting the kind of subdued looks of half-surprise that Bill had seventeen corners ago; instead I'm greeted with indifference as I approach the desk. Clearly I'm not the first fiancée permitted overnight access—this emboldens me slightly as I open my mouth for something other than a yawn, ask politely as the time will permit for your whereabouts.

Turns out I was close to you two hallways and six corners ago; I take the room number and the fake smile that Tammy—the graveyard shift nurse showing the most signs of life—gives me as I turn on tired heels and resume my search for you.

Having dissected the finer points of the madness I'm returning to, I've accepted my fate by the time I reach your room. Entering the open door and letting the blackness of your resting place overtake me, the symbolism is both recognized and appreciated.

It takes my tired eyes time to adjust to the pitch of the room; momentarily I'm able to discern that you're sharing the space with *another* probably-sleeping patient.

I gather that there's a small bathroom to my left, and that the right and the rest of the tiny area is home to your bed, closest to me, your roommates' bed, invisible behind a drawn curtain intended for mock-privacy, and the host of whirring and beeping machinery whirring and beeping beside the bed you rest in.

Rest, relatively speaking, because I know you well enough to know that it just doesn't come easy to you under the best of circumstances—and that this situation certainly doesn't qualify.

So *no*, I'm not surprised to find your probably-should-be-sleeping eyes open and already resting upon mine, which, having appropriately adjusted to the darkness I've literally and metaphorically entered, instinctively know just where to fall also.

You reach for me, extended arms strained somewhat against the confines of the tubes and wires they're entangled with, and within moments I'm resting inside them as though the last month never happened.

You pull me closer, and suddenly I'm navigating not only the relative darkness of the room, but the confines of the small and already-crowded hospital bed.

I hold you back as hard as I can, trying to re-establish a dominant position as I writhe to get underneath/behind you; you remain silent, kissing my hands after they've found and interlocked with yours. I exhale for the first time in two forevers, comforted to have found you and thankful the blood pounding in my ears has begun to slow a once-frenetic rhythm.

I close my eyes and tell myself it's only for a moment; knowing I'll have to open them and engage, eager to learn what landed you here and eager to hear what tempted you to text me that image of your hospital bracelet after all this time…but the new rhythm is soothing and my eyelids are heavier than I anticipated…and so you don't protest when they *stay* closed, curled up underneath/behind you in a hospital bed clearly not big enough for the both of us.

…

Supraventricular Tachycardia.

It's a mouthful and it's what you have—you've told me that it is an abnormally fast heartbeat, caused by some abnormal circuitry in the heart. *Overlapping signals*, or some such thing, because you *love too much*, if I'm to believe your self-diagnosis.

There's a post-it note by your bed; scrawled across it, in your *not-nearly-as-pretty-as-the-rest-of-you* penmanship, is a record of your latest Creatine Kinase levels.

The normal range—according to the data scrawled on the left side of the post-it; anywhere from seventeen to one-seventy. I couldn't tell you seventeen to one-seventy *what*—you're still sleeping soundly on-top/beside me—but the post-it note between the end of the bed I've just woken up in and the desk your water rests on details that your levels are on the decidedly *high* range.

The right side of the post-it, just under

My levels

in un-pretty handwriting?

One thousand thirty-seven.

My free hand—the one not wrapped tightly around your gently-heaving torso—fumbles for my phone on the desk above the post-it; I hastily get off the screen indicating three missed calls from Sugar Baby Sousa. I google

elevated creatine kinase levels

and discover that,

yes,

one thousand thirty-seven micro-grams per liter of blood is absurdly high; thankfully a few hundred thousand less than the highest levels ever documented, which—as it turns out—proved to be definitively fatal.

I feel my heart rate kick up a notch as I google *causes*, learning quickly that one form of creatine kinase—CK-MB—occurs within hours of a heart attack. You're still sleeping soundly, the rays of light filtering through cheap hospital room curtains doing little to disrupt what is probably the most peaceful rest you've had in weeks.

I'm watching you intently, alternating glances at the array of diagnostic equipment your tethered to and my web browser in hopes of translation. You don't look as though you've had a heart attack—although, admittedly, I would have no idea what you would look like if you *had*.

My mind—racing in part due to a lack of restful sleep and the after effects of a nightly adrenaline overload—is telling me to regret the time apart, extrapolating based on google findings that you may not have much time left, and that it may-or-may-not-be all my fault.

Without realizing it, you've effectively made me feel absolutely fucking horrible for my time apart dalliances with Sugar Baby Sousa—I chastise myself for believing that *this* breakup was more significant because of duration than any of the thousand breakups before.

The overprotective, territorial, almost-as-irrational-as-you part of me feels the all-too-familiar urge to hover over you in the hospital bed; to send any entering nurse—or even the mystery roommate still snoring in rhythm to the beep-beeping of your monitoring apparatus—running in terror should they attempt to wrest you from the peaceful sleep I've sacrificed all feeling in my left arm for.

So I watch you breathe, fighting both the tingling in the arm you're lying on and the tugging at heartstrings I thought you'd cauterized long ago, marveling at how one photo of a hospital bracelet could send me careening headlong into a fate I'd just gotten my weary head around avoiding.

...

I'm thinking of texting Sugar Baby Sousa—to tell her that I'm okay and that I'm back with you and *this time for good* and that I'm so sorry for what happened last night

and

I'm thinking of how well she's going to take that news

and

I'm thinking of chewing my left arm clear off

when you shift your weight slightly from your resting place atop it

and

open your beautifully dark big black eyes.

They fall on mine, filtered by horrible-hospital-curtain-daylight, for the first time in thirty restless sleeps, and they tell me without telling me that

yes

you've missed me, too

and

yes

you've forgotten about whatever soul-crushingly important reason you had to run away from me in the first place.

And so the first words we move our mouths to share have less to do about the time apart, and more to do with what led you *here*.

You tell me you hadn't been feeling well and for a couple of weeks; worried about your latest failed love and promise of marriage, all the while burdened by looming Project Management projects I can only pretend to comprehend. So it was worries from work, compounded by stress from fucking Humberto your entirely inappropriate boss, multiplied by loss of both attitude and sleep that composed the calculation to make your little heart beat the exact number of beats to have you call the ambulance the way you did *two* days ago.

"Two days ago?!"

I choose the tone of my surprised/angered response very carefully; not wanting to accelerate a clearly-taxed heart and not wanting to devolve what has been a pleasant—circumstances notwithstanding—reunion into a multilingual verbal sparring session.

"I didn't want to bother you, Mico."

This is both a lie and a guilt-inducing stab at already frayed nerves; it goes without saying that, regardless of the constantly-revolving state of our love affair, I would be by your side instantly given the situation.

I offer assurances in hushed tones; beside us, behind the horribly tacky hospital curtain, your phantom roommate stirs, awakening from an impressively long slumber. As my eyes return to you from their startled departure at his stirrings, they stop just before yours to rest on the just-discovered array of gifts adorning the tabletop north of the note with your ridiculous CK levels scrawled on it.

I notice a pleasant-looking bouquet of flowers, recognize Gatto's appropriately perfect handwriting on a card stuck between two *very* in-bloom roses. I smile at this—almost surprised to learn he wasn't the one to drive you here; hell, I'm surprised he's not holding vigil from a chair in the corner.

I suppose I'm comforted, knowing you live with someone so unabashedly good; I'm certain that, should we ever drift apart permanently, you'll be cared for in my absence.

So the flowers get a pass—it's the teddy bear beside them that draws my gaze and instantaneous ire. It's inappropriately large, for one thing—long white fur and stupid, almost-crossed eyes, it resembles the kind of gaudy prize one would present to a ten-year old after winning some *everybody wins* game at a local fair.

So ostentatious is this bear, looming over the bed from a vantage point reserved for Gatto and his constant and *not-entirely-unfounded* worrying, that I'm troubled by the fact I hadn't noticed it until now.

I don't need to read the poorly-scribed message attached to the card attached to the tiny ear to realize who it is from; the only individual relentlessly douchey enough to present you with such a horrendous prize is your employer.

I can almost picture him leaning over the hospital bed to hand it to you, sweating from the relatively minor exertion and penetrating your nostrils with fumes from inhumanly-applied amounts of *Drakkar Noir*, amongst assurances that you'll have anything you need and reminders to—under no circumstances—contact me.

Yeah, Humberto is a motherfucker—the presence of his also-grossly-overt gift telling-me-without-telling-me why you waited until last night to reach out and let me know about your stay here.

I make a mental note to punch him in the face, which appeases the resurgent blood-pounding-in-my-ears long enough for my focus to shift back to you. Our small talk resumes without further needling; we're both aware that one wrong word could easily tear us apart for an ever-increasing, it seems, amount of time—and so we are careful in how we catch up, intertwined as we are in a tiny hospital bed.

Classically, we're oblivious to both the awakening of your phantom roommate and the litany of nursing staff entering periodically to attend to him; focusing instead on communicating *verbally and un-* where our priorities lie.

We're officially back together by the time your test results arrive; this latest battery disclosing that your mysteriously risen Creatine Kinase levels have returned to some semblance of human normality. You're wearing the ring I perennially keep in my pocket by the time you're collecting your things to leave—the fact that you're proudly engaged again almost makes you grabbing that goddamned teddy bear okay. A quick call—and multiple assurances to Gatto that *no*, you won't be needing him to come pick you up—and we're headed for the hospital parking lot and *home*, your place, because I maybe forgot to mention there's a still sleeping *likely* girl at mine.

…

Sugar Baby Sousa looks at me with eyes that aren't yours.

The tears that fall on her perennially-and-more-so-now cheeks, however?

They are, unfortunately, decidedly familiar.

And so I'm thinking about the amount of times I've watched them fall from *your* black rimmed little eyes; getting used to watching them fall from *hers*, too.

I don't cry because

I've haven't cried *tear one*, faced with a million, it seems, of these moments—because my father told me that men don't cry.

It's hard, however, to hear her call me

"Asshole"

the way you usually do, when the tears are coming from *your* eyes, and not start to think that there might actually be a ring of truth to it. I mean, I could always brush it off as the crazy Colombian in you—she's neither jaded from years of mistreatment or nearly South American enough in lineage to dispute her validity in the calling me of it.

So I take the name calling that comes, having returned home mid-morning after the night I mysteriously disappeared without a trace. I'd spent the remainder of my time away holding you in your bed; returning home with hopes to climb into mine only after your assurances that you would be returning to a work you hadn't seen in nearly a week, thanks to your sudden and mysteriously onset illness.

The girl still in it—*my* bed—came as a bit of a surprise; I guess I figured her school or my mid-night departure would incentivize her to rise and remove herself from what was already an awkward set of circumstances.

So a quick and recognizable heart pang followed the switch of the bedroom light; one benefit of a bachelor apartment with an office converted to a sleeping area is near-perpetual blackness, even mid-mornings like the one I returned to slip said-switch on.

I dismissed it—this involuntary physical manifestation of the knowledge that Sugar Baby Sousa was still there waiting for me, having done the *opposite* of your usual running away—and commenced with the

We're back together

and

I'm sorry, Sousa, truly

that led to the tears commencing and the asshole-calling.

The whole thing isn't easy,

breaking up with someone I care for and probably shouldn't break up with in favor of probably marrying someone who probably can't wait to break up with me

again,

but I give it my best try,

making mental note to remember that my heart and my head are arguing quietly as to whether or not this is the right thing to do, the latest mistake in an increasingly long *line of.*

So

Sugar Baby Sousa looks at me with eyes that *aren't yours*

and in between tears they tell me

You're making a mistake

before her pretty pumped up pretty little lips move to mouth

You're making a mistake

the last and only expletive-free words she throws my way before leaving me alone the way we're both suddenly sure I deserve to be.

...

So we're in Niagara Falls, and we're at this restaurant.

Wait, wait, let me back it up...

*I rented us a room for a night on short notice—the room, you should know, cost over *halfathousand* dollars—*halfathousand* dollars I don't have.

We drove up earlier in the day; most of the two hours was spent singing and horribly and horribly off key to whatever songs came on the radio in your Range Rover—the only thing I loved more about you than you. The sun couldn't have been shining any brighter, and it couldn't have been any warmer, and you couldn't have looked any better with your hair dancing in the wind to the off-key tunes your lips were moving to.

To paint a picture, it was *perfect*—

--what could go wrong, right?

We checked in, and I noticed in the checking that I was getting decidedly proficient at it—meaning maybe I'd been checking in a little too often. As the guy behind the desk confirmed the booking, I caught myself contemplating the amount of times in the relatively short amount of times we'd been dating that I had stood on the other side of some counter and listened to this speech...and then you put your hand on the small of my back the way you did when the

world melted away

the way I wanted it to.

And instantly it was less about hotels and checking into them and more about you and ripping whatever you were wearing *off* and *instantly*, and the only thing more soul-crushing than not being able to was not being able to right now, because we hadn't left the lobby yet.

I think you batted your big brown eyes at me, and I can't remember exactly, but I bet I appreciated it—and then we completed the checking in and began the trip to the hotel room.

I'm sure I carried your bags because I always carried your bags, and I'm sure my arms hurt by the time we reached floor ten, but nowhere *near* the ten times my dick hurt not being able to hide it inside of you.

See, you had this way of walking down hotel hallways, a shift and a sway and an echo, maybe, off of close quarter poorly-wallpapered walls...I remember my hand shaking as I fumbled in vain with the key card on the door, and I remember it having nothing to do with the eighty-seven pounds of luggage in my arms. I attacked your lips with my lips the moment we crossed the threshold; we tripped over your ridiculous assortment of getaway essentials and fell laughing onto the halfathousand-better-be-steam-cleaned carpet.

You took the bruise on that big fat ass better than you had any right to; of course, it just started forming when you finally escaped me and removed yourself to the bathroom, presenting a swollen and-not-just-from-the-fall cheek a half-second before shutting the door cruelly and

literally

and

figuratively

on my plans to have my way with you before we left the room.

You emerged a dreadful forty-three minutes later and *just* as the appetite in my stomach was roaring as loud as the appetite somewhere south; I remember having mind to chastise you for what had become routine disregard for the concept of time when I caught a glimpse of the black cocktail dress you had slithered into...

...and my angry admonishings retreated into whimpered whispers.

You looked at me, and your look had more fuck than fight back in it,

so I took your pretty little hand in mine and walked

without a word

right out of that room and into the restaurant that would ruin the rest of our time here, a place whose magic had wilted faster than my inclinations to scold you.

...

So we're in Niagara Falls and we're at this restaurant…

…and I'm not two bites into whatever health-conscious half-meal I've managed to order when you part those pretty lips to let the darkness out.

*There is a pattern to this too, I've learned. Your eyes are black—like, horse on the farm I grew up on black—and they manage to get blacker still when the storm clouds you call brain cells decide it's time for rain.

Picture me sitting at some too-expensive-for-my-modest-salary restaurant and savoring bite two of some sandwich when I sense the electricity in the air…I stop, mid-chew, and offer my best 'baby-don't-not-here' face and go down in a blaze of glory, because

"Joo son of a beetch"

despite the summer sun, the forecast calls for rain at table twelve.

By now, and in retrospect, one should realize that it's not a plot hole but a matter of fact that both your mood and opinion of me could change like so much weather—doubtless, the reader will be just as surprised as I was to learn that a day that had started so beautifully was about to end as anything but.

You'd discovered something, or so you believed, on the phone you held in your tiny little hand at the table and about me—and in the discovering of said something you'd decided that here and now was as good a time and place as any to confront me regarding said indiscretion, imagined or no.

The confronting began the way it tended to—with words in increasingly indiscernible Colombian accents and the now traditional throwing of the engagement ring. I caught it—again, this was a time numbering nearly our table, so twelve, and growing up boxing had given me nothing if not hand-eye coordination.

That, and the ability to take a beating—although I admit I would have preferred the physical kind to your preferred

"Joo fucking scumbag coward"

public chastising.

By the time the waiter came to embarrassingly ask

"Is everything okay?"

meaning

Please keep it down

and you answered

"Oh, sure—everything is juss fine, I juss have a cheating pieces of garbage—

etc.

etc.

I'd decided that time-number-table

so twelve

was a touch too many.

I remember getting up from the table and feeling the all-too-familiar feeling of my heart remaining seated. I remember the wild in your black eyes and the half-smile on those pursed lips, corners already crawling into that indescribable position your mouth made when you secretly respected me for standing up to you the way Former Fiancée #3 never would. I remember paying the war-shocked waiter and apologizing for the disruption; I remember the lady with the man with the Tommy Bahama shirt calling me

"bastard"

under her breath as I walked by, a stern half-stride ahead of you.

I also remember not being mad at her comment—she had problems enough being with a man bold enough to wear that parrot-covered travesty to lunch.

Your engagement ring burned a familiar hole in my pocket as I strode as forcefully as I could back to the *halfathousand* hotel room we'd checked into a mere two hours before. The soundtrack to floor ten was wailing, and in incomprehensible versions of Colombian as you continually reminded me of what I can only imagine were my failings as a man.

I half-listened only to protect the back of my head from any slapping that might be coming, accentuations to a fight you felt as passionate fighting as you had twelve-thousand, two-hundred and twenty-two fights ago. The venom stayed in your voice as I packed our bags, deftly dodging the toiletries you tossed at me from the bathroom and that goddamned beautiful black dress.

I stole a glance only when the bags were appropriately packed, this mental snapshot of you jiggling furiously in that toothpaste tube gown, resound in both my desire to leave you forever and spend the rest of said life missing you horribly.

...

We're in the parking garage some half-hour later; it's getting dark out and I'm tired of fighting and you're apparently *not* tired of fighting and we're waiting for the valet to bring your beautiful Range Rover-- the only thing I love more about you than you. You've mercifully worn your voice ragged from yelling—and believe me, I still can't recall what this one was about—although I do recall remaining steadfast in my desire to leave both this horrible, horrible place and you as well.

Which won't happen without driving you home first—and maybe you recognized this and maybe you were just saving up to go another round, a round in the privacy of your goddamned beautiful ride on the ride home. So we're waiting, and it's silent and it's summer and it's sundown and it's goddamn beautiful too—and I'm probably stewing about blowing *halfathousand* for two hours of nothing when you reach your tiny hand out and hold onto mine, and all at once

nothing

is all I'm thinking of,

because I'm holding your tiny hand right back.

...

Just like that, our ride appears and we're off—and for the first dozen kilometers or so it appears the fight is off, too; cancelled or at the very least postponed for some better day. We're not singing and horribly and horribly off key to whatever songs come on the radio in your Range Rover—the only thing I love more about you than you—but we're not screaming at each other either. I take the peace and quiet for what it is—so *bliss*, driving along the darkened-yet-still-busy three lane highway and thinking to myself

It's over

for the thousand-thousandth time.

So when you reach your hand back across the circular shift knob on the center console of your ridiculously expensive SUV to hold mine, I take it for what it is, and what it is is bittersweet. Maybe we're both tired, or maybe we're both tired of fighting, but we actually manage to sit in silence for what feels like an hour.*

It was twenty-four minutes.

Minute twenty-five, and you look at me and I catch the storm clouds rolling in behind the black of those eyes, reflected in the glow of oncoming headlights. The war starts softly, the way it tends to, with a comment uttered under your breath and in a language I sometimes wonder if even *you* really understand. My strategy, borne more of exhaustion than any deliberate attempt to antagonize, is to remain silent, and let your words cascade against my flesh—metaphorical body blows in the ring that is your Range Rover.

This continues for a mile marker or two; your tone intensifies as I reach for the radio knob, your reflections and dissertations on just what I'd done wrong at the restaurant revealing themselves in tandem with the notes over the speakers. In moments like this, I often wonder just how your mind works—circling from what I imagine must be self-righteous anger, to demure hand-holdings, and right back around the bend again. Maybe it's the face I make in moments of levity; maybe it's my admitted and timeline- questionable 'infidelities' lingering on your brain from weeks when I honestly believed you when you screamed

"Eeet's over!!"

the way I can imagine you're *about* to.

I tighten my grip on the wheel, straining to focus on the road and the headlights and the everything-else except your somehow-still-sweet sounding voice; hell, maybe I've gotten so used to be yelled at that your admonishings have become lullabies.

And lullabies are for sleeping; I let out a yawn because I think I would really *like* to—a mistake I recognize an exhale too late. Colombian women perceive moments such as this as an insult; before I can mask my gross insubordination, you scream

"Pull over"

like you really, really mean it.

Now, we're three lanes away from anything resembling 'pulling over,' and so I *don't*, more interested in getting home *and fast* than continuing this decidedly one-sided conversation parked alongside the highway we're travelling one-hundred-thirty-kilometers on.

You insist, offering another

"Pull over, right now Mico!"

And this one has some *ass* in it; out of the corner of my still-focused-on-the-road-where-it-should-be eye, I catch the shift your body takes as you lean in dangerously close to me and the operation of the motor vehicle we're speeding in.

Now, I've known you long enough—been engaged and not engaged and engaged again with a certain violent frequency—to understand that you mean business when your weight shifts. Now, I want to make it clear that while I understand the severity of the situation, my rational mind assumes that you're not crazy enough to unleash the fury that follows while we're travelling at one-hundred-thirty kilometers down a darkened yet still-busy super highway.

Naturally, I am wrong in this assumption.

In a flash, your cartoonishly small hand reaches for the odd-design-choice shift knob in the center console of your Range Rover—the only thing I love more about you than you—and the vehicle turns off.

Immediately.

In the fast lane of a three lane highway.

You say something, but I can't quite hear you—can't hear, or don't care, *because the vehicle is rapidly de-accelerating and the lights on the instrument panel and-- more importantly-- the headlights outside the vehicle are off and dark and I'm one-thousand percent sure we're about to crash and die which is funny because if I was paying attention I would have heard you say*

"I can't live without you"

which doesn't mean we shouldn't live, *at all.*

It takes another two-thirds of *a very important second* for my eyes to flash into the rear view mirror, more out of the absolute certainty that we're about to be rear-ended by the next vehicle travelling one hundred-thirty kilometers in the fast lane we're suddenly nowhere near travelling .

It's funny, because in the third that follows, I tell myself

We're about to die

We're about to die

We're about to die

We're about to die

We're about to die

We're about to die

We're about to die

We're about to die

eight times before we *don't*; don't because I push the ignition button beside the steering wheel, and

miraculously

your Range Rover—the only thing I love more about you than you—starts right back up. My foot, glued to the accelerator, and my eyes—glued to the headlights gaining on us still-too-rapidly—won't do anything other than their pre-delineated tasks; once we've adequately reached travelling velocity, the foot remains, but the eyes race towards yours.

Which remain big and black and crazy, moving as fast as your lips, which are moving to create more words that sound suspiciously like

"Pull over,"

the *last* thing we should do after your moments-ago attempt to kill us.

I'm in shock, *probably*, and you're in shock, *hopefully*; hopefully because it means you're not completely insane when you reach your cartoonishly small hands back across my side of the cockpit, this time resting baby-carrot-tiny fingers on the leather-bound wheel of the expensive vehicle I'm trying desperately to operate with a modicum of safety.

Before I can react, you wrench the wheel violently in the direction of the ditch three lanes to our right—three lanes across traffic which suddenly is trying to avoid us, because we're heading there right *now*. I hear tires squeal and horns blaring as my mind races, all

We're going to die

We're going to die

We're going to die

again,

because you're apparently trying your hardest to ensure we do.

I appreciate the whole *so-crazy-in-love-I-can't-live-without-you* vibe our whole relationship is built on, but I think I'd much rather just kind of quietly recognize it, rather than attempt to prove its validity.

So I go with it, the violent trajectory our vehicle is travelling on, rather than attempt to jerk the wheel back the other way. Thankfully, the traffic around us seems to have sensed something was…off…about the luxury SUV spontaneously stopping in the fast lane, and has given us enough berth to safely reach the right hand lane.

At this point I karate chop your hand (*as delicately as I can) off of the goddamn steering wheel and regain control of the vehicle like the man I am. You appreciate this—the subtle sign of aggression and subsequent reminder of my dominant alpha position—because your fight back has more fuck than fight back in it,

"Pull over asshole"

becoming

"Baby, please just pull over"

and your tiny little baby carrot fingers gripping the area where my dick *would* be, if you hadn't scared it away rather than, thankfully, any part of the vehicle required for its operation. My adrenaline is screaming, vocalizing notions of

"Leave this crazy bitch right now"

and

"Please just get home alive and then never ever ever see her again"

and,

"Goddamn she looks good right now"

oddly; or *maybe not*, because your tiny little baby carrot fingers are gripping the area where my dick is slowly re-emerging.

I'm changing lanes and catching feelings, and, by the time we're back at home in the fast lane, I'm strangely in agreement with your inclinations to pull off at the next exit, my change in mood not doubt influenced by the massaging of your tiny baby carrot fingers and the lull of your Goddamned Colombian accent.

If I were of a sound mind, I'm sure I would recognize this as just the *latest* insanity *in a line of*; clearly my path should remain on that far left lane and rocketing home and as far away from you as I could possibly be. I curse my weakness and my testosterone and my endorphins—and the deadly cocktail the three have cooked up for me as I put on my signal, crossing three lanes properly this time and pulling off, Exit 232 and right, down some dimly-lit side street probably named Destiny.

…

"I can't live without you Mico"

clearly,

and whispered softly into my now-throbbing ear;

now throbbing because I've just pulled off the side of some dimly-lit side street and parked the car and you've just stopped chewing on it.

My dick is back, and majestically, and it's throbbing too—throbbing because it wants to escape the confines of the pants I've so mercilessly sentenced it to, and throbbing because I'm sure it realizes this is *usually* the part with the make-up sex.

I say *usually* because my rational mind—as little of it there is left, leastways—is still reminding me that this is the deranged Colombian *still-ex-*fiancée who tried to kill me just two roads ago.

The rest of my mind—the unsound parts—correct me, technically tried to kill

us

and because we can't live without one another; and to a tortured writer's mind,

Goddamn that's hot.

We're pulled over and whispering—or at least comparatively, as the octaves have reached something sensible, and words like

"Never wanna see you again"

have turned to

"Can't imagine never seeing you again"

and before I recognize what I'm doing, I'm slipping the ring back on your delicate little baby carrot finger.

There's a madness to this, I realize, and the night outside seems to heave a sigh, and the sigh it heaves is stretched out over the silence of the abandoned road we're safely stopped at. I strain my ears through the open windows of your Range Rover—the only thing I love about you more than you—and I can make out bugs buzzing and they're buzzing things like

Leave her forever, you just almost died

and

You spent over halfathousand on a room you didn't stay more than an hour in

and

an hour ago you were speeding on a highway headed for freedom

but right now they can all go to hell, because you're looking at me with those big black eyes. I'm under your spell again, and we promise each other that no one understands the love we have for each other because no one else feels love as deeply as we do. The adrenaline is coursing through my veins and my heart is pumping in my ears and when you threaten to kiss me, the drumming drowns out the bugs and their sensible whisperings and when your lips touch my lips the touching is all that matters—car accidents and expensive hotel rooms be damned.

By the time I press the ignition on the dash and by the time the tires trace the highway on the road home, we're singing horribly and horribly off key and any talking between is spent marveling at the madness our true love has made.

We're crazy and we're wrong and we're hurting each other—and we agree, and somehow it's okay; okay because in the history of men loving women there has never been a man who loved a woman more.

...

It's been a long night after a hard day, and I'm counting on tomorrow being better as we reach the halfway mark of an eventful drive home. You're fading in the passenger seat, a tiny hand still held in mine, and I'm reflecting on the events that led us here, all new levels of understanding and 'we're-fucked-but-at-least-we're-fucked-together.' I'm alternating my focus; the road ahead and then your raven black hair dancing out the open window as you try not to fall asleep, the gentle breeze just barely audible as it dances around the cabin between notes from the speakers.

My eyes are heavy—if not for the racing of my mind and the racing of the tires all around me, I'd surely close them too, the way yours appear to have, just now. I'm envious, I'll admit—your seeming exit from a day that started blissfully happy and turned miserably angry and climaxed in near-death only to provide a denouement of understanding. I can't make sense of it; maybe I'm done trying to, focusing instead on imaginings of my parent's reaction when I recite *this*, latest in a line of tragically eventful weekends. I can see the disappointment on my father's face, reflected on and warped back against my own features by the glass of the windshield; all at once unable to bear it, my eyes fall to the tiny illuminations of your ridiculously expensive dashboard. The

you're almost completely out of gas, motherfucker

light is on, and so my adrenaline—just having fallen back to sleep, by the way—electrocutes my testicles, snapping me from my fever thoughts and encouraging me to focus on the whole 'getting home safely' thing once more.

I half-remember a service center sign some twenty kilometers back, instantly vigilant and scanning for a sign of such presence. I receive confirmation some five minutes up the road—praying to a god I don't believe in that we have the necessary fuel for the remaining seventeen. Determined, I attempt to calm the adrenaline still stinging my balls by turning up the radio, humming along to a country song, blissfully unaware that humming to the *next* country song will result in the evening taking a turn for the tragic, once more.

...

You're still in love with me as we hit the service center parking lot; hell, you've got the ring back on your tiny baby carrot finger by the time we separate to relieve ourselves in the 'his' and 'her' restrooms. I'm standing at the urinal and missing you, oddly…and while I fully realize that this means I'm crazy too and while I realize that this is my opportunity to paint you as the villain, it just wouldn't do justice to our relationship and the truth in these pages.

So maybe there's a bit of villain in me, too, when I pull out my phone with my not-occupied hand and realize that I've got a text message, and that it's not from you.

Now, given the insanity of the night and our turbulent engagement, I'm imagining there's some justification in responding to Sugar Baby Sousa when I look at my phone, there in the men's room, and I type

I miss you too

and hit 'send.'

And it's true, and I do miss her—and I miss the admittedly alien calmness and consistency of our brief times together—pleasant and honest and abbreviated by my returns to you and your Colombian goddess-ness. It's weakness and it's wrong and it's technically emotional-cheating because you've got a ring freshly back on your little baby carrot finger, but part of me is tired and wants a little peace, so I follow the

Can I see you soon?

that follows

with a

You're goddamn right you can

before re-packaging myself *expertly* with my good hand and returning to you and the storm clouds already rolling behind those big black eyes.

It takes me the better part of a minute to realize that I've made another mistake—this, in addition to the incorrect sing-along to a lyric of a song I apparently had no business singing-along to, is about to push my night back into 'almost-get-killed-or-wish-I-was' territory. The text, you see, from Sugar Baby Sousa came through on my phone—and, thanks to the wonders of modern technology, and something called an iCloud—on my iPad.

The same iPad you had resting in your purse on your trip to the ladies' room.

So I meet you in the lobby, and I pretend really hard that the

I'm going to kill you motherfucker

look on your face isn't a

I'm going to kill you motherfucker

look at all.

You say something that sounds suspiciously like

"I need cigarettes"

on your way to the shop that sells cigarettes; I'm a half-step behind and reaching for a hand that isn't there, because the

"I need cigarettes"

is pushed through lips amidst words like

"Joo are a lying, cheating scumbag."

And I'm in shock *not* because you're onto my restroom infidelities, but more because I'm bewildered by how you *could* know; all at once the adrenaline that had only recently subsided is shooting electrical current through my tired testicles. I've realized the hand to hold *won't* be coming and that the hand I prefer to hold might not be wearing the ring that only just went back on your tiny baby carrot finger as you reach to point at the terrible little cancer sticks you can't seem to quit.

And maybe the irony would make me smile—how you can quit *me*, so easily and so often, but can't quit the things you turn to when quitting me leaves you leaning on crutches both metaphorical and not…Would smile, but I'm still half-guessing at what has you so angry and *after* we seemed to have resolved our latest dispute; still unaware of the evils of iCloud and my own culpability in the latest turn our evening has taken.

As you slide your well-worn debit card into the debit-card-machine, you pause—just long enough to turn to me with venom on your puffy little lips and say—

"I weesh joo were dead, joo motherfucker!"

Maybe the truth hasn't hit me yet; *maybe it has and I'm just tired*—either way, by the time the bewildered cashier turns from the other side of the desk your cigarettes rest on to face me, I'm pivoting on my heels and leaving the both of you to your terrible transaction. I've decided that the comfort of your parked Range Rover—the only thing I love more about you than you—is the sanctity I need to try to make sense of the events of the day. I'm reaching for the service center door, thoughts of

in love

and

out of love

and

in love

stomping across my troubled mind, even as I enter the night and the cold night's air.

So the cold hits me fast; the sound of your shrill-yet-somehow-still-sexy Colombian voice hits *just as*, and maybe harder. Had I mind to realize you've followed me—meaning left the cigarette shop mid-transaction—I might offer more than the continuing walking away I'm offering…it's not until I hear you say

"I'm calling the police you *sohnofabeetch* thief"

that I slow my pace.

Again, I'm slow on the uptake—call it too many adrenaline dumps for one evening—but amidst obscenities are accusations—and the accusations are screamed for the audience that is anyone-within-earshot. So I'm turning and back towards you and realizing with relative abject horror that you *actually* think I'm in the process of stealing your Range Rover.

This means that the phone you're reaching for is to dial the police; the sigh I heave is more

Not this again

than

Oh my fucking God you're calling the police!!!!

I know better, and so my pace back towards you is twice the pace I paced in the getting away from you. You're done dialing what I can only assume is a very specific three-digit phone number, and the phone will reach your ear, tragically, well before I do and I'm panicking *kinda* until…

The cigarette shopkeeper explodes into the night behind you, having left the cigarette shop to hand you the debit card you'd left in the debit machine. *God Bless his intervention*, all

"Miss, you forgot your card—

before you drown him out with a

"Joo thief motherfucker"

and the rest of the *usual* that follows from your pretty pumped up pretty little lips.

Yeah, you make him stop in his tracks, but mercifully his tracks stop a few feet from you, and the act of reaching for your just-found debit card has you lowering your police-calling hand and the phone in it. I take the opportunity and close the distance to you, your pretty little back to me, talking in decidedly more-hushed tones to the shopkeeper. He looks amazed, you should know, that you could turn from spewing venom to whispering the pleasantries you're mid-whispering as I grab your arm and turn you back towards me.

I catch his eyes just as mine fall to yours—in that moment, I can tell that he's clearly never dated a Colombian—the

"Are you alright, miss?"

he so graciously offers is matched with a resounding

"Fuck off!"

from both of our well-worn lips.

There in the eye of the storm we've trapped ourselves in, I take the next moment to appreciate that, no matter the calamity we cause, while we're perfectly content to notify absolutely everyone in the immediate vicinity, we'll attack anyone who dares interrupt our admittedly misguided passions. The shopkeeper, doubtless realizing this as well, takes the hit on the chin, turns on his heels, and leaves us to our madness.

I hang your phone up for you. You're appreciative, as now you're unencumbered, beginning the task of unwrapping your delicious little cancer treats from their plastic prison.

You're still mad as hell, and I'm still yet to discover how this techno-bastard iCloud betrayed me, but we're somewhat cognizant of this latest little scene we've caused; I catch the hint of a smile on your pumped up pretty little lips as you attempt to hide the wind from the lighter you're reaching towards them.

Maybe I smile too; either way it starts to rain all around us, there in the parking lot of the service center we've so callously destroyed, and neither one of us bother to notice. We laugh for the time it takes to become adequately soaked, and then we retreat, back to the relative sanctity of the vehicle we only *nearly* almost died in, the last time you decided you couldn't live with or without me.

...

You're behind the wheel literally and metaphorically, and by the time we hit the on ramp to the highway, you're back to breathing the fire you'd only just stopped breathing a half-soaked half-cigarette ago.

"Mico."

Your inflection indicates that the preceding was *not* a question.

"Yes?"

"Why were you singing along to that song?"

*This, as I have mentioned, was apparently my *first* mistake; a mistake made before we pulled into the service center and before I pulled out my phone in that service center men's room and before you pulled out my iPad in that service center ladies' room.

"It's a good song"

is *not*, apparently, the correct answer and the look you shoot me from your admittedly terrifying position of power behind the wheel makes me wonder if we don't die tonight, after all.

"Was I too loud? I'm sorry, baby, I thought you were sleeping"

is true; in truth, I should have known that you were playing possum—no way, after the excitement of the evening, that you could have fallen asleep so easily. Now, the only thing more frightening than your I'm-calling-the-cops-again-motherfucker voice is this, your reserved, measured I'm-clearly-baiting-you, less accented tone.

At this point, I know you're mad about something, but I'm not yet convinced you somehow-magically realized I was up to my old tricks in the men's room—you've yet to educate me on the evils of the Apple Corporation—so I'm rolling with the punches, our sparring match now more mental warfare than verbal assault.

I know something's up and I know *you* know something's up—still, my answer has more

"I just like the sound of it"

than

"You caught me red-handed, you're right I'm a cheating scumbag"

in it; so I go with the former, clench my teeth and prepare for the worst.

The crash doesn't come—you maintain both your composure and control of the Range Rover, and we travel the majority of the remainder of the drive in silence. I'm sure as hell not humming to whatever sad song comes over the radio, and you're remarkably calm considering the sum of moments that directly preceded this one.

Maybe I'm too tired to tell myself there's more to your strange silence—maybe I'm so frayed at the edges that I'm missing the obvious—but I take the moments of precious peace to reflect on the harrowing events of the day, feeling my body relax, no longer bracing for impacts both physical and verbal. I can see your mind churning—hell, if the radio was playing any lower, I'm sure I'd hear the waves crashing against the metaphorical shores of your wild imaginations—but I really do appreciate the peace...and so I finally close my eyes, confident that the next battle will begin exactly when you want it to.

Some seventeen songs pass and pass uneventfully, and before my eyes open we're drifting back into our city, gliding on streets that can't-tell-don't-care for our troubles. The streetlights kiss my eyes open, and the gentle inertia of a slowly stopping vehicle rocks me gently to consciousness. I scan my body hurriedly, and, finding no apparent stab wounds, am appropriately astonished to discover that you've pulled over in the parking lot of your bank branch.

The neon sign is humming and your voice carries the tune, beside me as you lean over, purring

"Half of *halfathousand*, right?"

in the kind of tone that belies a night's worth of conflict.

In the half-moment it takes to pinch myself you glide gracefully from your captain's chair, disappearing into the atmosphere of three-something in the morning, reaching the door to your bank branch and the ATM within before I can convince myself that *no*

this isn't some sweet dream.

You're gone all of two minutes, and the whole time I'm relieved/terrified; still half-asleep as you emerge and glide right back into the captain's chair, starting the engine and resuming the journey as if the stop had never happened.

The intention has me convinced I'm dreaming—after wanting to kill me and then loving me and then wanting to kill me again, could you really be admitting your part in our tragic evening? Are you really about to reimburse me for the half of the cost for the hotel room we never really got to ravage? These questions and more roll through my troubled-still-sleepy mind as we pull away and towards the sanctity of my apartment building. We talk, probably, but I'm still shaking the fog as you pull up to the roundabout in front of the entrance to my building, five floors below a bed I had no intention of sleeping in tonight.

You tell me you won't stay; that you're tired too, and that you need a night to yourself following the madness of the day. You assure me that we're still in love and together and engaged—hell, you even kiss me on too-tired-to-kiss-back-lips. Had my wits been anywhere north of my balls, I might catch the subtle difference of wanting to sleep alone after trying to kill us because time apart is a fate worse than death, but hey, it's after three am.

I find my feet, put them on the pavement outside your Range Rover, and begin my journey to the back of the vehicle, intent on opening the hatch to retrieve the bag I had stuffed with the necessary provisions for our weekend away. My plan—if one could accurately call it a plan—is to successfully retrieve my items, circle the remainder of the vehicle, and plant a goodbye kiss on your lips from outside the driver's side door. At this point, I'd love to collect the half of *halfathousand* you've stopped at the bank to withdraw, sometime after the next goodbye kiss but before the actual goodbye.

As I reach the handle to the back door of the vehicle, I'm reminded that my trust in the sanity of certain Colombian women is entirely foolhardy. With dexterity that belies the ungodly hour, you thumb the lock to the hatch, effectively barring me from my toothbrush and my clothes and my shoes and the rest of the entirety of my possessions. With a sweetly accented

"Fuck joo"

and a wave of a middle finger from a driver's side window I have no hope of reaching, you step on the gas at *least* as hard as you can, leaving me alone and tootbrushless in front of my apartment, three am on a morning attached to a night I'll never forget.

...

To say that I wake up poorly would indicate that I slept at all. Still, the sun is trespassing on the floor of the apartment I open my tired eyes in; I'm foggy and irritable as I round the corner to the kitchen and the coffee.

It's almost noon—by now, I should be in the Falls and doing tourist shit—maybe I'd be on the Maid of the Mist, soaked and shivering and with you and somehow *still* happier than the comforts of home and the alone I can't quite believe I am yet.

I thumb the kettle with the callousness of you and the door locks some seven hours ago, scrolling through missed texts from Sugar Baby Sousa that I'm not yet aware you've probably already read. It's great to hear from her—especially on days attached to nights when you leave me and the promises of a life together—but this morning I'll admit that the message I was hoping to see was from you.

I want you to know that I'm thinking of responding to her and in a way that's more thought-out than the *you-just-tried-to-kill-me-for-the-first/ last-time-I'm-leaving-you-for-good* that I knee-jerked texted her last night.

Hell, maybe I'm about to, but the kettle goes off at the same time that the phone in my hand does, steam and ringtones tag teaming my urges and reminding me that I'm still technically yours and you're doubtless calling to remind me. I hit that *accept call* button right quick, not looking at the number that called and fully expecting to hear that it's

joo

--I mean you—

and that you're sorry for both squealing the tires on the roundabout at my apartment building and the intention to get away from me that drove you to do it; fully expecting to, and suitably disappointed when I hear

"Hello, son"

and that it's my dad calling, instead.

*This is startling for a couple of reasons. I love my old man—and he loves me—but we love each other in that distinctly bro *only-call-to-discuss-football-picks-feelings-are-four-letter-words* kinda way…meaning phone calls outside of football season are limited to deaths in the immediate family.

So I'm assuming the worst, answering tentatively and with the reservation of a man who's been through enough drama, thank you, for one twenty-four hour period.

It's

"Hey Pop"

back, and with guarded inflection; his

sigh

on the other end of line does nothing for my confidence.

"Muneca came out to see me today."

I almost drop the phone.

I process the insanity of his statement in the time it takes to clear my throat; I'll admit that one of the few optimisms mused as my head hit the pillow last night was calling my family to recount the events that very nearly led to their only boy's death. It is not without resignation that I realize she's probably already given her decidedly-different and Colombian-hued version; I'm half-expecting my father to tell me *I'm* crazy as he parts his lips on the other line to continue.

*Notice I'm not at all surprised that the woman who basically told me to go fuck myself with the last breath breathed in my direction has woken up super early and gone to tell on me to my parents.

"What did she say?"

when I can already imagine; the fact that I haven't yet had my morning coffee only adds to the horrible, horrible rumbling in the pit of my stomach. I sigh, again, subtlety indicating my displeasure at the situation, as though hoping to color my father's recounting of the morning in a favorable light.

I brace, ready for

"She never wants to see you again"

or

"She says that you're with another woman and she never wants to see you again"

or

"She says that you're a piece of shit and you're with another woman and she never wants to see you again"

or any variation of the theme I'm a millisecond from hearing...

"She asked me for your hand in marriage"

and so I do the only rational, logical thing I can do...

I pass out.

...

I wake up, which I assume is a good thing, some two-minutes and thirty-seven seconds later. I know this, because I'm apparently still on the phone with my father, and the time elapsed is two-minutes and thirty-seven seconds after the seven seconds it took for him to tell me the most ridiculous thing he's ever told me.

He says

"Hello"

the way, I'd imagine, he has been, and for the duration of the time I've been lying spread-eagle on the cold kitchen floor. My head hurts, maybe even more than my stomach hurt a moment before I passed out in the first place—the goose-egg I can already feel forming at the back of my head tells me this is likely my fifth concussion.

Meaning I've still got a good five to go before I start worrying, so I tell dad

"Don't worry"

and that I had a bad connection; when he asks

"Did you pass out and hit your head on the cold kitchen floor?"

or something decidedly similar,

I lie and say

"I'm fine"

and ask him to repeat himself instead.

Because I thought I heard him say that you drove all the way out to Aylmer— the tiny little town I'm from—to ask him for my hand in marriage, which is emasculating not only because it's a traditionally *male* thing to do, but because I've already successfully asked *your* parents the same question.

That I was the fourth guy to do so is unremarkable; later, when you'll tell me that I was the only one of your handful of fiancées you cared enough to travel all the way to their tiny little hometown and ask such a question will give me reassurance comma none.

I ask my old man what he said, and I'll admit that I'm relieved/sad when he tells me he told you

"No"

and that

"you two make each other literally ill"

and that

"I just don't think you're right for one another."

I ask him how you took it, this news that really shouldn't come as a surprise to you—*or anyone who has ever been in our general vicinity*, for that matter—and he sighs, again, in a way that tells me it might be hereditary, before mentioning that

"She told me that you were in love and she would fight to stay with you, no matter what"

which *I* take to be as vaguely threatening as it sounds. There's more, he tells me, and of how you swore that we could work out our differences and build a life together—and while I admit it's comforting, set against the backdrop of the alone I woke up in, I'm not entirely sure I see our future the same.

"We argued for a little while, and she left"

is how he leaves it, but not before mentioning that you peeled out of the laneway in your Range Rover—a perfect interlude to the recounting of my night that I spend the next half-hour recounting to the rhythm in the pounding of my aching head.

He laughs along to the parts that are laughable, offers fatherly advice when fatherly advice and common sense dictate that I stay the hell away from you-- the way I fully intend to--there in the kitchen attached to the morning I passed out in, confident that it might finally be over and that we need to stop this before one of us gets hurt the way I kinda just did.

As I tell him

"I love you"

awkwardly and maybe for the fifth time in my entire life,

I'm thinking about the bump on my head and how it hurts and how I don't want to hurt you, blissfully unaware that I'm in the process of doing just that…

…because you're lying on a kitchen floor of your very own, and the ambulance is on the way.

…

It's been a few Wednesdays since the Wednesday Sugar Baby Sousa took me back, against her better judgment and against, I'm sure, your wishes.

So it's a Wednesday, and it's a Wednesday with Sugar Baby Sousa—which means I couldn't rightly tell you *which* Wednesday. I guess the days kind of bleed together when there's no wars in them; all I know is that it's been double digits since the last of the days and wars with you in them, and my life is settling nicely into the normalcy that comes with being with someone who is perfectly content being with me.

We talk about you, sure—she listens the kind of intently women listen when the story is about other women, laughing at the parts that are tragically comical and laughing at the parts that are tragically tragic.

She assures me, with the pressing of her pillowy lips and the pressing of her perfect little body, that the choices I made/you made for us are the right ones, quieting the wars that occasionally well up in me with battles beneath covers.

And she's good at this and good for me—and so the days that pass pass with her in them; over at my apartment and on everyday that eventually ends with her sleeping over the way her parents don't really know about.

She's young and almost *too*—but her eyes are big and her ass is big and she's the kind of kind that hasn't been spoiled by silly boys like me. And so I take care of her, and she takes care of me—and we keep things the *light* of her hair, just one more opposite/reprieve from you and the darkness something in my stomach tells me might not be over with yet.

...

Expensive, again

Sugar Baby Sousa looks at me from her perch beside the window of the ridiculously expensive hotel I'd stayed with you in, just two months ago.

And the look in her big, kinda blue, kinda green eyes couldn't be more different than the look that had been in yours, having looked out the same window on some similar floor and with the banality of someone who had seen the Toronto skyline countless times before.

Her eyes are expressive and wide and wild, scanning the sunset and the reflection of the skyscrapers opposite with the wanderlust of someone who's never been somewhere and appreciates the change.

And I've spent all mine—change—coming here with her just two months after coming here with you, figuring washing away the stain of our latest can't-even-remember-over-what catastrophic end with a weekend away in my favorite close-by city is just what my breaking, slowly soul needs.

Dejan the doorman—himself married unfortunately or fortunately to a no-doubt-equally-tempestuous Colombian as I've learned from my previous stay with you—looked both confused and bemused by my latest arrival, showing up with a just-twentysomething bombshell in a Honda Civic; stark contrast to my last five or so stays, pulling up with a Latina Goddess in a Range Rover.

I wonder if he wonders what I do as I watch her undress, frame silhouetted by a sinking sun on a *three-and-change night* skyline…musing football stud or super-middleweight boxing contender or maybe not-quite-famous-yet-but-kinda-close singer…something to justify the frequency and the beauty of the women I'm running away from reality to spend time with.

This emboldens me the way watching her wind to the music I softly play from surround sound stereo speakers emboldens me; I'm feeling downright immortal for the first time in days without you in them when she joins me in the bed I'm wrecking literally the way I'm probably wrecking my life metaphorically.

Some magnificently spent thirty-four minutes later she removes herself from bed, adjusting pretty pink pretty little panties on her way to the much needed cleansing the shower in the middle of the ridiculously expensive hotel room is sure to provide. Her walk away gets me wondering, and, emboldened by the faux-immortality fucking a maybe-just-twentysomething provides, I pull my cell phone from it's slumber on the nightstand beside the bed I've just literally wrecked. I'm not realizing I'm wrecking something *else* when I find our last conversation some five-most-recent-conversations-deep in my message history, and reach out for the first time in double-digit days, inciting a shower-long conversation that ends with my typing

What color are your panties?

and being pleasantly surprised with

green

and the photo of you in *just* them that you send to prove it.

Moments later I'm laying with her and thinking of you, already well on the way of wrecking the quiet salvation time with her and not you offers a breaking, slowly soul. I'm half-asleep and maybe dreaming, running metaphorical tracks in the direction your head-on train is barreling down, caught in the headlights and maybe relishing the impending collision.

...

Monster(s)

Sugar Baby Sousa is over and she's looking at me with those big, beautiful kinda-blue, kinda-green eyes—and they're filling with the kinda tears I *lied* when I swore to her I'd never cause.

The lips below them are uttering softly-spoken urgings—something about *staying* and with her and *being together* and not returning to the darkness so perfectly manifested in your hair and your eyes and your skin.

And I can't take my eyes off of hers

and I can't take my mind off of yours

and so I'm standing somewhat numb in the kitchen I cracked my stupidly stubborn skull on, praying to a God I don't believe in for clarity I know isn't coming.

And the worse part is the slowly roaring realization that, if you're a fucking monster, than I'm a fucking monster too—equally capable of chewing through the flesh of the fools foolish enough to maybe love us.

Maybe it's got something to do with how we keep crashing into one another— time off only time taken to lick wounds and prepare for the eventuality of the next crashing; recognition of a monster, *same* fueling some desire to see who's fangs can gnash hardest.

So it's Godzilla v Mothra, *again*, and Sugar Baby Sousa is just another petrified apartment dweller in the cardboard Tokyo we stomp on the way to each other.

Hence the kitchen floor and the standing on it and the first tear tickling a slightly trembling cheek, having escaped from kinda blue, kinda green eyes en route to staining the same floor my blood stained the *last* time I tried to stay away from you.

She says something, Sugar Baby Sousa, about understanding and I know that she most certainly does *not*; her overriding innocence and unwavering dedication to being simply better than you are or I am meaning her whittle little lies are worded to wound her and spare me—just one more stark contrast to the wounds littering my skin and caused by your heavily accented shouting.

She speaks the kind of softly that makes hearing the kind of impossible it is to take my eyes off of her—knowing full well that the picture of the hospital bracelet illuminating my phone—again—is enough, without context or text or any explanation at all, to tear me from her the way it is about to, not recognizing patterns or the absurdity of a second time as I collect my coat, and leave her to the darkness of an apartment we all know I kinda simply *wait* in.

...

I told her—Sugar Baby Sousa—in the moments between the text of the hospital bracelet and the running out the door, that she could stay *behind* it, invited to deal with our breakup in the sanctity of the apartment we'd shared for the beautiful dream the weeks without you allowed.

I figured this would be easier for her than banishing her back to her parent's house—not really wanting to be the explanation behind the tears she would doubtless crash through the door crying. I even agreed to allow her a friend or two to commiserate with, thinking-without-thinking that maybe the fallout would be more palatable if it wasn't alone.

All of this occurred within moments of receiving the first text or photo I'd received from you since the second or third Niagara Falls disaster—within these moments I'd managed to verify that *this* no-context-hospital-bracelet-photo was different from the *first* no-context-hospital-bracelet-photo and I'd managed to break up with Sugar Baby Sousa and I'd managed to ensure that the coat I'd grabbed on the way out the door was the coat with your ridiculously expensive ring hidden within it.

The only words I'd uttered—aside from the only ones that mattered

It's over

were the foolishly uttered urgings to,

under no circumstances

contact me at the hospital I would be convalescing with you at.

As I race a familiar route en route to you, I'm *not* thinking about how foolish breaking up with a just-twentysomething girl who cares for me in favor of a woman who certainly *sometimes* does is, and I'm not thinking about leaving a about-to-be-resentful just-twentysomething in an apartment full of potentially incriminating evidence of my indiscretions.

I'm not thinking *anything*, turning the left turns towards you on adrenaline and instinct—the adrenaline and instinct that have put me in messes like this for the past two years…

…and the adrenaline and instinct that are about to put me in trouble again.

…

FamiLIAR

I'm laying in the hospital bed you've called home for, as I've learned, the past twenty-two hours…

…and I'm twenty-two seconds from sleep when my phone screen illuminates the darkness violently.

As you stir beside me, shaking off the hold sleep has struggled to provide you with for days, the last of things I'm to learn tonight is just how much I fucking hate the iCloud.

…

(*Nobody really understands it—this tech-shrouded geek-talk verbiage posing as explanation for just where the fuck pictures and text chains that have no business being stored or saved go to be stored or saved. I'm vaguely certain the guy at the store where I went to pick up my phone covered it—*certain*, like of how I was that deleting old conversations to cover conversations that shouldn't be happening at certain times covered tracks best left covered.)

As text after text after text appears across my home screen

--all screaming the headline

Sugar Baby Sousa

I'm half awake and fully-realizing how wrong I was.

…

I'll learn, much later on, that the iPad I left on the kitchen counter you were mourning our relationship beside contained a full backup back-dated some two weeks before…before, as in before I deleted our incriminating

What color are your panties

and subsequent photographic proof

conversation.

The date stamp on said conversation—date stamped the kinda-memorable date we went to stay in Toronto together—was probably incriminating *enough*; the text chain just under the photo of you in green panties and only?

Downright damning.

I miss you.

I miss you, too.

Come see me?

Can't. Away for the weekend.

--with her?

Well?

.

.

.

With her?

Yes.

That's fucking great. While you're asking me for naked photos?

Sorry—

--I'm all fucked up.

When are you back?

Monday.

.

.

Come see me Monday?

Yes.

I miss you Mico. I fucking hate that I miss you…

…but I do.

I miss you too, Muneca.

You're done with her after this weekend.

.

.

.

Right?

Right.

Motherfucking type it.

I'm done with her.

Looking back, leaving the iPad on the kitchen counter you were mourning beside?

The *least* of the sins I'm laying beside you in a hospital bed completely unprepared for, and yet about to pay for anyways.

…

I suppose I should have put notifications to bed, before climbing into *yours* in this hospital; the realization hits me in bursts of screen messages illuminating the surface of my phone and projecting across an otherwise blackened room and shattering the just-restored serenity of an already tired and tumultuous relationship.

You react the way you're programmed to; sitting up when you shouldn't and allowing your heart rate to race the way you'd just finished telling me your physician said you *really* shouldn't, opening dry from severe dehydration lips to breath the air that will power the insults that are sure to follow your first forthcoming word.

And before I know it and maybe deservingly so, I'm reading text messages about what an asshole I am and listening to sweetly accented variations of the same; dodging chastising from beautiful women I'm trying really hard to love and being reminded *times-two* that I'm not doing a very good job.

I draw breath to explain, allowing my fingers to race across the phone's busy surface while attempting to do the same; telling you the truth, and that I ended it with her before coming to see you here after weeks without word

and

telling her the truth, and that I've admittedly overlapped contact with you in her presence, maybe not really over you the way I told her I was in times together.

And I'm *not* texting her in anger and over how she logged into my should've-been-put-away-better iPad and browsing my text message history, violating the trust I perhaps foolishly put in her when I allowed her access to my apartment in lieu of grieving

and

I'm *not* speaking to you in anger and over how you expect me to continuously draw me to your side with admittedly dramatic photos of hospital bracelets and only, negating weeks apart and with no contact and for always completely insurmountable circumstances.

No, I'm just lying in a hospital bed in the middle of the night *taking* it, punishment probably deserved for loving you too madly to know how to get away from it and for maybe starting to love her for foolishly thinking I was maybe worth saving from it.

So it's madness and *again* and were I not equally as much a part of the problem, I might draw breath to sigh and just kind of admire the absurdity of it all.

Sometime around the time you say

"Joo are the biggest piece of shit cheating scumbag I've ever met"

and

sometime around the time she types

*You two deserve each other—I tried to show you someone could fucking care for you without making you feel like a fucking child**

(*albeit with slightly worse spelling and slightly more curse words)

I tell you to

"Stop"

and

I text her to

"Stop"

and I proceed to attempt to take control over a situation I have absolutely no control over.

I do this very, very carefully, texting her

I'll text you back in a minute

and

No, I understand

when she quickly replies

Don't you fucking dare stop talking to me to make up with her—I'm around all of your shit, do you understand?

turning to face you and urging you and your really rapidly beating heart to calm down.

I climb out of the hospital bed slowly, careful not to upset the array of tubes you're carefully connected to and careful not to upset you into lashing out at me physically while you're so carefully connected.

…

I offer you my hand, part peace-offering and part *I-don't-think-you-can-physically-get-yourself-out-of-bed*, urging you gently to stand and with the intention of taking you anywhere but here and where you're currently raging in.

You put your tiny hand in mine, and the frailty in the touching both breaks my heart and reaffirms *why* I'm so foolishly fucking madly in love with you.

You're weak, Muneca, standing softly on softly-shaking legs and reminding me that, underneath all of your fierce Colombian bravado you're a woman with a heart exposed and hurt previously and really, really not for having it broken the way I guess I kinda have been.

And just like it has been, in hotel hallways and in expensive restaurants just after dinners ruined—on different islands in different countries and on boats in the middle of big, big oceans—we're quietly walking hand in hand, hurt and silent and both fully aware that there isn't anywhere in the world we would rather be.

There are differences this time, sure—you're attached to a portable tower steadily supplying you with some form of intravenous drip, and the wheels squeaking against otherwise abandoned hallways are ensuring *this* walking together isn't really silent—but the hand holding and the significance and the symbolism aren't lost on me as I head towards the twenty-four hour cafeteria we both unfortunately know just how to get to.

I'm hoping that hot coffee tastes better than the saline your hand is ingesting on the other side of that tube; that a subtle change of scenery and the presence of anyone else will temper your potentially-dangerous-for-you-this-time heart racing admonishings.

I'm hoping that the time it takes to get there—walking at a pace slower than our usual, despite the presence of an extra four wheels—will allow my rapidly racing thoughts to settle, and to concocting some discernable solutions as to how to get out of this latest self-inflicted disaster.

I'm nowhere closer as we step onto the elevator, standing silently

still

still

and not making eye contact, for fear of betraying the wall the words we're not speaking would certainly create and neither of us really having the strength to go another round the way the night and the bed and the constantly illuminating phone screen have certainly demanded.

So we've got three floors to descend in silence and I've got

Three

minutes tops, between the soon to be open again elevator doors and the cafeteria our next battle could entertain in and

Two

floors now and scrambling, maybe wanting to continue to tell you the truth and weather the storm and love you no matter how really fucking hard and forget about the

One

person who knows I'm fundamentally fucked up for playing a part in this and willing to love me anyways, currently dissecting my apartment while I'm waiting to come up with some goddamn idea of what to do.

The doors open

tragically

and I'm nowhere closer to a solution, figuring I'll just have to figure it out as I go the way I *have* been, countless fights and two years of fighting them.

You could call the elevator ride we've just gotten off of a descent fully into madness, or a descent into hell, or a descent into a cafeteria; all I know is that I'm still holding your hand and I still really really love you and that I'm really really sorry that this realization is costing me heaven, sanity, and the chance of happily digesting the food I'm about to eat in attempt to distract you.

…

You're chewing half-heartedly on a half-heartedly buttered half-heated bagel and, watching you chew, a new realization—that this is the first solid food you've attempted to eat in twenty-four hours—is breaking an already-breaking heart. I suppose I hate everything about this; the hospital gown doing it's damndest to dial down your beauty, the hospital lights reflecting off of the sheen of your severely dehydrated skin, the IV attached to a slightly shaking bagel holding hand that is attempting to do something about it.

I'm across the cafeteria table, awash with piss poor cafeteria coffee and metaphors of descents and the kind of self-loathing that can only come from involvement with too many women.

And the result of my actions is staring back at me, between half-hearted bites of half-heated bagels, batting big brown eyes and swallowing hard in between questions of

Why

and a distinct and utter lack of attempting to understand my probably half-hearted rationalizations.

I try my best, explaining that I left her in my apartment to grieve the death of a relationship I was probably half-invested in, telling you that I spent time with her only to ease the pain of losing you again and forever

and then again *again* and forever

and so on—and maybe I half-believe the lies I move my lips to lie.

The truth I keep to myself; that I really did/do care about her and that she made time together the kind of easy that time together *should* be, sitting across a cafeteria table and really regretting what was probably my last best chance at storm-free weather.

You're listening to me explain that I'll take back my apartment key and delete her phone number and avoid her at the gym and you're analyzing my inflections with the predatory gaze of someone who has been hurt by words spoken from lips just like mine.

I tell you that she's infatuated and only; wait for

You pursued her to stroke your pathetic little ego

to explode from your pretty pumped up pretty dry pretty little lips, but it doesn't come, half-hearted chewings paired with weakened resignations replacing the vitriol I've become so accustomed to.

I show you the text messages because you ask to see my phone, fully prepared to deal with the fallout of her more spiteful opinions of you and our relationship, figuring

You told me that you were only with her the last time because you didn't know how to tell her it has to be over

would merit an explanation I'm only half-prepared to attempt…but you simply chew on the rubber posing as your dinner, scrolling through the youthful exuberance played out on the screen with the *fight-back* of someone who really doesn't have any *fight-back* left.

You hand my phone, red-hot with spirited and still-incoming chastising, back to me, and your lack of

Fuck you

and

Eet's over

coupled with her texts of

Fuck you

and

it's over

has me saddened and admittedly confused; maybe I'd just gotten so used to her being calm and somewhat understanding and you being anything but that makes this role reversal so alien to me.

I delete the still-incoming and entirely one way conversation, hoping it represents my intention of cutting off communication to her to *you* and hoping it represents my intention of cutting off communication to her to *me*, too.

I promise the kinds of things I need to promise in order to keep your heart rate down and get this fucking IV out of your arm and get you out of this depressing hospital cafeteria and that unflattering hospital gown—and you look at me between chewings with the intensity of someone who probably desperately wants to believe me.

So in the time it takes for you to finish what is unfortunately your dinner, we've reconciled for the second time tonight and for the first time since the girl I left in my apartment decided that me leaving to come rescue my on again/off again fiancée wasn't okay.

I take your slightly-shaking hand in mine and we head for the elevator; the rhythm of your IV cart playing background to the soundtrack reverberating between my ears, singing songs with guilty lyrics and heartbreaking melodies. I came down here expecting a battle you're physically/mentally/emotionally unable to fight, weakened by your Tachycardia and my equally irrational abilities to love you desperately and leave you *just as*.

And maybe your weakness has defeated me in a way your violence never could; as the elevator doors close around us, my thoughts are of protecting you and only, and, for the first time since the very first war we waged, I leave my justifications for my actions in the basement with the bad coffee.

...

The Oddest of a few

We're in the hospital

--which is kind of a semi-regular thing with you

--and we're finishing up with what has turned out to be an entirely too-traumatic seemingly non-traumatic at all procedure.

You've just had an IUD* inserted

(*^Intrauterine device)

in order to prevent a potential pregnancy we both know we're nowhere near stable enough to weather.

The doctor

--who'd assured us that said procedure was routine and relatively non-invasive and entirely, one hundred percent safe

--is sweating profusely and looks as though he's just performed a five hour quadruple bypass.

I kinda sympathize, having been there

(--not performing the routine and relatively non-invasive and entirely, one hundred percent safe procedure)

--no, having been there in terms of surviving the multi-lingual assault he's just survived having performed the routine and relatively non-invasive and entirely one hundred percent safe procedure on *you*.

You're looking at me with one of those

this is all your fault

looks,

all my fault for not wanting to have a baby with you, given the tumultuous nature of our *almost-kinda* relationship.

My mind is hazy, given the tension of the two minutes *tops* procedure, but I'm relatively sure that we both agreed that this particular course of action was in our mutual best interest.

And while I wholeheartedly sympathize with you—I wouldn't want a stranger shoving something up my private parts either—I can say from previous experience with girlfriends past that, while the whole process is invasive and painful and horrible and stressful—it is *not* the attempted murder you're claiming said doctor just performed.

But I'm here in the supportive partner role, and so I help lift you from the doctor's chair/bed, and I turn to thank the eager-to-exit doctor after listening to the after care routine you won't, and before I know it, I'm walking down a hospital hallway and listening to you complain in tongues I really should start to learn.

I'm already picturing the rest of the afternoon—tending to you while you lay in bed cursing the invasions to your body that my reckless love has led you to—when you turn abruptly down a hospital hallway I know for a fact doesn't lead to the parking lot we're parked in.

Had I time, I might lament the fact that I've been in this building with you or looking for you or because of you enough to understand the convoluted floor plan…but I'm occupied instead with wrangling you and your suddenly determined escalation in pace.

"Baby"

in my calmest, most sympathetic tone

"the car is this way—"

"I have one more stop to make"

you answer, cryptically and tersely and without a turn of your head.

I should find the change in your tone alarming, less

wounded victim

and more

but, having weathered multiple swings in both your mood and weather, I'm painfully oblivious to everything save the fact that you've clearly made subsequent plans.

Without telling me, and so I'm following you blindly and having to pick up the pace, appreciating how the seemingly unendurable pain of the entirely too invasive procedure has given way thanks to an apparent need to be somewhere *else* as fast as humanly possible.

I clue in by the time we get off the elevator you've led us to, third floor labelled

Dr. Glavas, Cosmetic Surgery

with a great big arrow pointed in the direction you're racing down.

You're through a set of glass double doors a minute later, flashing your health card to a receptionist who seems to know you, and surprising one of us by saying

"I have an appointment with Dr. Glavas;"

Dr. Glavas being the name on the wall outside the elevator; the name right above the *Cosmetic Surgery* sign and corresponding arrow that led us here.

You're ushered past the waiting area and towards a closed door; I'm without instruction and wondering with a glance at the many unarmed waiting room chairs if my part in this little adventure is to end here.

I'm half resigned to my fate, chauffeur and *only*...but then I realize that you're not even bothering to look back at me and so

fuck it

I'm heading to the mysterious closed door at the end of a dimly-lit corridor too, *supportive partner* meaning I'm part of *all* today's procedures, informed of or not.

The receptionist opens the door and you sway your ample hips through, the jiggle from behind the fabric of your previous-procedure-inappropriate sundress reminding me why I put up with your volatility. I'm half-surprised when the door is held open for me as well—on the other side rests a doctor's chair/bed just like the one you were so dramatically *forced* onto minutes ago, as well as a couple of waiting-room-similar seats, one of which I follow you wordlessly to occupy.

The receptionist, satisfied in the accomplishment of her task, exits without a word, her lack of

"Dr. Glavas will be with you shortly"

indicating to me that you know the routine.

So I sit bewildered—bewildered and silent and on purpose—wondering if you will do your driver, if not your lover, the kindness of explaining why in the hell we're seated here.

You don't

doubtless part of my punishment for subjecting you to the horror of extreme birth control modalities, and so the five minutes that pass pass painfully.

You busy yourself with your phone, texting and smiling at the texts returning, texts clearly not from me, and smiles at texts back clearly meant to evoke jealousy or at the very least, wonder.

And I am,

wondering

but more about what in the fuck is wrong with you, failing to mention that you've had a subsequent meeting planned and—given the theatrics of your previous appointment—that you're able to walk, let alone sit comfortably, waiting at some plastic surgery clinic the way we so surprisingly are.

I'm lamenting the turns my afternoon has taken, extrapolating proposed effects on the rest of my life and mourning the death of any hope of normalcy, when the door swings open frenetically, revealing an overly enthusiastic Dr. Glavas; Dr. Glavas because

"Dr. Glavas!"

escapes your suddenly animated lips almost as enthusiastically as he's entered the room.

Now, I kinda figured, what with his name on the hallway and the glass door and all, but the second reveal—based solely on the falsetto in your voice when speaking his name—confirms my suspicion that you know one another, meaning—at the very least—you've been here before.

Looking at him, I guess it kinda makes sense—as far as Cosmetic Surgeons go, he's beautiful; a thick head of curly, salt-and-pepper hair atop a mysterious-ethnic-descent-conceived square jaw, an elegant and expensive pair of wire-frame glasses accenting perfectly symmetrical, probably-cosmetically-enhanced features.

He smiles warmly, his doubtless-collagen-enhanced lips parting to reveal a dazzling smile—I spend the length of your probably doctor/patient protocol-inappropriate hug scanning the emoting his face does for wrinkles that just aren't there.

If he's had work done, it's *good*—I'd put him at forty, but it could be five years north or five years south, his age suddenly as mysterious as his ethnicity.

Following the entirely inappropriate and increasingly confusing embrace, he turns to introduce himself with a smile and a handshake; to my surprise, both are unerringly warm and confident.

Despite the confusion I'm feeling about the situation, I'm appreciating the gesture he's making that you probably should have, and so I match the warmth in my smile/shake back, relieved somewhat to meet another man in your life who doesn't give off the rapey-vibe your boss/best friend/sponsor does.

He doesn't ask who I am to you, and you don't offer, and so, as he settles down atop the doctor's bed/chair the way young, roguish doctors do, we're both listening intently for your explanation as to just what the fuck we're doing here.

"I'm tired"

you begin, echoing a sentiment I suppose I've just kind of gotten used to living in "and eet's"*

(*^it's)

"showing on my face"

it's not

"right here, under my eyes"

eyes you bat, unnecessarily and for dramatic effect, somehow feeling the need to arch your back and push the tits already threatening to escape today's procedure-inappropriate sundress up around the eyeballs you're only half interested drawing attention to.

Dr. Glavas moves closer, to investigate

your eyes

and the areas you're pointing to, I hope, and I don't blame him; looking for bags that aren't there and probably already calculating the best way to tell you so.

You're adamant, however, carrying on about imaginary wrinkles and marks and mars, and he's doing a great job listening—listening the way I'm increasingly *not*, my mind searching madly for events of the past week and any possibility that you mentioned this appointment and I missed it.

I'm coming up empty, forced back to the moment the moment he reaches into one of the many cupboards beside the waiting room style chair you're waiting in and produces a needle wrapped in a sanitary shrink-wrapped package; a needle that looks at least twice as terrifying as the thumbnail sized device you were fretting over in the *last* doctor's office.

At the sight of this one, filled with a magical, mystery ingredient labelled

Juvederm

or

Fountain of Youth

or

Chemical Concoction for Your Face

you're practically salivating, a far cry from the traumatized victim leaving the south wing of the hospital some minutes ago.

Dr. Glavas explains, in a well-practiced, soothing tone, that he will make a series of small injections into the skin of your cheeks, illustrating with a rub and an application of some mystery freezing cream I don't recall seeing him produce that the affected areas will not hurt and the effects will be dramatic yet natural-looking.

Your

"As natural looking as before?"

revealing far more about your history with Dr. Glavas and your seemingly God-given beauty than you'd offered in silent walks down hospital hallways; I suppose that, given the affinity expressed between the two of you, I'm happier with the frequent-secret-plastic-surgery rendezvous than anything potentially romantic.

So it is relief

(?)

washing over me as we wait for the freezing adorning your already-puffed-up cheeks to take hold, small talk about Dr. Glavas' wife and kids putting me more at ease with what is turning out to be only the *second* most fucked up situation of the day.

I suppose I'm equal parts grateful/concerned; on one hand appreciating the disillusion of the veil of perfection so carefully erected in the monkey-dance that is courtship—that need to present oneself as perfect, an avatar/idea where a living, breathing, flawed human being should be.

Concerned, because the veil of appearances is one you subscribe to/protect ferociously—the constant turbulence of our particular dance leading naturally to thoughts of self-doubt…could your casual indifference in allowing me to participate in today's events mean you no longer desire to impress me?

Heady thoughts, for sure—and I'm thinking them, lost in my own world, alone beside you in *really, what a pleasant surprise* Dr. Glavas' office…until the syringe emerges from the shrink-wrap to land slowly in the soft skin a half-inch under your eyeball.

At this, I'm horrified enough for the both of us—equally and if not more so than watching another man between your legs inserting something, *surgically or not*, into an area I've gone through seven hells to claim.

You remain perfectly still

because the procedure demands it

as an inch-and-a-half long needle disappears into the flesh of your puffy cheek; the cylinder attached delivering a vial full of clear, viscous *tar* into the skin of the face I'm so (sometimes) fond of.

Dr. Glavas expertly maneuvers the submerged needle, firing a stream of slowly-disappearing goo into areas encompassing the totality of your right side—foolishly, I assume that the contents will prove plentiful enough for both sides…but, as your face greedily laps up the very last ooze of miracle, I'm learning that you're a *two* syringe girl.

He practically leaves the needle hanging, empty and exhausted, from your *no-more-beautiful-because-this-whole-process-is-unnecessary* face, expertly maneuvering his free hand to administer a cotton swab to the tiny hole the needle so eagerly created.

After a surprisingly thorough smoothing of the tissue with his surgically gloved hands (--the boxer in me recognizing the tactic literally borrowed from a cut-man smoothing out swelling in a fighter's corner between rounds--) it's on to the tearing of the shrink-wrapped home of needle *two*, this one disappearing and *too* and into the side of your face I'm seated closest to.

My bird's eye view of this, the latest and possibly-as-if-not-more barbaric looking procedure providing much welcomed insight into the machinations of your admittedly cobwebbed thoughts; how procedures designed to have a direct positive impact on your perception of beauty are to be welcomingly weathered; how procedures designed to protect your irrationalities—but having no perceived impact on your appearance/worth to the outside world, are met with equal parts derision/revulsion.

So I'm learning volumes, even as you're *taking* them, to the face and in place of the learnings couples generally do by communicating.

Dr. Glavas finishes, spent as the needles after practically putting an expensive Italian loafer onto the arm rest of your waiting room chair, so hard was he massaging the mystery plastic into your beautiful face.

You converse pleasantly—with him and not me—while he finishes throwing away his torture tools. I answer the few, for-prosperities-sake questions he throws my way, admiring his disposition and silently wondering if I might in fact need work *too*.

I curse Dr. Glavas and his smoothness with a smile and a handshake, appreciating how soundly he must build his referral business based on equal parts effortless charm and undetectable, efficient work.

You finish the impromptu-to-me appointment with a warm embrace goodbye—I'm watching awkwardly yet still sufficiently disarmed, and before long I'm accompanying you and your surgically-enhanced and alarmingly rosy cheeks to the reception area and the waiting receptionist, electronic payment terminal in hand.

The amount you pay for the procedure you've had turns *my* cheeks red, too—it's close to a thousand for two syringes and the time in Dr. Glavas' admittedly pleasant company. As we wave a final goodbye I can almost understand why you attempted to keep this from me—ten paces from the clinic and the spell we've both fallen under, I'm snapped back to the reality that you've just spent a ton of cash on something—temporary aggressive swelling aside—probably completely undetectable.

So it's walking in silence, time down hospital hallways spent marveling at your clearly tenuous grip on sanity; and, once again left doubting my own, somewhat-willing participant in the madness that is time spent with you.

The car door closes some five minutes later; relieved to be free of the hospital and planned and not-planned appointments, it's another seven before you part your pretty pumped up (probably surgically enhanced) pretty little lips to speak to me.

"Now, *there's* a man."

It's accurate, sure; as Cosmetic Surgeons go, Glavas is by far the best (only) I've met. Your tone betrays a sense of antagonistic intent; I do my best to not take the bait, my

"Yeah, good guy"

designed to diffuse your forthcoming fury.

"Successful, gorgeous—he's not much older than joo, joo know."

"Oh, yeah?"

"Jes.* Fuck, his wife is lucky."

(*Yes.)

"Sure is."

"I mean, if I had a head on my shoulders, I would steal him away—did joo know he lives on a horse farm?"

I did not—and, you know damn well that I grew up on a horse farm.

And that I miss said horse farm.

And that, if I were a more successful man, I'd be living on a horse farm.

I grip the wheel tighter, put my right foot a little more firmly on the gas pedal. I know where this conversation is headed, as surely as I know the roads back to your/Humberto's-*likely* house.

Emboldened by my silence, you flip the passenger seat mirror, mock-examining your results and feigning indifference when you offer

"Why do I keep wasting my time?"

under your breath and poking,

metaphorically

the way you're poking

literally

at the bruises forming on your ever-swelling cheeks.

I pretend to not-hear, turning my head the direction of my wheel, left and away from you

literally

reminiscing on the more ridiculous aspects of an increasingly ridiculous day, running out of metaphors and road and wishing I was

literally

anywhere else.

"I need a man like *that*."

I grit my teeth, resolve to avoid this latest and most direct attack. By the time you offer your next comment, however, I fail miserably.

"Instead of these *losers* I'm always supporting; I mean, *fuck*, I'm the woman, I should be the one taken care of."

Your words are leverage and cruel and effective; your emasculation—usually subtle and simmering and understood—now brought aggressively to light, a verbal reminder of the omnipresent fact that you make much, much more money than I do.

Now, despite the fact that you might have had some…assistance…in your somewhat-deserved ascent from dishwasher to Project Manager, I understand that your traditional Latin American values dictate that the man in the relationship remain the primary breadwinner. My pride does too…now under a familiar and semi-constant attack, I fail in my efforts to restrain myself.

I wait until you reference Humberto as your last best relationship before surrendering to rage justified by your outright absurdity.

My retort includes at least two

fucks

and one

spoiled little bitch,

incendiary and by design and now relishing the combat I find myself in, a day of ferrying you to appointments both dramatic and secretive bringing out the worst in my admittedly lacking sense of restraint.

My rebuttal to your

"Joo fucking loser"

covers a variety of timely topics; clandestine appointments with—and inappropriate conversations about—really, fight-proof Doctors and your general lack of respect for your chauffeur/sometimes-love and your continued need to remind me of my somewhat lacking social status and my annoyance with the more princess-like aspects of your personality like going to get you fucking Starbucks every morning and *more*, words like

Never see you again

and

tired of this bullshit

and

fucking tired of this bullshit

telling you and *really* the things I should have been telling you all along.

To write that you pull on the door and attempt to exit a vehicle travelling sixty kilometers down a rush-hour London road might seem absurd were it not a logical extension of your flair for the dramatic; the

"Good luck with the rest of your life, joo fucking arrogant dirtbag"

preceding the pulling of the handle has me seriously considering leaving you in one of two congested Southbound lanes, four-fifteen on a Friday afternoon and two traffic lights from the left hand turn that might rid me of you forever.

I rationalize that normal couples don't make trips to the doctor's office that turn out quite like *this*; beside me, you've abandoned the dramatic gripping of the door handle in favor of gesturing wildly—gesturing wildly the way you usually do before the *flailing* starts.

The rest of the horrifying drive home continues this way, causing commotion in congestion, giving fellow drivers stopped at the red lights we unfortunately stop at quite the show. As luck would have it, the swelling on your artificially-enhanced cheeks has discolored to the point of bruising, adding the

oh-he-beats-her

dynamic to our impromptu-in-traffic stage show.

I'm dodging limbs and accusatory glances from similarly windows-down contemporaries, suddenly wishing it was a few months north of July and a few miles from the onlookers we're crawling along with.

By the time we reach your laneway, the outcome of my evening has been painfully illustrated, thrashings telling me before your words that you'll be making an all-too-familiar walk up alone. I watch your hips sway towards the door, moving furiously and illustrating to any and all outside or within-earshot neighbors that you're displeased for the thousand-thousandth time.

My duty as chauffeur fulfilled, I put the car in reverse, cursing the spell your hips and the ass attached have wrought upon my poor soul, maybe only half-understanding that *I'm* the crazy one for already looking forward to the inevitable make-up.

...

I'm cooking steaks and theories.

You're over, and it's rare and we like them medium and we're *back* and after the latest and *maybe-longest-who-the-fuck-can-tell-anymore* breakup…I'm watching you from the patio and through the smoke of the barbecue, dancing in the living room of my apartment to some song we're crazy enough to believe was written for us and *only*.

And it's not true and maybe tonight it'll do; both savvy enough to realize the good moments mean more, because history has shown they're to be few and fleeting.

I'm *starving*, having worked late and met you here, the allotted and appropriate dinner time relinquished to catching up and the first bottle of red we downed some bottle-and-a-half ago. So it's late—and I don't care and you don't care—because the magic is working for us tonight and we're both clearly relishing the delay of the inevitable death one wrong word could/will cause.

The jeans you're wearing move impossibly as you sway your ample hips to some song I can't/wouldn't hear anyways; I divert my gaze painfully and just long enough to avoid burning the steaks we've waited far too long to taste. The cool of a late August evening fails to bite my skin—I thank the wine for the subtle numbness, keeping the blood from surging south of my waist the way you're trying your damndest to make it.

Yeah, everything is going smoothly; having learned to breathe somewhat slowly in moments like these, I finish the steaks—perfectly—and make my way back through the living room/dance floor. Your eyes betray an appreciation for my otherwise-completely-lacking culinary skills; I set my kill on the table, pausing only to place whatever salad I could care less about into bowls I could do without too.

I'm practically salivating, the scent of the meat competing violently with my every-other-senses and need to ignore everything but you. I place the steaks on the center of the table, fully intending only a fraction of a moment to let them cool…

…and then you look at me like *that.*

...

We destroy my apartment, ruining everything but the meat we ignore, biting into each other and with the anxiety of two people who may very well never taste one another ever again.

There's violence in the sex we endeavor to create, this the first of five times this evening, and easily the most bruising. We communicate all too effectively this way—thrashing and clawing, your nails digging into the naked flesh of my back and tracing words like *yearning* and *love* and, most likely, *hatred* too.

The madness of your lips against mine numbs the sensation your claws are creating; I'm fumbling, eyes closed, through the living room you used as a dance floor minutes and emerging seductions ago, searching desperately for something to bend you over.

If I was proud of the steak I spent seven minutes searing—the steak cooling on the counter I couldn't give a fuck about now—then this, the first of five times I take you, is my fifty-three minute masterpiece.

By the time the evening ends and the steak is in the trash and we go to bed starving and yet satisfied, I'm already cataloguing tonight in the proverbial win column, weighed favorably against an ever-increasing series of evenings that have ended in a loss, and of you, and—usually and according to the words you hurl—forever.

...

You're talking to me about wedding plans for a wedding we both know won't happen.

And I'm pretending to be engaged in the conversation the way maybe I'm pretending to be engaged; going through the motions as though our pending nuptials are anything other than some foolish romantic ideal. Maybe I thought the act of engagement would calm the storm behind your eyes, offering assurances that, despite the violence of our days together, we have some hope in hell of enduring our all-encompassing madness.

As you look up at me from the laptop displaying pictures of churches in Colombia, I think we both understand how futile these preparations are.

…

In the months since coming back form the cruise, tanned and tired and supposedly betrothed, we've managed to spend more time apart than together. You've thrown your ring at me more than a half dozen times, asked for the one on my finger back just as many. We've sworn to never see one another again in multiple tongues and with the entirety of colorful language available in our combined vocabulary.

So you'll forgive me, eyes falling to the list of churches in made up places like Bogota and San Andres, if I lack the enthusiasm of a likely-going-to-go-through-with-this groom to be.

You're pretending *hard* today, in love and with the idea of me being married in your hometown, likely-probably trying to gauge my current level of commitment by glancing through potential venues with the finality of a bride-to-be and believably.

Of course, it's equally possible that tonight's little exercise—fueled by particularly passionate make-up sex/hate fucking and the delicious bottle and a half Malbec/Cab Sauv that followed/is following—is simply another of your calculated games. The cat-with-a-ball-of-yarn bemusement written across your appropriately intoxicated features certainly lends credence to this possibility;

regardless, I'm swallowing hard sips of California red, eyes scanning desperately and maybe for an escape that isn't there.

Don't get me wrong—the idea of being engaged to you, maybe partially in hopes of meeting your apparent commitment level requirements, maybe partially to show you I love you enough to stay despite your probably bi-polar levels of bullshit—is something I'm still *very* much interested/invested in.

The idea of actually going through with it—the whole *marriage* thing?

Forgive me if the turmoil of the past two years has left me anywhere close to the assured it would take to go through with it the way we're pretending to.

And it doesn't mean we're not madly in love

as I scroll through the first three churches, careful not to swipe past without a modicum of feigned interest

and it's not as though the foolhardy dreamer in me doesn't pretend hard enough sometimes to make it a possibility, however faint

no

no

too remote

but with each church and the clicking past it, the anxiety gnawing at the base of my brain seems to gain appetite. And the wine, while thankfully appreciated for the numbing of my still-clicking fingertips, doesn't seem to be satiating the way it should

no

no

no fucking way

and so a dozen churches with increasingly incoherent names come and go, leaving you with only a few dozen more in the much smaller list of Colombian towns qualified to witness our unholy union.

Were I sober, I might muse that there seems to be a church on every corner in Colombia; you're throwing options and increasingly indignant looks my way, a never ending sea of

Primatial Cathedral Basilica of the Immaculate Conception

and

Catedral Nuestra Senora del Carmen

and

Cathedral of Our Lady of Chiquinquira

peppered with looks that could almost and *most likely will, one day* kill.

I pick one, more for the sake of picking than actually basing my choice on location or the resplendent detail of the frescoes adorning the inner sanctum, and turn the laptop slowly to face you, maybe a little afraid that my choice will be met with the derision you seem so intent on offering.

After painfully extended moments of tempestuous eye scanning and a few investigative finger clickings, your big black eyes shift from the screen to mine, and the first hints of what *couldn't* be a smile crack the façade of your ridiculously well maintained/significantly moisturized face.

We're pretending hard today after all; potential catastrophe averted, I exhale deeply, and am beginning to ponder what is sure to be a time consuming recollection of the evening's events and how they led us *here*, one wrong church away from argument, when you leap over the laptop and tackle me.

The act takes me by surprise, yet my body relaxes almost immediately after contact—our violence is always verbal with a hint of physical—this tackling is indicative of an overly aggressive need for contact in moments of happiness.

So I take you in my arms, feeling your kiss explode across my lips, physical representation of your pretending hard tonight satisfaction with my level of commitment.

The act of tackling has toppled the bottle of Malbec, equally surprised by your impromptu/welcome assault and empty, thankfully, and rolling on the carpet we fall to roll beside. The Cab Sauv, probably not empty and equally eager to topple, is saved by the dexterous fingers previously occupied with the unclasping of your bra.

After minutes well spent rolling against the debris your passion created, I pick your now-naked body from the floor and the dangers of rugburn the carpet was sure to create, placing you not-delicately atop the table usually reserved for the dinners we have here at your home.

So it is with absolutely no fear of bacteria that I eat off the table and from between your legs—granting the dinner table a sorely lacking sense of purpose, having stood solid for but a handful of meals in the two years together and hundreds of dinners spent *anywhere else*.

You moan a sense of appreciation, and the table chimes in with a rhythmic series of creakings, ever increasing in frequency and fighting to match your pleasured wailings.

I move the laptop to safety, not bothering to adjust a contortion wrought by your hurried leapings, and then set to work, urging the symphony of creakings and wailings ever onward as I endeavor to fuck my frustrations away.

...

We finish, mercifully, some twenty-two minutes later.

I step away from the table you're sprawled across, covered in sweat and sex and vindication, standing on still-shaking legs and admiring my handiwork. It takes minutes—minutes filled with post-coital kissing and delicate maneuverings around questionable and still-fresh stains—to realize that we've managed to move the dining room table some four feet across the dining room.

The realization comes only after you rise from the table top, adorned with many of the aforementioned questionable and still-fresh stains and turn to note that the table is now resting against the back wall. The realization sets in slowly, my head still swimming from post sex endorphins and the adrenal fatigue twenty-two minutes of really good and really rough sex has left me recovering from; staring somewhat dumbfounded, I can't help but admire you and your body's ability to distract me entirely from traversing geography.

We laugh at our unknown interior decorating sensibilities, promising to return the dining room and the table to some semblance of normalcy before Gatto and Gatto's breakfast are served atop it, three hours and counting until the morning makes tonight a memory for the *pleasant* column.

Minutes and the quick shower within them later, you're sleeping peacefully atop my chest and I'm close behind, the endorphins relenting slowly and reminding me—just before sleep takes me too—that despite how this evening ends, I was only one wrong mouse click from shattering the illusion of peace we found sanctity in.

...

In case you're not exhausted enough (and to recap)

Here's some typical days of the week in my time with you.

…

It's a Monday

It's a Monday, and

I'm collecting the totality of my items from your home

--so a toothbrush and a sweater you'd worn home a week ago

and I'm looking your poor mother in the eye on my way out the door

and even though she doesn't understand one fucking word I say

and even though I don't understand one fucking word she says

we both kind of understand that this isn't the first time I've been kicked out of your/your boss' house

and we both kind of understand it likely won't be the last.

...

It's a Tuesday

It's a Tuesday and

your mother is down from Colombia and she's over at my apartment

and you are too,

and the three of us are cooking something Colombian in my kitchen.

And even though I don't understand one fucking word she says

and even though she doesn't understand one fucking word I say

we're communicating beautifully over too much wine and the kind of from-the-belly laughter that tells us both that this—*meal, and*—is going to turn out okay.

...

It's a Wednesday

It's a Wednesday and

your mother is looking in the window of some expensive storefront

here in the middle of some expensive weekend away,

and we'll likely buy her whatever has her so interested on the other side of that window

--because money matters about as much as *anything* when we're together and feeling the way being away together feels

--so not at all.

And even though she doesn't understand one fucking word I say

and even though I don't understand one fucking word she says

she knows by the laughter that follows

the presentation of the bag holding whatever it is she wanted

that moments like *this* are worth more than the next ten trinkets

we'll stop in ten expensive stores to buy.

...

It's a Thursday

It's a Thursday and

your mother is looking at the look on your face; and while she may not understand the

Fuck Joo

you're moving your pretty pumped up pretty little lips to scream

she understands the look you're contorting your face to in order to scream it.

My response is measured, more

We shouldn't be fighting in front of your mother

than

Fuck you, too

and even though she doesn't understand one fucking word say

and even though I don't understand one fucking word she says

she understands that this kind of behavior isn't normal from two people who claim to love one another the way we do.

…

It's a Friday

It's a Friday and

your mother looks tired.

She's down from Colombia for the third time in the two years we've been kinda together, and, in those three times, she's witnessed our love and the apparent absence of; watched us kiss under the open sky and watched us hurl words like weapons in kitchens too small for the arguments we filled them with

And we're in a kitchen

yours

and even though she doesn't understand one fucking word I say

and even though I don't understand one fucking word she says

I nod my head and offer her the kind of hug that says without saying

Goodbye

and because, after fights like the one she's just witnessed

I'm unlikely to be fiancée number four by the time she's standing here next.

...

Last

This is our last fight.

And I can't remember what it's about or what caused it or why we're waging it the way we, exhaustedly, are...but this is the last time that you'll look at me with that storm in your eyes.

This is the last time we'll hurl words meant to wound, flail limbs intended to hurt, each trying desperately to show the other that we're more raw, this time, than the previous time and the time before that and the time before that.

I'm tired

and

you're tired

and the fucked up thing about it is that we both kinda silently understand that two people can love each other completely and wildly and horribly and still be completely and wildly and horribly unable to make that enough.

So time stops, because time is tired too, doubtless having better things to do than to watch two people who clearly love one another go the ten thousandth round of a never ending fight.

You're frozen in the middle of throwing an just-emptied wine glass, mouth agape in a scream carrying some terrible insult I've heard seventy-seven times before.

I just kind of sit and watch, wondering how someone so beautiful can turn a phrase so ugly. I count the lashes protecting your big beautiful black eyes, maybe move close enough to look for light on the surfaces they protect. I'm in range, your glass likely to hit me somewhere hard enough to do the damage you're hoping it will. It's worth it—this last study of the face worth the years some might call wasted.

If I look hard enough, I can make my heart skip the same beat it skipped the first time I stopped and stared; telling me without telling me that the years haven't and maybe wouldn't have taken the feelings that caused this and every fight in the first place.

I can admit that I'm scared—and I've been scared—of losing something I value so very much; scared the way you're scared. Someone said…or maybe some movie told me…that you're careful with what you love.

Time—being the motherfucker that it is—decides to let go, right around the time you do.

Your wine glass shatters on the wall just over my left shoulder

--because you're careful with what you love

and your scream stops, right around the time the first tear you're crying collects on the ridge of your still-quivering lip.

It surrenders for you,

because the words you hurl are just words, after all

words like these ones and the ones after, the ones to attempt to rationalize why I turn on my heels, look at you one last time

and walk out your front door

nothing left but words like these,

the ones after the ones I wasted in my failed attempts to save you.

So I love you

because I really really do

and I wish you the best

with your Fifth-Fiancée-First-Husband

and the daughter (!) you've had since I wrote the first word, some eighty-five-thousand and five years before this one; and I'm wishing you a life without storms and I'm happy you're happy and I'm sorry for the words here that might hurt and I'm sorry

that every single time there's lightning on a dry day

your heart will skip a beat and you'll think about me.

www.ingramcontent.com/pod-product-compliance
Lightning Source LLC
Chambersburg PA
CBHW071545110726
47908CB00007B/1995

* 9 781775 087618 *